Diana's Eclipse

Moons of Mystery Book Three

S Bolanos

CHAOTIC NEUTRAL PRESS LLC

CONTENTS

Series

S BOLANOS

<u>CONTEMPORARY ROMANCES</u>

Ulwich Preparatory Academy

Our Last Fall (MM)

Our Secret Winter (MM)

Our Epic Spring (MM)

Oak Haven Romance

One Brave Thing (Enby/M)

All the Hype (MM)

1

—◆○◆—

CAPTIVE AUDIENCE

FIVE DAYS SINCE THE murder on campus. Five days since I'd tripped over a literal dead body. With an *arrow* sticking out of it. Five days and not so much as a peep on the local news, in the Blackwell Hollow Times, or even the university rag. I blinked down at my notes, but all I could see was the lifeless body of the young man, the dense fog I'd disturbed, curling around his naked body as if to eat it.

I shuddered and reflexively felt the back of my head, which I'd hit, then promptly blacked out after tripping over said body. Most everything after that was a blur, before as well, if I was being honest with myself. I remembered leaving the library after studying with my friends. I remembered it had been dark; the fog obscuring damn near everything. And the fear. I definitely remembered the fear... and running.

Had the young man been running too? And why had he been naked? Had the police determined his identity yet? Did his family know about the horrible accident? *Was* it an accident? Everyone knew pledge hazing could get out of control. So much so that they were trying to pass laws to ban it. But to shoot someone in the back with a real arrow? Surely that went

1

beyond hazing. Then there was the howling. Goosebumps crawled over my flesh as the cacophony of cries I'd heard that night filled my head.

"You okay over there?"

I jumped in my seat, sending my forgotten pen rolling across and off the table. "Huh?" I asked, looking up at Jennifer while simultaneously trying to regain my bearings.

"You've been reviewing last week's notes for ages, but I'm pretty sure you haven't seen a single word. Is everything alright?" Her dark braid fell over her shoulder as she peered down at me, her brown eyes bright with concern.

I set my pen down and leaned back in the mercilessly stiff chair. Sadly, all the cushier chairs on the study floor had already been taken by the time I'd arrived. The logical part of my brain said I should drop it. Maybe I hadn't heard anything because there was nothing to hear. It was possible the police had already caught the culprit and didn't want to cause a panic over an accident, albeit a horrific one. But the hunter part of my brain, the one trained to look at the darker underbelly of this world, didn't believe that for a second. No one "accidentally" shot someone with an arrow like that. The school should have been a buzzing hive of paranoia. The media should have been running a constant commentary. I should have been brought in for more questions. And what about the howling? How was it that no one else had heard it? Or if they had, why was no one talking about it?

"Anna?"

I blinked and refocused on my forgotten study companion. "Hmm?"

"You checked out again." She set her pen aside and leaned forward. "What's wrong?"

I waffled for another few seconds, debating the wisdom of discussing this in the middle of the school library, but after a quick look around, I mirrored her move and leaned forward. "Have you heard anything about the other night?"

"What night?"

For a second, I feared I'd imagined bumping into her after the paramedics released me. I already knew my memory of the night was a little fuzzy, but I was positive she'd been there with her... cousin? Taking a gamble that I hadn't made up the whole encounter, I dropped my voice. "Have you heard anything about the murder?"

She shook her head, but didn't tell me I was nuts. So, there was that, at least.

"What about..." I trailed off, not sure if I should actually ask or not. Near as I could find out, no one else seemed to have registered anything else out of the ordinary that night.

She placed a hand on my shoulder. "Hey, whatever it is, you can tell me. I can't imagine what you're going through."

I worried my bottom lip, still debating how wise it was to ask. Maybe I'd imagined the howling and the feeling of being chased across campus. I took in her open expression and went for it. "Do you remember hearing any... howling that night?" I finished awkwardly.

The concern melted from her face, leaving it eerily neutral. "Howling?"

I chalked up the unusual response to her being freaked. "Uh, yeah... The night I found the body, I heard howling—like wolf howling—everywhere." I neglected to mention that it had seemed like the howls were following me.

"Wolves... At Blackwell..." She raised a disbelieving eyebrow.

"Yes, I know. There aren't any wolves in Blackwell Hollow," I cut her off a little too loudly, my exasperation getting the better of me. "Ugh. I'm sorry." I dropped my head onto my arms. "It just doesn't make any sense."

"It is weird that Joey never made the news."

I slapped the table in my rush of enthusiasm, earning myself several reproachful glares. "Where did you hear that name?"

Jennifer blanched. "I-I'm pretty sure I heard an officer at the scene say something."

"Did you catch a last name?" I asked intently, leaning over the table far enough to breach her personal space. "Tell me you got a last name."

"Mannis," she blurted. "I think they said Mannis."

I slumped back, ruminating over the information. How had the police identified the body at the scene with no ID? Had the victim fit an earlier missing report? Had his family been looking for him this whole time? I supposed it was possible I hadn't looked far enough back into missing person reports in my quest to name the poor soul I'd discovered. But if that was the case, then it was *definitely* murder. Had Joey also been running from the howls? What could he have done for someone to want him dead bad enough to kill him in the middle of campus? And why, for Goddess's sake, was he *naked*?

"So... I'm going to go."

I blinked, realizing that not only had I checked out again, but I'd seriously upset my friend. "Jen..."

"No, it's fine. I... I think I've been staring at notes too long. Need some food and rest. That's what I get for burning the candle at both ends," she added with a chuckle that sounded forced.

"I could join you. We could hit up that Korean joint on sixth." I packed my things to reinforce the statement. "My treat."

She offered me a wan smile. "I appreciate the offer, but I think I'm just gonna eat what I have at the dorm and pass right out."

My backpack drooped to the floor. "Are you sure?"

"I think so. I'm zonked. Rain check?"

It was either take the olive branch and let it drop or insist and risk making a scene. Despite my uncertainty of simply letting her go, I valued our friendship more. "Of course. Next time. But I think I'll call it a night as well. I'm clearly not getting anything done."

She laughed a little more naturally. "You have been a little spacey. It's good to know your limits. See you in class?"

"Like I could miss it," I said with an ironic laugh. "As for these," I indicated the notes I'd been unsuccessfully studying, "hopefully they're enough to get me through one of Doctor Ruth's infamous exams."

Jennifer grimaced good-naturedly, and I felt like things were back on better footing between us. "They really are the worst."

"They really are," I echoed. "Why did I choose to major in Poli-Sci again?"

"Because you can't help but want to fix the world." She gave me another genuine smile, then made her way toward the stairs and the exit.

After a minute or two, I started off in the same direction, only to get sidetracked by a display of ancient Roman literature. It wasn't until my back started to ache from the weight of my backpack that I realized how long I'd been standing there. I let out a low groan and stretched. Between the renewed running in the mornings and late nights of studying, my body seriously needed a break, or even better, to get laid.

"Ana!" a familiar voice shout-whispered. Sure enough, my friend Kora was shuffle-running toward me, with Millie and Hyacinth following at a more moderate pace.

I suppressed a wince. Even from this distance, I could see the challenge in Hyacinth's dark eyes. Whatever Kora was rushing to tell me about, there would be no getting out of it.

Apparently, my introverted ways would only be tolerated for so long.

Kora slid to a halt, causing her blond hair to swing dramatically. "Perfect! Looks like you're heading out, too."

"Uh, yeah. I was going to head back to the apartment before that storm is supposed to roll in."

"Not anymore, you're not," Kora said, looping her arm in mine and plucking the book from my hands. "You're coming with us to check out that local band everyone has been raving about."

"I am?"

"Told you Anna wouldn't let us down." Kora gave Hyacinth a smug look, and I resigned myself to what I already knew was a bad idea.

I let out an exasperated sigh as I unlocked my apartment. The door closed behind me and I rested my pounding head against the cool wood. Not only had going out been an epically bad idea, the band had been sub par, *and* I'd gotten stuck in the storm.

As if to emphasize my misery, thunder cracked loudly overhead. I pushed away from the door, eager to get the stale smell of beer and overly-perfumed college students off of me. Thirty minutes later, I was tucking my feet under me on the couch while rain pelted the windows. Lightning back lit the curtains and thunder followed, hot on its flash.

I burrowed deeper into the warm blanket and turned up the volume to hear what the B-list actors were talking about. Thunder cracked again, somehow even louder than when I'd gotten back from the bar.

"Good grief. This storm's gotta be huge."

No sooner did the words leave my mouth than there was a solid thud against the door. I immediately straightened and watched the entry. Money bought a lot of things, including an apartment I didn't have to share, but it didn't guarantee safety. And while I'd gotten one girl's number at the bar, I wasn't expecting anyone tonight, and there was no way the others would have braved this weather just to continue hanging.

There was another muffled sound that was hard to distinguish against the backdrop of rain and the crappy show I was attempting to watch. I quickly muted the television and listened intently. A few tense seconds ticked by, then I heard it again. An odd shuffling sound just outside the locked door. And was that—a whine?

I cautiously approached the door, triple checking that it was in fact locked, before peering through the peephole. All that was readily visible was the small patch of concrete immediately in front of me and the shrubs that hedged my sad excuse for a porch. Other than that, there was only the expected cascade of water.

I wet my lips as I reached for the lock, the clack of the dead bolt withdrawing infinitely smaller than the thunder. After a deep breath, I twisted the knob and cracked the door. I peered through the thin opening. The fresh smell of rain bombarded my senses while the flying water dampened my clothes for the second time that night. Even with the porch light struggling against the gloom, I couldn't make out anything that could have caused the sound. I shook my head, mentally berating my paranoia, and made to close the door.

Suddenly, a soft whimper drifted up, defying the madness outside to be heard. Without thinking, I flung the door open. And there, tucked up as close as it could get to the exterior wall, was a mud covered *something* curled into a ball, giving me the most pitiful look.

"How the hell did you end up out here?" I asked, equal parts concerned and furious that anyone would leave their animal to fend for themselves in this kind of weather. I searched the storm-tossed night, stubbornly hoping I was wrong and that their owner was actually desperately looking for them. But there was only darkness. When I glanced back at the animal, it had uncurled and inched closer. Now that it was standing, it was significantly larger than I'd assumed. Best guess was that it was some kind of dog, though I was doubtful about the breed, especially given the size.

It stood at least three and a half feet off the ground with a coat that was nearly black from what I could see poking through the mud. In fact, if it hadn't been coated head to tail in the stuff, I suspected its coat would be on the bushy side. As it was, the matted fur clung to the canine's body, emphasizing a slim frame that bordered on bony.

Considering the fact that I'd grown up with Irish Wolfhounds, it wasn't the size of the beast that gave me pause so much as the extra sharp teeth that glinted in the porch light. I took a wary step back. No matter what anyone said to the contrary, there *had been* howling that night. Maybe there *were* wolves in Blackwell Hollow after all. Or... I had an even more dire thought. Or werewolves.

At my movement, the animal looked up and caught me with a soulful pair of brown eyes—very domesticated brown eyes. That, plus an accompanying whimper, and I couldn't help but dismiss my paranoia as just that. This was clearly a lost pet, scared and seeking refuge with humans. Besides which, werewolves were significantly bigger–bulkier–than their mundane canine cousins.

While I was wavering with the wisdom of inviting a strange pet into my apartment, a fresh crack of lightning turned everything a blinding white. There was a loud yip, and I looked down to find the filthy creature huddled against my legs.

"Guess we should get you inside," I said with a defeated sigh.

With no further prompting, the large dog slipped past me, emphasizing my belief that it was not only domesticated, but well trained. I followed, shaking my head and pulling at my now very damp shirt. Once the door was firmly shut against the elements and locked, I turned to find my unexpected guest appraising me. At least now, I could tell it was a he.

I let out a sigh. "First things first. We need to clean you up."

The second I registered him shifting his weight, I reached out to stop him, but I was too late. He violently shook his body, sending mud and water careening across the small living space.

"No. No. No." My aggrieved cry was too little, too late. I gestured at the substantial mess he'd created. "Are you serious? Thanks a lot."

His tongue lolled out in what could only be described as a canine grin. The expression revealed even more of the teeth that had given me pause earlier.

"You seem harmless enough," I said, more to myself than him, as I skirted past to acquire a towel or three. When I returned, he was nosing around in my backpack. "And what exactly do you think you're doing?"

At the question, he scrambled backwards and barked at me, causing me to jump.

"Be quiet, you, or the neighbors will report me. And then where will you be? Back outside, that's where. And me with you, because the complex has a strict no-pets clause."

His ears fell, and he glanced at the windows as a timely peal of thunder accompanied a fresh flash of light. He whined again and turned those puppy-dog eyes back on me.

"Come on. Let's get you cleaned up."

Much to my surprise, he dutifully sat.

I approached slowly, mindful of keeping my hands in sight, lest he decide I was a threat after all. Rather than shy away from the touch, though, he remained perfectly still while I administered the wet cloth, his sharp gaze tracking every movement without so much as a twitch. Each stroke of the towel removed clumps of muck to reveal a glossy dark coat beneath. Despite my initial assessment that he might be skin and bones, he seemed, in fact, quite healthy. The muscle wrapping his sides was sturdier than it looked and there didn't seem to be an ounce of wasted meat on him.

At last, all the mud on him was gone. That said nothing for the state of my living room, but I was too tired to deal with the haphazard splatter. I dropped the final towel and stood up. "There. All better."

He barked, quickly glanced back at the door, then gave a softer yip.

I couldn't help but laugh at his obvious remembrance of being quiet or else. Oh, yes, he was incredibly well trained. Someone would definitely be looking for him. Once again, his tongue lolled out happily and he nudged my hand. I hesitated a second before drifting my palm over the incomprehensibly soft fur on his head.

"I don't know what I'm worried about. If you were going to eat me, you would have done it by now."

The look he gave me on a human could have easily been described as rakish.

"You know, you're exceptionally expressive."

He cocked his head to the side and stared back at me.

"And probably hungry."

He immediately stood and wagged his tail.

"I'll take that as confirmation. I'll warn you, though, I don't exactly have dog food."

His face scrunched up, and he made a sound at the back of his throat reminiscent of disgust. I chuckled and ventured around the tiny peninsula separating the miniature kitchen from the living space.

"Let's see what I have," I mumbled to myself. The fridge opened with a clink of glass as jars jostled against each other in the door. Suddenly, a large furry head wedged itself past my legs to stare into the fridge with me. I looked down at him. "And what do you think you're doing? Get." When he didn't move, I tried again. "There's no way you know everything else I'm saying and don't understand this. Now, go on. Go. Out of the kitchen."

He simply looked at me with those enormous eyes and returned to perusing the meager selection.

"You're a piece of work."

His tail swished at the rebuke, smacking me in the backside.

Rather than argue with a creature that clearly couldn't be argued with, I reached in and grabbed the carton of eggs. In short order, I'd scrambled up all that remained of the dozen. I kept a small portion as a snack for myself, then lumped the rest into a bowl.

I stood clutching the medium-sized mixing bowl full of still steaming eggs, unsure of how to go about giving them to him. He seemed to understand my hesitation and took several steps back before sitting down and waiting patiently to be fed. I set the bowl down and he let me move a few steps away before approaching.

As he investigated his meal, I leaned against the wall. "Where is your collar, I wonder? Surely, an owner diligent enough to train you so thoroughly wouldn't risk you getting out without one. I suppose I could always take you to the shelter to see if you're chipped."

He snorted into the bowl and snagged a mouthful of yellow without looking up.

I glanced over to the windows where the rain was still coming down. "Guess you'll be sleeping here."

His tail gave a lazy wave while he remained focused on his dinner.

"While you finish that, I'm gonna change into something warmer than soaked pajamas. Then it's bed for me."

I waited a second, curious if my declaration would be met with yet another strange response. When none was forthcoming, I pushed off the wall and walked into the bedroom. I snagged a fresh pair of pajamas and slipped into the bathroom to clean off any remaining mud from myself before changing. Feeling substantially better, I returned to the bedroom to find the mysterious canine lounging on my bed.

"Oh, no you don't."

His tail gave a small thump as he settled deeper into the comforter.

"Nah-ah. That's my bed. You can sleep on the floor. Out there." I pointed aggressively back out to the living room.

He looked from me to the open door and stood up. Then promptly spun around and settled down facing the other way.

I rubbed my forehead as I tried to figure out what to do. Did I dare try to move him over or, heaven forbid, attempt to push him off? Just looking at how much room he took up was daunting enough. Finally, I gave it up and walked around to the side. The moment I came into view, his eyes tracked me, causing the hairs on the back of my neck to stand up. Whatever breed he was, he was undeniably intelligent.

Werewolf.

I stubbornly squashed the persistent whisper. I'd studied werewolves my entire life. They were killers, barely more than rabid animals. They didn't cry about mud in their fur, get scared of a little thunder, or ask for pets. And while my companion had an impressive mouthful of teeth and was a hair bigger than even the largest dogs, he was not a snarling, hulking beast.

Satisfied that I'd curtailed a lifetime of ridiculous paranoia and determined not to show fear, I picked up the edge of the comforter. I moved slowly, holding the material like a shield between us, just in case he decided to take offense. When he didn't respond at all, I got in.

"Fine, you can sleep on the bed. But the least you can do is move over, you big brute."

He grumbled and shifted literally just enough for me to get my legs under the covers before resting his sizable bulk back on them. The move was both alarming and oddly comforting; he wasn't behaving that much different from the dogs I had back home. Within seconds, heat infused the covers, saturating my body with a warmth that banished the lingering chill from getting nearly soaked.

"I hope you're pleased with yourself," I mumbled before switching off the lamp.

He grumbled softly, but otherwise didn't move.

"I cannot believe I'm doing this," I said aloud, then closed my eyes.

2

THE DETECTIVE

I ROLLED TO ESCAPE the cold intrusion of my cocoon. Warmth was settling comfortably around me when the prod came again, this time decidedly wet. I yelped and sat up, grabbing the nearest thing at hand to defend myself: a glass dildo. Despite my unfortunate choice of weapon, I brandished it anyway. At least it had some heft to it.

Then the fog of sleep cleared from my mind and I realized the source of my rude wake up call. "Ugh, it's you."

Warm brown eyes studied me, then flicked to the glass phallus. His head tilted to the side, and he leaned forward. Whether to sniff it or take it, I wasn't waiting to find out.

"Absolutely not." I shoved the item into my nightstand drawer. "That's a people toy, not a dog toy."

His ears wilted, and he took a step back.

I sighed and rubbed my face. "Sorry. I'm not much of a morning person. Besides, a wet nose isn't exactly what I'd call a fantasy wake-up." I scowled at him, then softened my tone. "Suppose you would like to go out?"

His ass rose off the floor, tail already wagging, as he gave me the dog equivalent of a grin.

"Fine." I'd just tied my robe when my cell started ringing. Given that it was the weekend, there was no way it was my alarm, and anyone who knew me knew better than to call before ten. I quickly unplugged the device and checked the caller ID.

<Blackwell Hollow Police Department>

I quickly answered the call and put it on speaker. "Diana Harker," I said as I went to open the front door for my guest. First and best rule to avoid sketchy calls from likely telemarketers: Never say "hello". Not that I thought it could be one, but better safe than a victim of a credit scam.

"Good morning, Miss Harker. This is Detective Takashi. I hope I haven't woken you."

"No, that honor belongs to someone else." I glowered at my furry companion. Then the name registered. I vaguely remembered speaking with a man while medics checked my head. My hand stalled on the knob. Was he calling to say they'd caught the murderer? That Joey Mannis would get his justice?

"Detective, I'm surprised I haven't heard from you sooner. Not that I'm not glad to hear from you," I amended, struggling to regain my composure. The dog seemed poised to bark, but I held up a finger to silence him and he seemed to think better of it. He probably was anxious, as I hadn't actually opened the door. I did so, leaving it open, so I could prop against the jamb and let the cool morning air soothe my suddenly frazzled nerves. "How may I be of assistance?"

He cleared his throat. "I'd like to request your presence at the station."

"Oh. Um... What for?" I asked, a tad put out. That was *not* what I'd been hoping he'd say. He'd had weeks to conduct a followup interview. Why now? What had changed? I let my gaze follow the dark outline of the large dog as he sniffed around the open grass, but didn't actually do anything. He truly had a beautiful coat. It caught the light in the most mesmerizing way.

"Miss Harker?"

I frowned at the sudden tone of impatience. "Yes?"

"I asked if you'd like me to send a car. The sooner we can review your account, the better."

"What if I have plans?" While I didn't, certainly not at the unholy hour of eight on a Saturday morning, the question bore asking. Not the least of which, because it would give me an idea of how serious this impromptu "chat" was.

"Cancel them." His succinct reply made the hair on the back of my neck crawl. "I can have a car at your apartment in twenty."

I didn't like his insistence on sending someone to get me, nor the reminder that he knew where I lived. "I'm perfectly capable of escorting myself. Give me an hour." I ended the call before he could respond, my heart beating double time. I continued to stare at the dark device for a few moments, curious if he'd call immediately back. When the phone remained quiet, I pocketed it and shifted my gaze to my furry guest.

He'd wandered closer to the forest on his quest for apparently the perfect spot to do his business. As if sensing me watching, he lifted his head to meet my gaze. We stayed frozen like that. I couldn't tell if he blinked, but knew I didn't. Then, with the slightest incline of his head, he turned and slipped into the forest without so much as a cracking twig to betray his passing.

I rubbed my arms to quell the sudden bout of goosebumps and did my best to smother the sudden surge of unease. The image of dense forest slowly vanished from sight as I closed the door. He was going home. It was entirely likely that he'd just gotten turned around and frightened in the storm. It wasn't because he really was a wolf. Because there weren't wolves in Blackwell Hollow. And there definitely weren't any werewolves. I'd know.

Wouldn't I?

I took the transit to the nearest stop by the police station. I was tempted to annoy the detective by taking a longer route, but decided it was wiser to be quick. After weeks of scouring the news for any mention of Joey Mannis, it looked like I might finally get some answers. Top of that list was why the hell no one seemed to know about a murder in the middle of campus.

A full body shiver rushed through me as I stepped onto the sidewalk from the bus. I glanced around as casually as I could manage, given the unnerving feeling of being watched. Buildings every bit as old as the ones found on campus lined the main street. Plenty of people were already out tackling their weekend tasks. But none of the stray glances my way held the level of intensity that had the hairs on the back of my neck prickling.

Rather than let on that I was aware of my watcher, I moved with casual purpose toward my destination. People I passed offered either a polite head nod or nothing at all, more intent on their path. Despite my leisurely pace, no amount of stalling could make the microscopic downtown larger.

I walked past a full-sized statue of the town's namesake, Colonel Blackwell, high upon his podium and got a full view of the town police station. Normally, the rustic red brick and artfully crafted sign would have been charming. Except the intense gaze had yet to let up, following every turn I'd made since leaving the transit.

The glass doors edged in steel made a soft whisk as I pushed through. I briefly contemplated telling them that the original iron ornamented doors should have remained on instead of relocated inside behind a glass display case. But that would require explaining the Fae's aversion to iron, not to mention any spirits that might take grievance with the station and choose to linger. Plus there was that whole awkward bit of explaining that all those fairytale creatures were *real* and then some. But that was also a good way to get myself locked up.

I shook my head to clear the ridiculous compulsion. One small murder and suddenly I was back in the life, questioning everything and frustrated with humanity's ignorance of the world. My steps faltered at the unfortunate and downright callus thought. A young man had *died*. And whoever he'd been in life, he didn't deserve that. I'd walked away from my family legacy to escape that kind of thinking, and I had no desire to go back.

The much more inviting, modern doors shut behind me with an ominous suction of air as I met the gaze of the front desk officer. While the room was slightly warmer than outside, I seemed to have brought the chill with me. Mercifully, the feeling of being watched ended at the threshold.

"Hi, I'm Diana Harker. I'm here to see Detective Takashi."

Before the officer even responded, Takashi manifested out of a side room. He was young for a detective, but then, what did I know about how old homicide detectives should be? His dark hair was perfectly styled, without so much as a hair out of place, and his casual suit looked as though it had been pressed... twice. I may have been accustomed to attire that boasted more labels than sense, but it was obvious that Detective Takashi took his job very seriously.

"Miss Harker, perfect. If you'll follow me, we can get started."

I controlled the impulse to remain stubbornly in one place to force him to come back and followed the detective through the station. We approached what appeared to be his desk in the bullpen. Stacks of papers were organized into neatly piled folders perched on every available surface. I reached for the strategically placed chair when Takashi waylaid me.

"Oh no, Miss Harker. We'll be in here." He picked up the top couple of folders, clicked his pen, then led me into what was clearly an interrogation room. The door gave a decisive smack as it shut behind us. I stared at the sterile metal table with its equally utilitarian chair. Was I... a suspect? Suddenly, his insistence on getting me here ASAP made a lot more sense.

"If you'll please have a seat, this shouldn't take long."

I cringed as the chair made a wretched screech against the floor until at last it was far enough out for me to sit. Meanwhile, Takashi settled on the other side. The folders made a soft wisp as they settled on the table, followed by another whisper of air as he opened one to peer at its contents.

"What's this about, Detective?" I asked with cold neutrality, leaning into the lessons that had been pounded into me for as long as I could remember to cover my nerves.

The sharpness of his eyes betrayed the casual way he leaned back in his chair to study the folder he'd opened. "I know we took your official statement already, but I hoped that time to heal would help clear up a few things. Maybe even jog a few things loose?"

Okay. That wasn't so bad. This was just a formal setting to conduct an interview. I wasn't *actually* a suspect. It made sense in a weird way that he'd want to touch base to see if I remembered anything else. "Of course," I said, nodding. "However I can help."

"Excellent. I'd like to start with what led you to believe the victim was shot by an arrow." He pulled up a sheet of paper and perused the one beneath. "Your statement at the scene displayed a remarkable insight to what type of weapon could have been used."

"I mean, I saw it? Or, I'm pretty sure I saw it?" I hated how uncertain I sounded. This wasn't like me. Everything I did was with absolute conviction and purpose. From choosing a university across the country to avoid my family entangling me in their warped sense of legacy to dating or sleeping with whoever I wanted, regardless of gender. I thought things through. But I didn't *waffle*. That the head injury I'd sustained was making me question my memory was equal parts frustrating and irritating.

"Hmm." The detective's noncommittal hum, set my already frayed nerves on edge. "Perhaps it would be better if we did start at the beginning. See if any of your account has changed."

I internally bristled at the implication that I might have been lying originally. A man was dead, for fuck's sake. I took a deep breath and let it out slowly, dutifully reminding myself that this was about the head injury and nothing more.

"Whenever you're ready." He placed a recorder on the table and provided his name, rank, the case number, the date, my name and relevance, then gestured to me.

I straightened and did my best to exude a calm front as I recounted the horrific night. "I was studying with my friends at the library. We parted at about eight in the evening. They'd asked me to join them at a bar, but I declined, citing more homework. Truthfully, I just didn't want to go. Partying has never really been my scene. Guess I should have made an exception, huh?" I smiled weakly, but Takashi's face registered no emotion.

I cleared my throat and looked back down at the shining silver table. My gaze caught on a water bottle I hadn't noticed before. I gestured to it and waited for Takashi to nod before grabbing it and taking a healthy swallow.

"Right, so it was already dark as I made my way across campus. And a weird fog was thickening between the buildings."

"Why not simply drive back to your apartment?" he inter-jected.

I took another drink before responding. "I don't have a car and figured walking in the mist was better than standing around waiting for the transit. Plus, it let me stretch my legs," I added at his dubious expression. "I hadn't gone too far when the fog enveloped nearly everything. I'd completely lost sight of the library when I heard it."

He referenced his notes. "The... howling?"

"Yes." Cold washed over me as I recalled the fear I'd felt at hearing so many cries, the unmistakable sensation of being watched... hunted. "The howls got louder, closer, until it felt like they were all around me. I walked faster thinking maybe it was just the usual fraternity antics, but..." I trailed off. How did I explain the instinct I'd spent years honing beneath the careful, determined tutelage of my family.

He glanced at me, his dark eyes still not betraying anything. "But?"

"It felt dangerous. So, I ran."

"Why not call the police?"

I bit back a huff. Like that wasn't the *first* thing I'd thought of. "I tried, but sometime while I was at the library, my phone died."

"Convenient."

"Actually, I'd say it was about the furthest thing from conve-nient," I snapped, my bated anger pushing through. "Anyway, I recalled from orientation way back when—"

"Three years ago," Takashi supplied with a patronizing smile.

I fought the urge to grind my teeth and took another drink. "I remembered that the university is equipped with police call stands with a button you can press and keep moving to the next one and the next if it's not safe to stay in one place. So,

I went that route and hoped they actually worked like that." My hand shook as I reached for the water again and I opted to clasp them beneath the table. "I got, um, turned around in all the fog. The howling was everywhere. I'd just crashed headlong into a building when I heard an arrow being fired."

"That's unusual, isn't it? My understanding is that an arrow being released is damn near impossible to hear, especially once it's in flight."

"That's true. It's a little easier if you're familiar with the soft sound... and really close to the point of origin." It wasn't until the words left my mouth that it clicked just how close I must have been to the murderer at that moment.

The detective did that irritating hum again and gestured for me to continue.

"I dropped my backpack and started running again. Though by this point I was so turned around I had no idea where I was going, just that I needed to get away. The howling returned even louder. That's when I tripped. When I glanced back to see what I'd fallen over, I saw the naked body of a young man lying face down with an arrow sticking out of his back."

"What else?" he asked, leaning forward.

I shook my head. "That's it. I blacked out. Next thing I remember, some officers and a paramedic were helping me sit up and taking stock of my injuries. Then you showed up."

"What about the body?"

"I think there was a sheet on him already and the officers led me away."

His gaze intensified suddenly. "Do you recall seeing an arrow, then? Either under the sheet or possibly with an officer?"

My eyebrows scrunched inward before I could regain my composure. "You still haven't found the arrow?" This was bad. Like, *really* bad. Maybe I'd hit my head even harder than I'd thought. Maybe there'd never *been* an arrow.

"We found an arrow. I was hoping you could lend us some of your expertise, since you seem so familiar with them." Without preamble, Takashi flicked open the folder still on the table and slid it toward me.

I recoiled in shock, causing my chair to squeal in time with my alarm. "What the hell?" The image within the folder wasn't that of an arrow or, more appropriately, not *just* an arrow. Clipped to one side of the reinforced classification folder was indeed the image of an arrow—specifically a five millimeter carbon composite arrow with an X nock and aluminum insert. It was a common arrow for hunters on account of its durability and precision. It could have literally come from any hunter, myself included, if it weren't for the picture on the opposite side.

The same arrow, identifiable by the custom fletching, protruded from the back of a young woman lying face down in a bed of leaves. She could have been sleeping if it wasn't for the arrow—or the fact that she was stark naked. Only the tiniest trickle of blood and rigidity of her body hinted that the shot had been fatal.

"That's not Joey Mannis," I whispered, lifting my gaze to meet Takashi's.

"No, it's not." We might as well have been two stones facing off for all the emotion either of us showed. "Care to educate me about the arrow, Miss Harker?"

"If you want to know, call a hunter."

"I was under the impression I had." The steel that entered the detective's voice gave me pause. "Now, the arrow. And while you're at it, maybe you could enlighten me as to how you knew the name of our first victim after claiming to never have seen him before."

My family had taught me a lot of things over the years, most of which I abhorred. But never in my life did I think I'd actually need to *use* any of it, least of all how to withstand interrogation. Because now I knew for certain: this wasn't a formality or even a considerate follow up. I was being questioned as a possible suspect. Considering my suddenly precarious position, the best option seemed to be to tell the truth, or a version of it.

I pointed at the image of the arrow and relayed my initial appraisal. "This type of arrow is not only common, it's preferred in many circles. You can literally find it in stock at any hunting goods store or online."

Takashi made a note. "What circles might these be?"

It took an active effort not to let my agitation get the better of me. "Typically deer hunters. Your best bet would be to assess the model type, year of production, and most importantly, who does custom fletchings. While some people can and will do them themselves, it's not cheap and it's incredibly time consuming."

"Spoken like someone with the resources and experience to accomplish such a task."

"Let's get something clear, detective. I have significant knowledge of archery and hunting because it is a family tradition. Think of it like when women were expected to know how to dance, knit, and play piano."

His eyebrow lifted in obvious skepticism. "Your family has some pretty interesting notions about what constitutes an accomplished young woman."

"Can't argue with that. Furthermore, I haven't touched a bow in nearly three years." Since I'd come to Blackwell Hollow, as a matter of fact. "And to answer your earlier question, I know the name Joey Mannis from a fellow student."

"I'd like the name of this student," he said with a click of his pen, ready to jot the name on his notepad.

I narrowed my eyes. "And I'd like to know why his name hasn't been in any of the papers or on the news." I jabbed a finger at the image of the dead girl. "Will you be releasing *her* name? That's two bodies, Detective Takashi, and from where I'm standing, you've been sitting on your hands."

He set his pen down and leveled his gaze at me. "You, Ms. Harker, are dangerously close to catching an obstruction charge."

"And you have better things to do than fill out that paper-work," I said, meeting his glare with one of my own.

"The decision to keep this quiet was at the request of the family, who have suffered enough." He folded his hands on the table. "We're not your enemy here."

My flash of anger receded and I deflated. The family, of course. "I'm sorry. It's been a stressful couple of weeks. When you called this morning, I honestly thought it was to tell me I didn't have to keep looking over my shoulder."

"I understand, Miss Harker." Takashi straightened, snapped the folder shut, then stood. "That'll be all for now. I trust that you'll be as accommodating to any future inquiries." He arched an eyebrow.

I mirrored him and stood. "Of course," I replied, a tad more clipped than I'd intended. The chair gave yet another awful screech as I pushed it forcefully out of my way and turned to go. Should have known I wouldn't be able to open the door.

Takashi rapped on the opaque glass insert of the door and someone outside released us. He held the door open, heed-less of my irritated expression at being so casually dismissed. "Oh, and Miss Harker?"

Every bone in my body wanted to ignore him and keep walking, but logic won out. I was already clearly a person of interest, if not a full-on suspect. The last thing I needed to do was make matters worse. I glanced over my shoulder, working diligently to keep my expression and voice calm. "Yes, detective?"

"I wouldn't count on your family taking care of this for you." His not-so-subtle threat issued, Takashi walked away.

Whatever restraint I was exercising snapped. Fear and anger tumbled together as I stalked out of the precinct. It had never even occurred to me to call my family. Even now, I'd avoid it if at all possible. But if I really was a person of interest... I paused on the sidewalk outside as the fear briefly won out. Maybe I needed to. I was a Harker. We had wealth, status, and most importantly, resources.

No sooner did I hover at the brink of capitulating than I shoved the errant thought away. I didn't need them or the strings those resources came with. I could do this on my own. For all I'd tried to escape the world I'd grown up in, now I'd have to use every skill I'd shunned to clear my name. Starting with finding a murderer. It would seem I'd have had a better chance of outrunning my family legacy by standing still.

3

COFFEE & COMPROMISE

MY "VISIT" WITH THE detective hadn't gone at all the way I'd expected. And how was it that there were now two students dead and there was still nothing in the news? I could sympathize with Joey's parents wanting to keep things quiet; they were undoubtedly going through enough without adding nosey reporters in the mix. But what about the other victim? Did she have a name? Had *her* family been contacted? The way I saw it, privacy or not, two murders warranted informing the rest of the student population, if not the entire town of Blackwell Hollow.

What I couldn't wrap my head around was how the hell *I'd* become a person of interest. Because I knew about arrows? That was ridiculous. I could probably pluck ten students at random and at least a few of them would know the basics of hunting, which included the super common arrow the detective had shown me. Was it because I'd been at the scene of the first murder? That also didn't make any sense. I'd been unconscious when they found me, hardly in a position to shoot anyone. Which I'd never done in my life, fuck you very much. Hell, I hadn't even successfully shot a werewolf, despite my

29

family's best efforts. I shuddered as I recalled the catastrophic trip to Texas. Never again. I glanced around on the off chance the detective was nearby, then ducked between two buildings.

My only real consolation was that he clearly didn't have any actionable evidence. Otherwise, our chat would have been much more... thorough. As it was, I knew better than to leave town, even though he hadn't expressly forbidden it. What I needed was more information. A *lot* more. But it would be a cold day in hell before I called home about *anything* that might be construed as me resuming my duties. So I did the next best thing.

I tapped my foot impatiently while the phone rang. People passing by gave me strange looks, and I shrank away from the main thoroughfare into a side street. Finally, the line picked up. "Hyacinth."

"Well, well. To what do I owe the honor?"

"Are you still planning to go home for Labor Day weekend?" I asked without preamble.

"Yeah. And let me guess, you're not." She snorted her disapproval.

I rolled my eyes. "Look, I know you have... other things you're taking care of while you're there, and I wanted to ask a favor."

"Mmm, a favor, you say?" she purred and I could all but see her smug face. "You know the cost."

I pinched the bridge of my nose. The Van Helsings may not be the mob, but they weren't any better, either. I took a deep breath and let it out slowly. This was still a better alternative than calling my family. "A favor for a favor."

"To be called in at the time of my choosing."

"I know how it works," I snapped. "Now, if you're finished, I have a murder to solve."

Hye's exasperated sigh filled the line. "Just let the local constabulary deal with it." Her callousness rankled. Not so much as a question of who had died or why I needed to solve the murder. Small wonder we'd grown apart over the years despite being raised and trained together. Hell, I'd even had a crush on Hye, once upon a time, but now her heart was as cold as the corpses she hunted.

"Well, I'd be more inclined if I hadn't just become a person of interest."

She snorted. "Like you'd be dumb enough to leave a body where *anyone* could find it."

"Hyacinth!" I hissed a little too loudly, drawing the attention of some students walking by. "This is serious." Why did I think calling her was a good idea again?

"Okay, fine. You want me to take care of it then? Not like you aren't perfectly capable of dealing with them yourself," she added under her breath.

"I do not want you to *handle* it," I gritted through clenched teeth. "Why is it always fucking murder and mayhem with you?"

"Three of my favorite things."

When I realized what she was referring to, I groaned. "Just forget it. I'll figure it out on my own."

"Okay, okay. I'll stop messing around. What do you need me to do?"

I released a relieved sigh. "I need records of any nearby *were* packs that could have migrated to the area and any records of actual wolves you can find."

"Uh, my family doesn't have those kinds of records. Now if you want to know about the branch of Erzebet Bathory's line that settled in Maine, I've got you covered. But I've got shit all for werewolves."

"You don't think I know that?" I was really starting to regret this. "*My* family does."

There was a long silence. "And how do you expect me to get that information?"

"Howeve you have to." I grimaced. Depending on what lengths she had to go through would determine just how "big" the favor I owed her in return would be.

"Consider it done."

The line went dead, and I sagged against the brick at my back. Running a marathon was easier than asking a favor of Hyacinth. After taking a few minutes to settle my nerves after a trying morning, I stepped out of the sidestreet and ran smack into someone.

"Shit. Sorry," I said at the same time a deep voice asked, "Are you okay?"

The strong hand I hadn't realized was steadying me, relaxed.

I glanced at him and barely checked my surprise at seeing Jennifer's cousin. His lithe frame belied the strength he'd used to steady me and I found myself admiring the angles of his face and the way his dark hair swept over his forehead like a raven's wing for a beat too long. I forced myself to blink, giving myself a good mental shake for added measure. This was my friend's cousin, not someone I should be ogling like I'd never seen an attractive man before. And he had a name.

"Alexander," I said aloud the second my brain produced something useful that didn't have to do with wondering if he had a secret six pack to go with those muscular arms.

He smiled, the light shining in his deep brown eyes. "Xander. Please."

I stubbornly fought the urge to return the pleasant smile. Friend's cousin equaled off-limits. Not to mention he looked way too young for me. Which made me a perv on top of everything else. I cringed inwardly and scrambled for something to say. "I'm sorry. I don't remember your last name." *That* was the best I had? It may only be ten in the morning, but today needed to *end*.

"Yeah..." He released my arm to rub the back of his neck and made an abashed expression. "Promise not to laugh? It's pretty ridiculous. Literally no one in my family knows why or where it comes from. Honestly, it's kind of a joke at this point."

The smile I'd been containing escaped at his adorable rambling. "So, what is it?"

He groaned and mumbled, "Wolfsbane."

"Well, that's... different," I finished after an awkward pause. I couldn't help but wonder if he knew that wolfsbane, or monkshood as it was also known, was a poison. Specifically, a poison that had been used to eradicate werewolves back in the day.

He laughed, despite having asked me not to. "That's one way to look at it. Upside, there's not a million other people with the name. Downside, I can never get one of those cute little keychains with your name on it."

I stifled a laugh and grabbed onto the first question to come to mind. "So... what are you doing here?"

He raised an eyebrow. "I go to school here."

"Oh, like the local high school?"

He frowned, and I instantly missed his smile. "Uh no, at BHU."

I snorted a laugh. "Nice try." When his scowl deepened, I realized my error. "Are you even old enough?" I asked incredulously.

"For the record, I'm twenty and plenty of students attend college early." The wry twist of his mouth suggested he got this a lot.

I grimaced, officially feeling like an ass. Forget him not looking a day over seventeen, it was none of my business. Clearly, my conversations had rattled me more than I'd realized. In other news, at least I wasn't a total perv after all. "Sorry. I don't mean to be so rude. It's been a morning. Haven't even had coffee yet."

His expression softened back into a smile, and I mirrored it before I could catch myself. "What do you say we remedy that? My treat. Since I'm technically the one who ran into you."

"Are you... hitting on me?"

He let out a laugh that I fought not to take offense to. "Let's pretend for a second that Jenny *wouldn't* string me up by my tai– toes. What if I am?"

"Then I'd tell you that you're too young for me," I replied. Just because he was an adult and attractive didn't magically make him mature.

His eyebrows shot back up. "That so? And how old are *you*?"

"Twenty-four." At his obvious confusion, I added, "I'm a year behind. It was a hell of a time convincing my parents to let me come here."

He nodded his understanding, though I doubted he did. People who looked as carefree as he did with his youthful energy, raven's wing hair, and sunny disposition never grasped the pressure of familial expectations *or* fighting them. "Well, the coffee is still on the table. No strings, just company. If you're up for it."

I mentally berated myself. Xander was basically a kid and Jennifer's *cousin*. Clearly, my paranoia was bleeding into the more mundane aspects of my life. "Coffee would be great."

We meandered to a nearby coffee shop, placed our orders, and settled into a pair of cushy chairs. I watched with humor as he blew on his steaming cup before taking a sip with exaggerated care.

He glanced at me over the rim. "What?"

I shook my head. "Nothing. So, how long have you been at Blackwell Hollow?"

"This is only my second year. My original plan was to load up my schedule as much as possible, but... some family drama over the summer messed with that."

I set my mocha down and leaned into the cushions. "There's always next term or next year."

"Yeah..." He fiddled with the lip of his cup before taking a sizable swallow, this time without blowing the steam away. "Maybe." Despite the cautious optimism, his demeanor had dimmed.

"What are you studying, anyway?"

Instantly, he brightened. "Government."

"Oh? Are you planning to go into politics? Heads up, I'm taking a poli-sci class with Dr. Roberts and it's *brutal*."

He chuckled. "Yeah, Jenny has mentioned her, and I'm not envious. Though it doesn't look like it'll be avoidable."

I leaned forward to rest my hand on his arm and gave him a serious expression. "My sympathies." He barked out a laugh. When he sobered, he glanced at me and I realized my hand was still on his arm. I withdrew it as subtly as I could, sinking back into my seat.

"What major are you pursuing that you're taking that class?"

"Funny story. You know how every major has these required courses and you can choose from a short list how to meet them?"

His eyebrow climbed into an arch. "Yeah."

"Well, it turns out I don't know how to read."

"How so?"

"I signed up for the wrong class altogether," I deadpanned.

He drained the last of his coffee and set it aside. "That sucks."

"Tell me about it. My five year fast track for a masters in business administration is no longer fast at all. So, I totally get where you're coming from with the school schedule being all messed up. Of course, it probably doesn't help that I keep filling in hours with history classes. At the rate I'm going, I'll have enough credits to double major."

He let out a low whistle. "Damn, Jenny said you were smart, but that's wicked impressive."

I checked my double take. Despite his assurance that Jenny wouldn't condone him hitting on me, he'd still talked to her about me. And he'd somehow gotten me to open up. Granted, just about my classes, but still. I normally kept things much closer to the vest. This kid was entirely too easy to talk with. It was past time to turn this conversation's focus back on him.

"Why history?" he asked before I could do anything.

I squirmed in my seat, my passion for all things history warring with my discomfort at being the center of attention. How did I explain that history was the one part of my training growing up I'd actually enjoyed? Hours spent pouring over text after text and learning the supernatural truth behind major world events had instilled in me a passion to seek more. "I guess you could say I've always been fascinated by it. I'm a total sucker for documentaries and stories based on real historical events. There's so much we can learn from the past. Not that anyone seems all that interested," I added with a grumble that prompted him to laugh.

"Learning from past mistakes seems to be people's kryptonite." His smile glowed in his eyes, then he seemed to realize he was staring. He cleared his throat and leaned back. "You should go for it. Sounds like, at most, you're only a couple of classes away from having the double major anyway, and you're clearly very passionate about it."

I hid behind taking a drink to cover my inexplicable blush. How often had I wished for someone to *see* me, to listen to the things I cared about, and, what's more, support them? I cleared my throat and set my now empty cup aside. "So, government. Are you planning to go into politics?" I asked again, since he hadn't answered earlier.

He squirmed in his seat and dropped his gaze. "Not in the way you'd think."

"And what do I think?" I asked, unable to temper the underlying challenge.

His gaze flicked back up, and he released an awkward laugh. "Okay, I deserved that. Most of the time when I tell people I'm studying government, they assume I'm looking to become a senator or something."

"But you're not."

He shook his head, his smile softening into something more genuine. "I'm more interested in affecting things closer to home."

I blinked, unexpectedly surprised. "Wait, so you *want* to return home after school?"

"Of course," he said with a rich laugh. "We all have our roles to play and mine is there. I take it you don't want to return home?"

I scoffed. "I chose BHU to get *away* from my family. Only way I'm going back is in a tied sack."

Xander chuckled. "Good to know you view kidnapping as a valid form of transportation. But in all seriousness, I'm sorry relations with your family aren't great. Mine may consist of a bunch of busybodies sticking their noses into everything, but I don't know what I'd do without them."

My shoulders tensed while a strange sense of sadness wriggled in my chest. What would it be like to be close to family, to lean on each other for support instead of backup? I mentally shook the unexpected funk off. My family wasn't like others, and wanting that kind of relationship with them would always be a pipe dream. I reached for my empty cup and stood. "I should get going. Those assignments won't write themselves." Not to mention the research into wolf migration and missing persons I needed to delve into.

"Same," Xander said, mirroring me.

I held up the cup in a weird salute. "Thanks for the coffee."

"Anytime." Xander stepped closer, his eyes glittering with a dark hint of a promise that froze me in place as he relieved me of the cup. "And for the record," he said, his voice dropping, "I don't think you're too old for me." In the blink of an eye, his sunny disposition returned, and I felt like a rubber band snapped back into place.

"Dream on, kid."

He gave me a toothy smile, that missed being threatening by the sheer fact that it was also goofy. "Don't mind if I do."

4

Noteworthy Exchange

I GLARED AT MY phone as I reread the latest message from Hyacinth. I should have known better when she'd mentioned she was going back home for another transfusion. Like she would honestly get one and *not* go on a mission. Not that I thought her doing so would prevent her from following through on my favor, but it did mean that I'd have to wait for answers. Waiting had never been my strong suit, at least not when I was perfectly capable of tracking down a few clues in the meantime.

My bag made a satisfying zip as I put away the last of my books, then swung it over my shoulder. A quick scan of the student union revealed a cluster of underclassmen waiting not-so-subtly for me to vacate my table. I gave them a quick nod as I passed by and made my way into the crisp afternoon. Once outside, I debated where to start my impromptu quest.

The gleam of sunlight off the polished dome of a nearby building caught my eye. With a small smirk, I made my way toward the registrar's office. Time to see if my bluffing skills were still intact or if I'd gotten rusty without constant practice. I dipped into a restroom before anyone could spot me. There,

39

I pulled my hair free and finger combed it into what I hoped would pass as "professionally frazzled". Then I snagged the sweater Jennifer had loaned me the other day that I hadn't had time to return. Satisfied with the image of an overworked office aid, I stashed my backpack and slipped into the main lobby of the registrar.

Rule number one of bluffing to get info: act like you belong there.

Rule number two: act like you don't expect resistance.

Rule number three: expect resistance.

I strode with purpose across the waiting area, bypassing the greeting desk to head straight for a young, clearly busy staff member. As I closed the distance to their desk, I scanned for anything that could provide insight and lend credibility to the bullshit story I was about to spin. On the surface, everything seemed bland enough. The folders behind them were neatly organized. Their cup of coffee had a telltale ring of white at the top, betraying it had gone cold hours ago. The desk held the usual amount of clutter, including interestingly enough, an adorable hedgehog that might have been a stress ball. And what did we have here? Did my eyes deceive me or was that a picture of Dean Proctor discreetly tucked by the computer with a dart sticking out of his forehead?

"Georgia Lesande?" I asked, peering at the nameplate perched precariously at the edge of the desk.

The young woman's head flew up at the unexpected greeting. "Um, hello. Can I help you?" she asked, glancing around, undoubtedly for anyone else to fob me off on.

"I sure hope so," I said with a loud sigh. "I'm a new student advisor. One of my kids wants to change his major for the eighth time."

Georgia grimaced, clearly no stranger to this particular struggle.

"Yeah, one of *those*," I responded. "Anyway, we're supposed to have a meeting in about an hour to recalculate whether any of the electives will now count and I still haven't received any of his records." I glanced at the digital clock on the far wall and gave an exaggerated groan. "Forty-five minutes now."

Right on cue, she huffed her agitation at being the one to have to deal with this. "Who did you say you were?"

"Sorry, of course. Rachel Evans." I extended a hand, which she took. "I don't mean to be rude. It's been a heck of a day and I expected to have more than a few minutes to review his information before meeting." Rather than continue to elaborate, I shut my mouth. Too many details would only undermine my fabrication.

"Nice to meet you, Miss Evans," she said with a thin-lipped smile that didn't look remotely sincere. "Are you experiencing difficulties accessing the BHU Admin Burrow portal?"

I just barely didn't roll my eyes. Not because it wasn't an obvious question to ask, but because if I *had* actually been an advisor, it would have been the pinnacle of insult to insinuate I hadn't checked that first. "That's actually why I'm here," I replied with the most sickeningly sweet smile I could muster.

She lost her composure for the tiniest moment before she launched into her next bit to get rid of me. "If you're having technical issues, you need to speak with IT and submit a ticket."

"Oh, you misunderstand me. I'm here, because there's absolutely nothing wrong with my access. Oddly enough, though, I *still* don't have the information I put in for two weeks ago. Weird, right?" She narrowed her light brown eyes, and I feigned giving in. "Look, I'm really not looking to cause some big fuss, but I need *something*. Can you look up at least if I'm listed as his advisor?" I asked as conciliatory as I could.

Georgia stared intently at me for a moment and I could practically see the gears in her head turning as she considered my request. "There have been issues in the past when a student changed colleges." I stifled a cry of triumph and forced my expression to remain passive. "What's the student's name?"

"Joseph Mannis." I leaned forward to rest my forearms on her desk as if relieved, which conveniently put me in excellent proximity to the monitor. Hoping she wouldn't notice, I focused my gaze on my hands.

Georgia clicked around and typed until she finally gave a decisive double click. "I see Jeremy Markham listed as his advisor?"

I dropped my head with an exasperated sound. As I raised it again, I angled forward more and searched the screen for something useful like Joey's address.

"Excuse me," Georgia snapped indignantly as she tilted the screen away. Too bad she was half a second too late.

I straightened the rest of the way and held my hands up in surrender. "Sorry, got a little ahead of myself. At least now I know whose door to go knock on. Hopefully, this glitch will get fixed sooner rather than later. Good luck with the rest of your day," I said and turned to go.

Unlike most of the campus dormitories, 122 Fandell Way looked newly renovated. Its deep red bricks bore no trace of clinging vines or moss, and it wasn't actually *on* campus. And the address looked familiar because it was the same dorm Jennifer lived in. Which officially gave me a backup reason for being here. It also explained why Jennifer knew the victim's name, even though I was *positive* the police hadn't mentioned it at the scene. Especially with how the detective had reacted when I'd let it slip.

DIANA'S ECLIPSE

I strode across the narrow street toward the impressive five story building. As I neared the doors, though, my steps slowed. Despite our close friendship, I'd never actually been inside of Jennifer's dorm, only met her outside or nearby. How the heck was I supposed to find Joey's room or even get inside without a key card? Five floors was a lot of ground to cover, and not all students put their names on their door.

"This should be fun," I mumbled to myself as I stepped aside to wait for an opportunity to grab the door the next time it opened. Fingers crossed it wouldn't be hours. Mercifully, it only took about fifteen minutes before a resident came hurrying out. Luck was with me as there didn't appear to be an RA on duty and I was able to venture all the way inside and make my way to the shared recreation space.

I'd suspected the building had been renovated recently, but the room didn't resemble any I'd ever seen in a dorm. While some lounge chairs and sofas were present, the majority of the space had been structured to resemble a high school cafeteria, complete with the standard table-benches lined up in precise rows. What was more, I didn't spy the kitchen at all. Though there was a set of double doors beyond the line of open-counter displays.

Abruptly, I realized every occupant in the room was staring at me. Infinitely glad I'd opted to forego the dorm experience in favor of a private apartment, I resumed walking like I had every right to be there. I'd made it all of ten steps into the room when a nervous-looking guy with light brown skin and freckles decorating his nose approached me.

"Can I... help you?" he asked falteringly, his eyebrows hanging low in open confusion.

I brightened, projecting my "chipper cheerleader" persona. "Oh my goodness, yes! I tried buzzing at the front and Joey hasn't been answering my messages. Can you help me find him? I lent him my statistics notes and I need them back to study for the exam."

The guy paled, and the rest of the room took on an oppressive hush. "I guess you wouldn't have heard. Joey is... um." He paused to swallow and guilt wormed in my stomach. "Joey passed away."

I widened my eyes in shock and whispered, "What?"

"Joey Mannis died last month. Look, I'm really sorry about your notes. We can take you up to his room and try to help you find them."

I nodded absently. "Yeah, that would be great."

He waved back and a couple of others peeled themselves off of a bench to join us. Okay, kind of weird that I was getting an escort, but at least I'd be able to get into Joey's room. Also weird that all of them were aware of his passing when no one else was. Then again, he did live here.

As a unit, we made our way to the elevator. I paid attention to which floor on the off chance I'd have to come back. We got off on the fourth floor and hooked a right. A few doors down from a small lounge area, we stopped in front of room 437. I waited until they'd unlocked the door, then shrank back.

One of my escorts looked at me worriedly. "Are you okay?"

"Yeah, I just... I still really need my notes, but this is a lot. Can I maybe have a few minutes to..." I made a stuttering breath as if I was fighting back tears.

The small group shared a quick look and the guy that I'd initially interacted with gave a sharp nod. The student that had expressed concern gently guided me back toward the lounge area. "It's been a shock to all of us. Take all the time you need. Can I get you some water?" she asked after helping me sit.

I shook my head, projecting being in a daze. "No thanks. Just... some privacy?" I asked tentatively.

"I understand." She pointed toward the opposite hallway from Joey's room. "We'll be in Room 405 to give you some space. Just knock on the door when you're ready to go in and we'll give you a hand." I returned her smile with a shaky one and thanked all my lucky stars that they really were going to leave me unattended.

I waited until I heard the door closing, then got up to peer into the hallway. Reassured that no one was lingering outside to keep tabs on me, I tiptoed back to Joey's room. I let out a sigh of relief to find the door still open and slipped inside. Unlike Hyacinth, I'd never excelled at picking locks, nor did I keep a kit on hand.

I surveyed the room, not really sure what I was looking for. At first glance, it looked like any other student's dorm room, though it looked to be designed for a single occupant. Near as I could tell, the room hadn't been touched. Which was kind of odd, especially if his family had been notified. Given how much time had passed, I would have thought they'd at least *start* packing up his things. Not that I was complaining. This was my absolute best-case scenario so far.

Painfully aware that I was working on borrowed time, I began my search. There had to be something in here that could explain why Joey Mannis was running around naked on campus or why anyone would've wanted to hurt him. I started at the nightstand, but only found a retainer and a dead phone. From there, I inspected the desk where I learned that Joey Mannis was clearly into art, going by the numerous sketches of night landscapes and running wolves littering the surface. He was even halfway decent. It was a true shame he'd never have a chance to keep refining his craft. A check of the drawers revealed a mess of crumpled papers, most of which looked like receipts from the cashier regarding his tuition.

Curiosity piqued, I flattened one out to see if I could glean some information about his family. To my surprise, the receipt simply stated that his tuition had been paid in full by an undisclosed third party. I frowned at the paper, wasting precious moments to try to make sense of the minimal note. Finally, I conceded defeat and replaced the papers I'd removed. That mystery would have to wait. There was no telling how much "space" my escorts would permit me before coming to check on me.

I moved on to his chest of drawers, where I discovered nothing of interest except for a fleshlight hidden at the back. Increasingly frustrated, I turned back to the bed and laid on the floor to explore beneath. A canvas duffel bag that looked like it had seen better days immediately caught my attention.

"Now we're talking," I mumbled to myself as I pulled it out. I straightened, dusting myself off, and placed the bag on the bed with a thump. "What secrets are *you* hiding?" My fingers were centimeters from the zipper when a voice stopped me cold.

"What do you think you're doing?"

I smothered the reflex to freeze and forced myself to casually turn to face my accuser. To my surprise, I found Xander leaning beside the now open door, arms crossed, face clouded with an interesting mix of irritation and suspicion. "I could ask you the same."

He lifted a dark brow, which only highlighted his confident stance. "*I* live here." Clearly he meant the dorm, as I'd already found irrefutable evidence that this was definitely Joey's room and he wasn't sharing. "I'm only going to ask one more time. What are you doing here?"

No way in hell would he believe I was here to meet Jennifer or even to retrieve some notes. Not after he'd literally caught me red-handed going through Joey's things. All that was left was the truth... Or part of it. "What does it look like? I'm snooping."

His gaze darkened and suddenly I had the strange sensation that I was looking at a predator. I quickly dismissed the observation as ridiculous. A likely byproduct of the fact that he was effectively blocking the only exit. Even if he took it into his head to come at me, he was going to be in for a rude surprise. My fighting skills might be rusty, but I could easily take his lanky ass any day of the week.

"How did you find out where Joey lived?" he asked, his gaze softening slightly.

I gave him a wry smirk. "I'm clever. I take it you live on this floor?" Maybe it was pure coincidence, and he'd heard noise coming from the room as he passed by. Or maybe my little escort had sent him to check on me.

"No." The flat response made the hair on the back of my neck stand on end.

Refusing to give into the sudden impulse to bolt, I squared my shoulders. "What do you want? In case you didn't realize, I'm actually here for a reason and I *don't* need a chaperone." It was pure wishful thinking that the commanding tone would cow him into leaving, but a girl could hope.

His harsh expression morphed into a knowing smirk. "Oh, I realized." He affected a bored attitude as he lifted a hand to inspect his nails. "Wouldn't have anything to do with why you were at the police station the other day, would it?" He flicked his gaze back to me and I released a small gasp at being so effectively speared in place. "Didn't think I'd noticed that, did you?"

Shoving my surprise and flare of insecurity down, I met his penetrating stare. "What of it?"

He pushed away from the door and slowly stalked closer. And *stalking* was exactly what he was doing by the way he moved. "I'll make you a deal. You share what you learned there and I'll let this little transgression go." He smiled menacingly, and his entire attitude rankled.

"I don't see why I should," I replied stiffly.

He let out a soft breath and ceased his movement in favor of perching at the foot of the bed. "Because you're not the only one who wants answers." His shoulders slumped as he studied his clasped hands on his lap. "Joey was family."

"Is everyone here family?" I scoffed without thinking.

He glanced up at me, his eyes shining with sincerity. "Of course."

At a loss for a decent rebuttal, I sat on the bed beside the duffel and filled him in on what I'd learned from Detective Takashi, leaving out the small fact that I was now being treated as a person of interest and it was me, not Takashi, that identified the type of arrow and likely bow that had been used. Part of me kind of hoped that he'd fill in the name of the other victim, much like Jennifer had inadvertently done with Joey, but no such luck.

After a few minutes of tense silence once I'd finished my tale, he nodded his head and stood. "Thank you. I know it wasn't much, but thank you." He took a deep shuddering breath, then looked at me. "You should get going before the rest of the... house returns."

Not sure what to say, I nodded and reached for the duffel beside me.

"Leave the bag."

I hid a wince, stood, and made my way toward the door, which had remained opened for the entirety of our unusual exchange.

"And Diana."

I paused, glancing partially over my shoulder.

"Don't ever come here again without an explicit invitation."

I was tempted to ask how he would know if it was explicit or not, but decided against it and left without a backward glance.

5

SOUNDING BOARD

Irritation dogged my heels all the way back to the apartment. I didn't even contemplate going to my last class of the day or responding to the never-ending stream of messages in the group chat with Millie, Kora, and Hyacinth. All I cared about was getting some space and preferably quiet to review what I'd found and what I hadn't about Joey Mannis.

Once home, I let the information continue to percolate while I showered, changed into relaxed clothes, and made an early dinner of ramen. With an exasperated sigh, I pushed away the half full bowl. Not even the addition of broccoli and some leftover chicken could make it appetizing enough to maintain my attention. I snagged a notebook from my desk and worked on compiling the incongruent information. As I jotted things down, I couldn't help but talk aloud to myself. It was a habit my parents had abhorred, but one I fully indulged in the privacy of my unshared apartment.

"Right, so the registrar's office." I created a rough outline of what I'd learned from the helpful Georgia Lesande. While my primary goal had been to determine where Joey lived, she'd provided so much more.

I tapped the bottom of my lip with the pen as I considered my notes from the brief interaction. "Interesting that Joey has no record of any financial aid." While Blackwell Hollow University didn't have the steepest tuition, it also wasn't what anyone could call cheap. Most students had at least some kind of aid, be it student loans or scholarships. I continued to stare at the page in the vain hope that some kind of insight might fly off and smack me in the face. No such luck.

What I had was a glaring lack of information. And a headache. It was likely said headache that made me sensitive enough to catch the sound of a faint whine. I straightened and willed my breathing to a soft wisp of air so that I might hear better. On the verge of giving up the strain, the sound came again, slight but unmistakable. I tentatively approached the door, on alert for more extreme noises of distress.

I hesitated at the door, not sure if I was up for dealing with whatever trouble might be out there. But what if it was a kid needing help? Children weren't really commonplace at the complex, but that didn't mean there were never any around. Or it could be another lost animal.

"Might as well see what the fuss is about so I can get back to banging my head against the wall with a clear conscience," I grumbled to myself, then promptly reached for the door before I could doubt the wisdom of the action yet again.

A cool breeze brushed the loose tendrils of hair from my face as I took in the twilight bathing the greenery beyond my meager stoop. Then, on cue, there was another delicate whine. I glanced down and scowled.

"You again."

In response, my canine companion from before looked up at me and barked.

"None of that. If you've come for handouts, you're barking up the wrong tree." I crossed my arms to underscore the statement. To which he barked again, louder this time, dark tail fanning behind him in a slow wag. "Hey," I hissed. "Are you trying to get me in trouble? Shut it."

He harrumphed and looked for all the world like he had every intention of barking again. If I had to guess, it would be the loudest one yet.

"Fine. You win. Just no more barking." I stepped to the side and pushed the door further open. He waved his tail more animatedly, then promptly trotted his furry ass inside. I rolled my eyes. "At least you're not covered in mud this time. I'll have you know it took me days to get cleaned up."

He huffed as if he had any clue what I was talking about as I shut the door. When I turned around, I found him sitting primly in the center of the room... staring at me.

"What?" He merely blinked. "If you're attempting to insinuate that I don't have a life, you can stow it. I have one. I'm just a little preoccupied at the moment trying not to get pinned for murder."

He let out what I chose to interpret as a commiserate whine. I might have even believed it too if he hadn't immediately eyed my abandoned ramen.

I snorted and stomped over to the predominantly full bowl, then did a quick inventory of the ingredients. "Hmm, I don't think there's anything in here that could hurt you." I twisted to face him, only to find that he'd vacated his position in the center of the room and was now right behind me. Alarm trickled down my spine. No way I was *that* out of practice to not have heard him make so much as a whisper of sound.

He licked his muzzle and eyed the bowl hopefully. I dismissed the sudden flare of unease. Of course, he'd made noise. I was simply distracted by my murder puzzle, that was all. Still silently berating myself, I set the bowl on the floor.

"Try not to make a mess. And don't think this means every time you choose to show up, I'm feeding you. Despite all evidence to the contrary," I added in a mumble. Like before, he waited until I stepped back from the dish before lowering his head. This time, however, there was no mistaking that he kept me in sight as he ate.

With a sigh, I slid back into my seat. I was still staring at my pathetic collection of notes and massaging my temples when my companion finished eating. Admittedly, I was impressed with how much of a mess he hadn't made, though now he was once again sitting quite close and staring at me with intense brown eyes.

I chuckled as I suddenly realized who those eyes reminded me of. He cocked his head to the side at the unexpected sound and I leaned forward to give him some ear scritches. "You know, you're quite a handsome fella and have impeccable manners. Not at all like that busy body who kicked me out of the dorm. No." I ruffled the fur on his head, causing his ears to flop every which way. The adorable sight made me laugh again. "Well, to be fair, Xander isn't exactly hard on the eyes, but his attitude and poor timing could use a lot of work."

My companion gave a muted woof, and my smile broadened. "I'm glad you agree. But just between you and me, you both have the prettiest brown eyes. Yes, you do." He continued to let me mush his face and scratch around his ears.

The simple companionship helped settle something in me. Growing up amongst hunters hadn't been all that bad. There were some bright spots. The brightest being our dogs. My father hated how I persisted in treating them like pets instead of weapons, but our wolfhounds certainly hadn't minded, nor had they ever wavered on a hunt. Distantly, I wondered if any of them had ever seen a werewolf in the flesh. I certainly hadn't.

With a heavy sigh, I sat back with renewed determination. "Alright, let's try this again from the top." I grabbed a fresh sheet of paper, though I didn't expect to make many notes. "Facts. Joey Mannis was running naked on campus in a dense fog. Actually, scratch that. We don't know if he was naked before I tripped over him. So we have Joey running from... something," I waved a hand in the air, "the distinct sounds of howling. Jury's out on if it was human, synthetic, or legit. The twang of a bow, then a dead, naked Joey with an arrow in his back."

My companion released a small whine.

"Yes, I know. It's truly awful. No one deserves to die like that, and I seriously doubt he deserved to die at all. But the real question of the day is, where did the arrow go? It was definitely there when I tripped over him, but if Takashi is to be believed, it was gone by the time the police showed up." I tapped my lip thoughtfully. "What am I missing?" I shrugged. "I mean, obviously a lot, considering I'd smacked my head hard enough to black out for a few minutes."

I absently rubbed at the back of my head, the memory of that sizable goose egg still fresh in my mind. Then it hit me. "Howling. There was more howling after I tripped over the body. That's why I was backing away and ended up hitting my head." Suddenly, the order of events didn't seem so haphazard. Had the additional howling been a means to get me away from the body so the condemning evidence could be removed? "But if that was the case," I mused aloud, "why not take the body too?" I glanced at my companion. "What do you think?"

He sneezed violently. While it certainly felt like a response, I couldn't make heads or tails of how to interpret it.

"There's something about Joey Mannis that's bothering me. The receipt for his tuition I found. A third party covered it. Not financial aid, not a scholarship or foundation, a third party. How peculiar not to list the details." It wasn't like it never happened. Hell, my family funded scholarships all the time. But they did it through a trust and into a *named* scholarship, even when it was intended to only benefit a single student. "What sort of connection could Joey have that would pay for his education without the harbor of a trust? Maybe he was in the mob."

I let that sit for a moment, then barked out a laugh that startled my furry companion. "Sorry, that shouldn't be as funny as it is. I think all the death and being a damn suspect are getting to me. I left home to get away from this kind of shit not to be embroiled in it."

My fluffy companion tilted his head, as if confused. Which was fair, as I was pretty confused about everything myself. I gave him an absent pat and returned to my notes.

"Okay, moving on to Joey's room. Nothing of note really beyond some impressive wolf sketches. But that could mean anything, including that he just liked wolves. He wouldn't be the first artist." I glanced at my companion, who'd remained resolutely rapt as I continued to talk at him. "But do you know what's most telling?" He tilted his head. "Not one single shred of anything to indicate he was involved with a fraternity. If you ask me, that effectively negates the police's optimistic angle of frat hazing. Even if he was still pledging, he would have at least had Greek letters *somewhere* in his room."

I sat back, rather pleased with myself. "Definitely not a hazing-gone-wrong incident. I just wish I'd been able to get a better look at that duffel bag. I'm sure there was something in there that could've shed light on why he was running around campus in the first place. If only *Xander* hadn't shown up." This time, I was the one to huff. "And why did he? I suppose it's possible my 'escort' told him. But again, why?" I shook my head. "That kid definitely knows more than he's letting on. He did a good job remaining expressionless, but I'd lay good money that he knows the victim Detective Takashi showed me as well. And if I really was a betting woman, the second victim also lived in that dorm."

My companion gave an aggrieved whine, and I nodded.

"You're right, totally sus. And first thing tomorrow, we're getting to the bottom of it. Well, *I* am. I don't know what you do when you leave here. Can't help but notice that you still don't have a collar. So either you're a runaway, playing for handouts, or a miraculously well behaved stray. Or..." I let the thought go. I'd already checked, then checked again. There were no wolves in Blackwell Hollow and there hadn't been for almost a century.

The canine and I were in a bit of a staring contest when my phone rang, shattering the standoff. I blindly groped for the device and answered without looking at the caller ID. The list of people who'd be *calling* me was extremely short and Hyacinth was on it. Hopefully, she'd carved out enough time to do what I asked before traipsing off to go kill something.

"This is Diana."

"Anna?" a distinctly feminine and most definitely *not* Hyacinth voice asked.

I straightened up, incidentally forfeiting the impromptu no-blinking contest. "This is she."

"Thank goodness. For a second there, I thought you'd given me a fake number." A relieved sigh filled the line. "This is Leena. We met a couple of weeks ago at Devon's. I know it's been a bit, but I was wondering if you were still interested in going out?"

My brain finally made the connection and a slow smile spread across my face. Oh I definitely remembered Leena. Long, silky chestnut hair, hazel eyes, a sweet mouth with the perfect Cupid's bow, and thighs to die for. "Hello, Leena," I purred. "I was beginning to think you'd changed your mind." Certainly wouldn't be the first—or the last—time a beautiful woman had too much to drink and decided it was time to explore her bi-curious side. Not that I'd gotten any inkling of wavering from her.

"Yeah, sorry about that," she said. "A series of you've-got-to-be-kidding-me events kind of stole my focus. But now that I'm on the other side of that, I figured I'd reach out and try my luck."

"How about you tell me all about it say… Friday?" Not that I gave any shits about her excuses, but she wasn't the only one who could benefit from a timely diversion. All I could hope was that no one else popped up dead and I ended up in a jail cell before then.

"That sounds great. We could grab dinner at the Cellar then hit up the club across the street."

I winced at her mention of the club. It wasn't so much that I didn't like them as I wasn't a fan of claustrophobic crowds, smoke-filled rooms, tipsy assholes, and all the noise. Okay, I didn't like them, but they *were* good for getting up close and personal with a date. "Excellent. Pick me up at eight? I'll text you my address."

"Looking forward to it."

Feeling rather smug, I ended the call and quickly saved the number so I wouldn't be caught unawares again. I'd scarcely sent a message with my address when my furry companion started whining and dancing from foot to foot.

"What's up with you?"

He whined some more and drifted closer to the door.

"Oh, I see. Now that you've gotten what you came for, you're ready to bounce. Typical," I teased, even as I got up to let him out.

He slipped through the doorway with hardly the scrape of a claw, paused on the porch to look back at me, then melded with the darkness. Without the moon to illuminate the green space, I couldn't really tell which direction his shadowed figure headed, but it seemed safe to say it was back toward the woods abutting the complex.

Feeling lighter than I had all week, I gave myself a good stretch as I wandered back inside. It had been a while since I'd been on a date, but that was certainly something I wasn't ever worried about getting rusty at. I flashed suddenly to the broody image of Xander leaning against the wall, his dark hair fanning sexily over his intense eyes, his arms crossed to reveal subtle, yet clearly defined biceps.

I shuddered and shook off the intrusive thought. Even if Alexander Wolfsbane was hot, he was too young and my friend's cousin. Dating him was out of the question. However, I was not above using my own wiles to get information out of him. I'd seen the heated way he'd looked at me—even thinking about it now had goosebumps prickling my flesh. I also was positive he knew a hell of a lot more than he'd let on.

6

—◆○◆—

UNEXPECTED ALLY

WHAT WAS A NON-SUSPICIOUS way to ask my friend about her cousin? More specifically, where I could find him. While I pondered over a plan of attack, Jennifer filled me in on the latest drama plaguing her group project.

"I really don't understand why no one wants to be responsible for the minutes. It's literally the *easiest* part and I can't even write fast." She threw her hands up in the air, causing the sweater I'd returned to slide from the bench onto the bricked path.

"Couldn't you just record your group meetings and then transcribe them later?" I offered as I retrieved the thin material from the ground.

She shot me a look, her disgruntlement obliterated by a dazzling smile. "That right there is why we're friends. I mean, it's such an *obvious* solution. Not to mention, I could always put the recording through a dictation app."

I gave her a shrewd look after catching a hint of deviousness in her tone. "Wait, did you *dupe* your classmates by emphasizing the tedium of having to keep the minutes, then acted like some kind of martyr by taking on the undesirable task?"

61

"You make it sound like I had to do anything. They did that shit all on their own." A beat went by, then she threw her head back with an infectious and decidedly wicked cackle.

"What's got you two rolling?" Xander asked, intruding on our moment.

I finished wiping the tears off my cheeks from my fit of laughter. As I blinked the world back into focus, I had to smother a groan. How was it possible for him to look even better than he had yesterday? And while his suspicious, broody face was sexy as hell, his bright smile was a showstopper. It paired beautifully with his dark hair that shone with a unique iridescence. Shit, I needed to get laid. The last thing I needed was to lust after my friend's definitely-too-young-for-me cousin. Mentally shaking myself, I turned to face Jennifer.

She snorted. "Just sharing how I tricked my group into giving me the easiest job of the assignment."

Xander smirked at her. "You're too clever by half." His gaze slid to me. "I suspect your friend is as well." I was busy channeling innocent bystander vibes as I met Xander's unerring gaze and nearly jumped out of my skin when Jennifer turned to me.

"Oh! I nearly forgot. One of my housemates mentioned you'd come by the dorm. I didn't realize you had a class with Joey."

Shit, shit, *shit*. Why hadn't I thought of a plausible explanation for *Jennifer*? I fought the impulse to look at Xander. He knew damn well that I hadn't been there to collect my non-existent notes. Would he rat me out?

"Speaking of the dorm, I nearly forgot why I tracked you down," Xander interjected before I could go into a full on panic.

Jennifer shifted to look back at him. "Oh? You mean you're not just here to ogle my friend?" She raised an eyebrow at him and he made a face.

"Ha ha. No, I thought you might want to know that Noah is at the house."

"He's what?" I marveled at the way Jennifer's cheeks turned a dark pink while the rest of her face seemed to lose all color. "Please tell me you're pulling my tai- leg."

Xander shook his head. "Nope. Last I saw, Melanie was keeping him company and offering to show him around campus."

"Like hell she is," Jennifer growled. She shoved the sweater into her backpack. "Nosy bitch about to find out..."

"You, uh, gonna be okay?" I asked tentatively. This was a side of my friend I hadn't seen before. Normally, she was sweeter than sweet with the patience of a saint, albeit with a devilish mind.

She looked up from stuffing her bag. "Huh? Oh, yeah. Totally fine. Sorry, I'll have to catch up with you later." She shot Xander a narrow-eyed look. "*You* behave. Now, if you'll excuse me." Without further ado, she shot off the bench and across the quad like her ass was on fire, or more like she was about to set someone's ass on fire. I couldn't help but wonder if it would be Melanie's or this mysterious Noah's.

"You're welcome, by the way."

I returned my attention to Xander. "For what?"

He continued to stare after where Jennifer had disappeared, until he eventually shoved his hands in his pockets, shrugged, and looked at me. "For saving you from having to lie about being at the dorm yesterday."

"You didn't tell her." Not a question.

His eyebrows lifted. "Should I have?"

I didn't really have a response for that, so I didn't bother. "Is there really someone at the dorm? Or were you just wanting to corner me again? Maybe throw around some extra accusations?" I crossed my arms and scowled at him.

He at least had the decency to wince. "Noah really is at the dorm. Though I feel a little guilty about the wrath I might have just unleashed on poor Melanie. But, I, uh…" He rubbed the back of his neck, looking as awkward as he had the first time I'd met him, and took Jennifer's now vacated seat. "I did want to talk to you."

It was my turn to quirk an eyebrow. "Oh?"

"Yeah." He dropped his hand and looked at me sheepishly, causing his hair to drift over his penetrating brown eyes. I schooled the rogue impulse to brush it back and waited. "Starting with an apology. I was maybe a little harsh the other day. We've all just been on edge since Joey." He paused for a long minute, then added with a heavy sigh, "And Katie."

"Katie?" I asked as neutrally as I could manage.

He leaned back against the bench. "Don't pretend. We both know the only reason you told me as much as you did about your interaction with the detective was because you suspected I knew the victim."

"So she does—did—live at Luxom hall." Again, not a question.

He nodded again. "It's been… hard." Xander leaned forward to rest his elbows on his knees and scrubbed at his face. "The whole house is freaking out and they're looking to me for answers."

I frowned at the stress-filled statement. "Why you?"

His shoulders stiffened while his mouth opened and closed a few times without emitting any noise. Finally, he answered. "I guess you could say I'm kind of the RA." Well, that was dubious.

"I take it your dorm is a pretty tight community?"

He huffed a short laugh. "Understatement of the century." He leaned back once more and slowly turned his head to face me. "They, uh, also don't really trust cops."

"Can't say I blame them, given the fine display of competence I've witnessed so far," I said dryly. Like seriously, how do you misplace a fucking *arrow*? And trying to pin the murder on the poor girl that hit her head and blacked out? Not cool.

Much like Jennifer had earlier, Xander threw his head back and laughed. I stole the opportunity to admire the way the muscles in his neck flexed, their definition drifting past his collar to what his shirt suggested was an equally remarkable chest. The moment he lifted his head, I snatched my gaze away and ducked my head to hide the sudden flare of heat infusing my face. Fuck, was it Friday yet? I never acted like this, but I couldn't seem to keep my eyes to myself. At least my hands were behaving. For now.

I cleared my throat. "Was that the only reason you wanted to talk to me, to apologize?"

"It probably should be, but no." He rubbed the side of his nose as if he wasn't sure how what he was about to say would be received. "You clearly have an invested interest in getting to the bottom of this, and so do I. Maybe we could... work together?"

"What makes you think I need your help?" I quipped with a smirk. To be fair, I most definitely did, and maybe it would have been wiser to lean into that, but no way was I about to make this guy think I *needed* him.

Xander took his time standing up, then looked down at me. "You mean besides the fact that you snuck into my dorm and I know the victims?"

"From where I'm sitting, that makes you more of a suspect than me. Maybe instead of partnering up with you, I should call Detective Takashi and point him in your direction."

He shrugged nonchalantly, like I hadn't just implicated him in not one, but two murders. "You could, but then I wouldn't be all that motivated to show you the second crime scene."

I lurched forward, nearly careening into him in my haste to vacate the bench. "You know where Katie was killed?" So much for my projection of cool indifference. His subsequent smirk said he knew exactly what I'd been aiming for and that he'd totally caught me out.

"If I do?" he asked, the undertone of teasing unmistakable.

"Then I guess you have a partner in crime. Well, crime-solving." I held out my hand to shake on it. He stared at the appendage for an uncomfortable amount of time, until I was positive he wouldn't take it. At last, his fingers wrapped around mine and the jolt of heat that went through me had nothing to do with the warmth of his palm against mine. I attempted to quickly remove my hand, only to have him tighten his grip. My gaze flicked up to his face in time to catch the flare of his nostrils and his searching gaze, then he released me.

"Come on. Unless you can see in the dark, we better get a move on, otherwise it'll be too late to see anything."

I surreptitiously wiped my unexpectedly sweaty palm on my pants. "Where exactly are we going?"

He took off toward the campus transit system and I had to scramble to catch up. "You know the forest on the west end of campus?" he asked over his shoulder.

Of course I knew it. That forest butted up against my complex. Not that I was going to tell him that. "I know of it."

"Good. We're not going to that one."

Was he... fucking with me? Had Jennifer told him where I lived? He tossed me a wry smirk and winked when I missed a step. Oh, he was so going to pay for that.

Two transit stops and a three-mile hike through the woods later, my patience was wearing thin.

"Nearly there," Xander said from several paces ahead.

"That's what you said twenty minutes ago," I grumbled under my breath, though judging by his subdued laughter, it wasn't as quiet as I thought. Not that I was a stranger to wandering around aimlessly through trees or even averse to being in the forest. What I didn't like was not knowing where we were going or the fact that I'd let this scamp lure me off on my own with a vague promise of answers. I was better than this.

Xander paused to give me a chance to catch up. I wasn't exactly slow, but he walked between trunks and around exposed roots like he'd been born here. Add to that the fact that I was intentionally holding back—no need to let on just how competent I was out here—and my irritation was reaching critical levels.

"I swear if you're leading me on a fool's errand..." I let the threat hang, using my glare to add weight.

His laughter echoed through the trees, startling some birds. "Cross my heart, Diana, I'll get you to grandmother's house."

"Really?"

He shrugged, still grinning. "You're the one wearing the fancy red cloak. You're kind of asking for it."

I closed the last of the distance between us and crossed my arms. "And I suppose that makes you the big bad wolf?"

"Only if you ask real nice," he replied with a toothy grin.

"Still too young," I countered, rolling my eyes. "And why do you keep calling me Diana?"

He resumed his trek, this time intentionally keeping us side by side. "It's your name, isn't it?"

"Yeah, but no one calls me that. Everyone calls me Anna." Except for my family, but they were an imperious lot as it was.

"I'm not everyone." He glanced at me with a look I couldn't quite decipher. "Besides, why would you go by something as average as Anna when you're literally named for a goddess? Sounds like disrespect to me."

"It's just a name." I didn't realize how morose that had come out until he abruptly pulled to a halt.

"Except it's not. Diana is the goddess of the hunt, of wild animals, and the moon. Where I come from that means something."

"And where is that, exactly?"

If I hadn't been looking right at him, I might have missed the way his shoulders tensed and how he shook it off. "West of here."

"But still North Carolina?" I pressed.

After a tense moment, he ground out, "Yes." I'd heard people eat rocks that had less gravel in their voice... or reluctance. He took another few brusque paces, then pushed through a thick shrub. "We're here."

I followed, hot on his heels, and emerged at the edge of the forest. Nearly flat ground spread out before us for at least a couple of acres without so much as a tall weed to break the serene landscape. I glanced around, but aside from the abrupt end of the tree line, there was nothing remarkable about the area. It certainly didn't resemble a crime scene.

"And what exactly am I looking at?" I asked when he continued to stare at the blanket of leaves before him.

Without looking away, he gestured toward a spot about a yard from where we'd emerged. "That's where she broke through." Then he nodded toward the ground he'd been studying. "This is where she fell."

I squinted first at one spot, then the other. "How do you know that?"

He took a deep breath and looked up. The well of sorrow in his eyes was both unexpected and heartbreaking. "When I came here last, there was blood on the leaves and a bare spot where the body laid." He turned to go back toward where he'd indicated she'd broken through the foliage. "I want you to see something."

I spared a final glance at the spot that absolutely aligned with the image Detective Takashi had shown me and moved to follow Xander. He carefully made his way back through the brush, somehow managing not to disturb so much as a leaf. As I got closer, I could make out the small broken branches that affirmed his assertion. Once I was beside him again, he gestured at the trunk of a tree.

"What do you make of that?"

I inched closer until I could make out a hole puncturing the bark and sturdy wood beneath. The impact had shattered pieces of the bark and I could clearly see them scattered at the base. Using a fingernail, I pried off some of the bark still clinging on around the hole to reveal a familiar shape.

I released a slow whistle. "Whoever did this wasn't fucking around. The force behind this shot is incredible. Judging by the height, I'd say they were aiming for her heart."

Xander shook his head. "Katie was only five-four."

My eyes widened as I took in the mark again. "Her head? Shit."

"Precisely. What I want to know is what kind of weapon could leave a hole that deep without any other trace?"

"I mean, a rifle would fit the bill."

He shook his head again. "Wasn't a gun."

I snorted. While *I* knew that, how could he? "What makes you so sure?"

"No casings and no gunpowder."

I was tempted to ask how the hell he expected to find either out here, but that wouldn't lead me to any of the answers I needed. He'd done his show and tell. Now it was my turn. I scooted closer to the trail and pointed at the edges of the hole. "You see here?"

He leaned in close to examine the spot. "What about it?"

"This diamond shape is typical for an arrow. Given the overall size of it, I'd say it was shot by a compound bow from..." I glanced deeper into the woods, squinting to gauge a clear line of sight. "From as far as eight hundred feet. Could be farther, but I doubt it given how shallow the hole is."

Xander made a choked sound. "*That's* shallow? And isn't that kind of... far?"

I gave him a considering look and didn't bother to sugar-coat it. "An arrow shot by a competent archer with a decent compound bow can go up to a thousand feet with accuracy, sometimes farther. Considering they went for a headshot, I'd definitely qualify them as competent. As for the depth, the hole is slightly misleading, because a good portion of the damage to the trunk was done when the arrow was removed. Which means while they got lucky with their follow-up shot, they didn't shoot from close range, and line of sight gives them a clear shot at—"

"Eight hundred feet," he filled in, his shoulders sagging. "But why not closer? They clearly came this far if they removed the arrow."

"If they'd fired from even as close as ninety to a hundred-twenty feet, the arrow would have passed completely through the body. And from the image Detective Takashi showed me, the arrow was still in her when she was found.

My guess is the hunter got interrupted before they could retrieve the second arrow." I'd also hazard to guess the girl had been quick on her feet and shifted direction with admirable aplomb, given the positioning of the missed shot. Doubly impressive, given the arrow would have been damn near silent and the bow too far to make out the thrum of the released string.

"Katie," Xander growled, his jaw tight and his fists clenched. "She wasn't some *body*, her name was Katie. She had friends and family. People who mourn her."

Fuck,I hated my family and what channeling their lessons turned me into. A girl was dead. Had died a few feet from where I was standing. "You're right. I'm sorry. I get in my head sometimes and things feel more like an abstract puzzle to be solved than reality. Do you know why she was out here?" I asked tentatively.

All of his anger withered. "She was meeting her girlfriend."

"Secret rendezvous?"

"No. Nothing that sordid. They just..." He shrugged, looking morose, and finished quietly, "liked to come out here."

"Did her girlfriend see anything?"

"No. They got separated. Cindy made it back to the dorm, but Katie didn't. By the time we made it here, the cops had already come and gone." He slumped against a tree—not the one with the hole—and stared up at the overlapping canopy.

I bit my tongue to prevent myself from pointing out with yet more insensitivity that what he described sounded like a classic hunting practice. Divide and kill. Panic made prey reckless. I glanced at the tree again and the narrow hole she'd punched going through the underbrush. So close to freedom, only to have it ripped away.

"Sorry, it's been..." He rubbed his hands over his face. "A lot." Even in the dappled light, it was easy to see the dark, haunted cast to his eyes, the downward pull of his mouth, the weariness etched into his defined shoulders. For as young as he was, he looked infinitely older.

I started walking back the way we'd come. Maybe if I was lucky and kept a sharp eye, I could glimpse something that could provide a clue as to our mystery shooter. Xander joined me, and I waited a few paces before asking my next question.

"Do you know why Joey was running around on campus?"

He missed a step and winced. "It was my fault. We were... we were in a group. Playing around, having a good time." His lips twitched in an almost smile. "Not even the rain could put us out. Then the fog came, thickening until we couldn't tell which way was what. Before we knew it, we'd been herded onto the campus." His fists tightened at his sides. "It was my responsibility to keep him safe. I was so worried about corralling the others, that by the time I realized he was missing, it was too late."

That didn't explain why he was naked, but it did highlight why Xander was so invested in finding answers outside of the police. However, it also raised a shit ton of more questions. Like where had they started? How had they been herded? What about the howling? What had they been doing in the first place? Rather than press for any of those answers though, I opted to bide my time. If we really were going to work together on this, there'd be other opportunities. Right now, Xander was clearly dealing with a lot of darkness. While I'd been accused of being insensitive on more than one occasion, I wasn't actually a heartless asshole.

7

DATING 101

Worst date *ever*. Thank fuck Leena was pretty, because thoughtful, she was not. I should have known when she showed up nearly an hour late after texting to say she was running ten minutes behind that the evening was going nowhere fast. Maybe if I hadn't been so desperate to get my mind off of murder, I'd have had the wherewithal to call it at the beginning. Instead, I'd let Leena take me to dinner, where I'd ended up paying... for both of us.

Not that I had anything against buying my date a meal or taking care of the cover at the club—which I'd also done—or even plying them with drinks all night. But a conversation would have been nice, even offering to go Dutch or get it next time, anything but the blanket assumption. Not to mention some general awareness, like realizing that while you pounded back your fifth martini, I'd yet to have more than one. Clearly, I'd be driving us back to the apartment, then likely escorting her drunk ass to the transit, because I definitely didn't need that nonsense on my conscience along with everything else.

By the time I stomped up to my apartment door, I was in a dour mood and ready to lose Leena's number in a very real way. But first, I had to lose Leena, who had been stuck to me like Velcro since her third drink at the club. Admittedly, having her perky breasts pressed against me as we danced had been quite nice, almost nice enough to let me relax and go with the flow. She was an excellent dancer and knew exactly how to utilize her curves to drive a partner to distraction. Shame she hadn't stopped at the three drinks.

Sighing to myself, I dug out my keys, but intentionally didn't open the door. Much as I'd been looking forward to exploring beneath Leena's flirty mini dress, I wasn't in the mood anymore, and there was no way I was letting her misconstrue an open door as an invitation to come inside. I rested my back against the wall by the door, prepared to give my goodbyes and let her know the transit would be here in a few minutes.

"Tonight was fun," she said, dropping her voice into a sultry purr as she walked her fingers up my sternum.

I attempted a smile, but it felt like a grimace. "It was something, alright."

She smiled brightly, briefly reminding me why I'd given her my number. "I'm glad you agree."

Except, I really hadn't. I cleared my throat, but didn't get any words out to the contrary before her dancing fingers made it to my cheek. Her other hand skated along my side, bunching my top enough that she could slide a finger along the exposed skin. I sucked in a sharp breath, which she unfortunately mistook for the very invitation I'd been trying to avoid.

"Damn, you're hot. I don't know if I've ever been with a girl as fit as you." Her wicked smile said she had plenty of thoughts on how best to take advantage of my fitness. And for a horrifically traitorous moment, I leaned in.

"Is that so?" I arched an eyebrow in challenge. It wasn't that I believed she could really change my mind, but I was willing to give her one last chance. My eyes fluttered closed as she leaned forward to press her lips against mine. They were soft and plush and not even remotely timid. All the things I'd hoped for this evening. Against my better judgment, when she teased the seam of my lips with her tongue, I opened. Mistake five hundred and forty-seven of this godforsaken night.

She all but rammed her tongue down my throat as she pressed me into the wall. When I tried to pull back, she gripped my side more firmly and curved her other hand around the back of my neck to hold me in place as she continued to dominate my mouth in the worst way possible.

Finally, I got a hand between us and pushed her away all of a few inches. "I think that's enough of that."

She gave me a faux pout that instantly dropped her attractiveness to a negative twenty. "Aw, am I going too fast for you? I didn't take you as the shy type."

"I'm really not."

Lust flared in her eyes, and she closed the distance once more. This time, I pushed her away less gently. "Come on, don't be like that. No one likes a tease," she said, still using that obnoxious purr. And I was officially done.

"I think you and I had two very different evenings. You're very pretty, Leena." She visibly preened, and I fought not to roll my eyes. "But I have no interest in sleeping with you."

"Ah, I see. You're a second/third date kind of girl. That's okay, we can still make out. You have an *amazing* mouth." She grinned and used her hold on my side to close the distance again.

I glared at her and pushed away her hand on my side. "You're not hearing me. I'm. Not. Interested. Not in sex, not in making out, not in inviting you inside for a cup of tea and a cuddle. And further, I'm not a girl, I'm a grown-ass woman."

Her hand still on my neck tightened in response to my forceful declaration. It could have been a subconscious reflex or it could have been on purpose. Either way, I was done giving her the benefit of the doubt.

"I'd like you to remove your hand now."

Her mouth fell open in blatant disbelief. "What's the deal? We were having a good time."

"Again, you and I have very different perceptions about how this evening went. Now, you can either remove your hand or I can break it. Your choice."

"Are you fucking for real?" she scoffed, her sultry façade burned away by anger. This time there was no mistaking the intentionality of her tightened grip.

I was about to warn her she had three seconds to release me when a deep growl rolled out of the bushes to my right. She squeaked and scooted closer. As if on cue, a large canine stepped out of the bushes just enough so the porch light could glisten off its alarmingly sharp teeth.

"You didn't tell me you had a dog! Tell that thing to cut it out!" Leena once again drew from her infinite well of stupidity and inched closer.

My furry companion—which I was now fully convinced was at least some kind of wolf-hybrid—dropped his menacing growl another octave. If it weren't for Leena's damn hand still on my neck, the hairs would undoubtedly be standing on end.

"Call your fucking dog off!" she screeched.

"Yeah..." I drawled. "Not my dog, and honestly, I wouldn't test him. There's really no telling what he'll do." I met her panicked gaze with a steely one. "You should probably take your hands off of me."

She immediately snatched her hands back, curling them against her chest, and I finally felt like I could breathe again. "Please make him go. I'm sorry I got carried away. Vodka makes me do stupid shit."

I refrained from pointing out that only one of her five drinks had contained vodka. Taking a chance, I dropped my hand to my side in what I hoped my fluffy friend took as a placating gesture. While his terrifying growl lightened, it didn't disappear altogether, nor did he stop baring his teeth.

Leena whimpered, effectively putting the last nail in her coffin. If the evening hadn't been such a disaster, I could have fucked her, if not tonight, another time. But I didn't *date* prey. Ever. Some family lessons never died.

My phone buzzed with the alarm I'd set. "You'd better hurry or you'll miss the transit."

She flicked her frantic gaze back to me. "The transit?"

"Well, you certainly can't drive. The stop is in front of the main office." This time I didn't bother holding back my eye roll. She gave the canine a wary glance, though he'd finally stopped growling. "Go on. He won't follow you."

He flashed his teeth in what might have been intended to be an innocuous smile, and I had to choke back a snort of laughter.

Leena did not find it in the least bit amusing. She took a wary step backward, then another, then she turned and bolted without so much as a "thanks" or "goodnight".

I shook my head and looked down at my furry companion. "Don't they know you never run?"

He sneezed in what I took as a scathing agreement.

"Right, so tonight has been a total clusterfuck." I slipped the key into the lock and opened the door. "What do you say to some tea and a cuddle?"

He stepped further out of the bushes to reveal a wagging tail, his tongue lolling out in a canine grin.

"Well, what are you waiting for? In you go." I gestured inside and couldn't help but chuckle to myself as he pranced past me. It wasn't quite the evening I'd had planned—not by a long shot—but all in all, a nice cup of tea, a fluffy cuddle-buddy, and some mind-numbing television wasn't a bad way to end the week.

I wasted no time changing into comfortable pajamas, then set about making a nice cup of chamomile tea. The moment the kettle whistled, I removed it from the burner and poured the scalding water into the cup. I was still staring into the depths of swirling steam when a sharp yip made me jump. I glanced over my shoulder to find my unlikely friend eying me. It was probably my imagination that it looked like concern.

"You know, I'm not entirely sure if dogs can have chamomile."

He blew harshly out his nose to tell me what he thought about that.

I gave a wry chuckle. "Fair enough. My friend Hyacinth says it's nothing more than dirty water, anyway. I'll fix you a small bowl and you can determine the truth of that for yourself." I pulled down a wide bowl that I typically used for pasta and made him his own dish of chamomile. On a whim, I even added an ice cube to help cool it down so he wouldn't inadvertently burn himself.

Cup in hand, I curled up on the couch and switched on the television. I flipped through several channels, dismissing them almost as fast as they loaded. In the background, my companion lapped at the bowl. I was still mindlessly flipping when he hopped up beside me. He spun in a circle that threatened to topple him off the couch before collapsing half on top of me with an exaggerated huff.

I grunted at the sudden weight. "Damn you're heavy. Don't suppose you have any preference about what we watch?" I flipped through a few more channels, then settled on a rerun of an old sitcom. With any luck, the station was running a marathon.

Time passed filled with horrible puns and a predictable laugh track. The tea steadily cooled to a bearable sipping temperature and the last of my adrenaline drained away. Finally, I set my empty cup down and glanced at where my companion had made himself comfortable. My hand hovered over his massive head. Given all he'd let me do so far, there was no reason to suspect he'd find head pets unacceptable.

I slowly brought my hand down. When he didn't so much as twitch an ear, I stroked back, reveling in just how soft his fur was. I released a deep sigh, and he angled his head to look at me. "Don't mind me. I'm just in a funk... and disappointed." I dropped my head to rest on the back of the couch. "My distraction from murder didn't exactly go as planned. What really gets me is how poorly I misjudged her character, though I suppose she could just be a phenomenal actress." I snorted. *Unlikely*. Far more likely that I'd missed the obvious red flags, because I couldn't be bothered to look closer.

I continued to stroke my companion's head and side while he gazed at me with what I chose to see as rapt attention. Once again, I was struck by how beautiful his eyes were and how similar they were to Jennifer's cousin's. "Xander never would have pulled that stunt at the door."

My hand froze mid-stroke as I registered what I'd said. Where had *that* come from? I shook my head. Intriguing as I found him, he was still too young, too... naïve. But then, who could I ever hope to find, to share my life with, that could understand the horrors of this world? Better to take comfort when and where I could without the expectation of permanence. Like this moment. I snuggled my companion into me and he made a contented sound in his throat that I agreed with whole-heartedly.

"Thank you for being here," I whispered into his ruff. "Even though I totally could have taken care of myself."

He grumbled noisily, as if arguing. I chuckled and squeezed him tighter.

"Just take the compliment."

8

Three's a Pattern

I DON'T KNOW WHAT possessed me to return to the crime scene Xander had taken me to, yet here I was, looking for clues long since reclaimed by nature. My scowl deepened as yet another low-hanging branch whipped across my face. Honestly, what was I even looking for? What could I possibly hope to find?

Leaves slid beneath my boots as I made my way deeper into the forest. With each step, I scanned for something, anything, that could provide guidance. If Katie and her partner had been coming here regularly, there would be signs, right? But if there were, I wasn't finding them. Even the broken twigs I found were at a height more befitting an animal than a human. So no help there.

Finally, I reached the area where I suspected the assailant had been when they loosed their fatal shot. I did a quick circuit of the borderline nonexistent clearing without success. Not that I really expected any. However, while the space to stand, and even draw a bow, was limited, it had a perfect, unobstructed sightline to the bushes Katie had pushed through. I took a stance where I considered it to be the optimal location and went through the motions. As I drew back my imaginary bow, I attempted to map the path Katie had taken. She was quick. And from the initial missed shot, smart enough to zigzag rather than run in a straight line. Which told me two very disturbing truths: Katie knew she was being hunted, and she knew how to avoid a hunter. Albeit, not so successfully, in this instance.

I dropped my arms and shook my head. "What were you really doing out here?" Unsurprisingly, the trees offered no insight. More frustrated than ever, I debated turning back. If there had been anything to find, it had either been removed already by the hunter or possibly the police, or washed away with the rain showers that kept popping up. Except I'd already come this far. Might as well go the rest of the way.

I plodded along, silently smug at just how quiet my footfalls were. Clearly, I hadn't lost *all* my training. And it was thanks to that very training that I caught the sound of voices before I walked into their owners crouched on the other side of some clustered trees. I scanned the area for a way to get closer without being spotted, slowly inching my way forward, painfully aware of how exposed I was. Damn trees with their pencil thin trunks weren't doing me any favors. What I needed was a way to get higher. While I searched for a way to accomplish that, I strained to hear what the voices were talking about.

"Grids are great and all, but the fuck does the detective expect us to find? It's been two weeks. No way there's anything here." The masculine voice didn't sound familiar, but labeled both people as officers.

A more feminine voice responded with an equal edge of irritation. "The only reason we're back out here is because of the new body they found."

"Fuck. Blackwell Hollow used to be such a quiet place."

A scoff. "Would have thought you'd be glad to be seeing some action."

An indistinct chuckle. "The only reason my wife agreed to me joining the force was precisely for the *lack* of action around here. Now we have three dead kids. *Kids*. It's not right."

I gasped slightly at hearing this latest revelation. Not two bodies anymore. Three, now. And I'd bet good money that they all shared the same fatal wound.

"Did you hear that?" the feminine voice asked.

"Probably some critters."

I silently cursed and glanced around more frantically. Unfortunately, all that was around were trees, trees, and... more trees. Which might not have been so bad if their lowest hanging branches also hadn't been a good fifteen feet off the ground.

A heavy sigh had me all but racing toward an uprooted tree leaning precariously against two others. "We should check it out, just the same."

I didn't pause to wonder if the felled tree could support my weight. My only consolation was that it still sported greenery higher up. I sent up a silent prayer that it wouldn't make too much noise and that I wouldn't fall through and break a leg. I might be unofficially a person of interest now, but I'd be formally suspect number one if I got caught canvasing the second crime scene.

A twig snapped close by. Too close. Scarcely daring to breathe and calling myself all kinds of insane, I scurried up the trunk, all but leaping to reach a limb that was only a mere *ten* feet off the ground. I bit back a hiss as my hands scraped the bark and hauled myself higher, already reaching for the next limb. By the time the officers stepped into the space I'd been occupying, I was easily twenty feet up and hopefully obscured by the foliage between us. Also didn't hurt that they weren't likely to look up—people never did, not in horror movies, not in reality.

Sure enough, the officers—a man of average height and an exceptionally tall woman—never lifted their gaze from eye level.

"Probably just a squirrel," the man said.

The woman sighed heavily. "Whatever it was, I'm taking that as our cue to meet up with the rest of the squad at the Medlin Aquatics Center. Fingers crossed they've already ditched the campus police. If you ask me, they need to do a serious purge of their ranks. Two of the murders happened directly on the campus—one out in the open and one inside a supposedly locked building. Clearly, they're more ornamental than useful."

"That's a tad harsh, Ridgeton," the man said with a scowl. "That there's been more years without incident than with, tells me they're performing their role perfectly. As a deterrent."

The woman, now dubbed Ridgeton, looked up toward the sky and I carefully scooted closer to the trunk. When she looked back at her partner, her shoulders were slumped and she appeared bone weary. "Why do you always have to be right, Carter?"

The man—Carter—snickered. "What would it take for you to tell that to the missus next time you come for lunch?"

They chuckled and continued to move away. I kept my silent perch until they were both out of sight and I could no longer distinguish the sound of their chatter. Rather than hop down immediately, I shifted to a more comfortable position, leaning against the tree, while I quelled the ache in my heart. Another body. Another life taken too soon from this world and another family left to grieve a senseless death. If the wounds matched like I suspected they would, that put the culprit in serial killer territory. I wasn't really sure what was worse, that there were likely to be *more* bodies, or that I was now even more qualified to solve this puzzle.

Right on cue, my phone buzzed inside my coat pocket. I took it out and answered without checking the ID. There was only one person it could be. "This is Diana."

"Good afternoon, Miss Harker. This is Detective Takashi." His voice was congenial enough, bordering on saccharine, but I could just make out the babble of lots of voices in what sounded like a large room. He was likely calling from the crime scene at the Aquatics Center and judging by the weird echo, I'd hazard he was by the Olympic pool.

I resisted the childish urge to ask if he'd found an arrow this time. "Afternoon, detective. How may I help you?"

"I was hoping to ask you some additional follow-up questions and wanted to make sure you were still in town."

I barely didn't snort. I had no doubt he had more questions, but that wasn't the real reason for the call. "As a matter of fact, I am," I replied, intentionally leaving out any description or clue as to my current whereabouts.

"Excellent. It may be awhile before I have an opportunity to sit down with you again, so I'd appreciate it if you didn't schedule any out-of-town excursions."

"And if I already have some scheduled?" I asked, unable to resist poking him.

"Cancel them." His flat response was exactly the confirmation I needed.

"Understood, Detective. I look forward to our next chat." I hung up without waiting for a response and promptly stood on my branch to survey the drop below. Now that I was "officially" a person of interest with loose orders not to skip town, I needed to know more about this latest crime scene. I couldn't afford to blunder into giving the intrepid detective potential evidence as to my involvement like I had during our first chat. And that meant getting my ass to that pool pronto.

My instinct that the murder had occurred at the indoor Olympic swimming pool had been dead on. Unlike the last crime scene I'd been party to, there were significantly more officers present. Apparently, three murders warranted a more serious approach. Though I was curious how they planned to explain such a large presence on campus. Looking at the flustered and decidedly green custodian, I almost felt bad for him. Odds were he'd only been doing his job when he'd gotten the shock of a lifetime.

I couldn't help but wonder if this latest victim's name would make the news or if it would prompt the release of the other two. Whatever path Takashi chose, no way could he continue keeping this silent. This place was too inaccessible for wayward students. People would want answers. And when they learned that this wasn't the first victim, panic would ensue.

I scooted closer to the edge of the bleachers I was hiding behind. Despite the increased police presence, sneaking in had been almost too easy, what with everyone more focused on the actual pool. I counted three major clusters: one by the door that was apparently the point of entry, one by the gurney with the bagged body, and the third that looked like the forensic team at the edge of the pool. If only I could get a look at the victim, I'd have a lot more to work with when I eventually met with Takashi, as well as another piece to solve my increasingly complex puzzle. Unfortunately, the general layout of the massive room didn't allow me to get much closer without risking being seen.

Confident that there wasn't much more I could glean from the situation, I slid more solidly into the shadows to make my departure through the side door I'd snuck in through. When my heel thumped into something solid that definitely shouldn't have been there, I froze. With exaggerated care, I slowly turned to discover what the foreign obstacle was. Before I could even register the need *not* to scream, a hand clamped over my mouth.

It took a second for my eyes to adjust to the darker pool of shadow the man stood in. When they did, I nearly released a muffled shout of surprise, anyway. It wasn't just some random guy that had snuck up behind me; it was *Xander*. And he looked pissed.

He jerked his head toward the exit I'd been intending to use anyway, then slowly removed his hand and stepped to the side, giving me barely enough room to squeeze past him. I held my tongue as I wove through the back of the folded bleaches toward the propped door that was miraculously still unguarded. The officers in the woods may have had a low opinion of campus security, but the police department wasn't exactly the pinnacle of their profession, either.

Outside, Xander stalked past me, heading toward the baseball fields. He'd gone several steps by the time he realized I was no longer with him. "Are you coming?" he asked over his shoulder in a low voice that made my skin crawl. Refusing to be cowed by his inexplicably hostile demeanor, I resumed walking after him.

It wasn't until we reached the visitor dugout that he finally stopped. His eyes flashed in the setting sun as he turned to face me, somehow looking even more furious than he had at the pool.

"Care to explain what the hell you were doing at *another* murder scene?" he growled, effectively getting my ire up.

I crossed my arms and met him glare for glare. "I could ask you the same."

His fierce gaze narrowed to slits. "Perhaps Detective Takashi would be interested in hearing about your presence."

"And maybe he'd be interested in learning about your connection to all three victims," I fired back. "We already have a second date lined up. I could tell him then."

Xander flinched, but didn't deny my assumption that he had a similar connection to this victim. The silence stretched between us as we stood glaring at each other. Finally, I couldn't take it anymore.

"Who were they?" I asked softly.

His lip curled in a snarl. "Don't you already know?"

I huffed my agitation. So much for compassion and understanding. "No, I don't. That's why I'm asking *you*. They'd already bagged the body by the time I got there."

"How did you even know where to be?"

"How did you?" I countered.

He took a large step toward me, bringing his angry face into my personal bubble, where I continued to hold my ground. "Damn it, Diana. This isn't a joke. I've now lost a third pa- family member and you *will* answer my questions."

This close to him, it was hard not to get absorbed in his deep brown eyes, even if they were sparking with fury. And it was probably my imagination, but he was hotter. Not just physically—because, yeah, that hadn't changed—but actually exuding more heat.

His nostrils flared, and I realized I'd taken a hair too long to respond.

I cleared my throat and attempted to gesture between us. "You mind?"

"No," he said in that same menacing growl that was simultaneously triggering my instinct to fight, as well as, unfortunately, my libido. No one had any right to look that sexy angry, least of all someone four years my junior that I had zero intention of pursuing.

Choosing wisdom over lust or violence, I took a half step back, then said in a voice that would have made my mother proud, "I'll answer your questions, but first you have to answer some of mine." I met his dark eyes with a calm expression and no trace of fear, though any reasonable person in my position would absolutely be afraid. After all, I was alone and unarmed with an obviously angry man. A young one at that, and arguably more dangerous for it.

He visibly composed himself before mirroring my half a step backward, putting a few more inches of much needed space between us. "His name was Dimitri." He shifted his gaze off to the side and added quietly enough that I had to strain to hear, "The curfew was supposed to keep him safe. I should have known he was missing." Xander squeezed his eyes shut, betraying the pain he was clearly trying to keep in check.

Against all logic, I couldn't help but reach out to him. "It's not your fault. You couldn't have known." I'd hoped settling a reassuring hand on his shoulder might help relieve some of his tension, but his shoulders remained firm stone.

"It's my *job* to know. My responsibility. Some leader I make. I can't even keep twenty people safe," he snarled, then straightened up as if he hadn't meant to say so much. He shrugged off my hand and turned a once more furious gaze on me. "There, I've answered your damnable question. Now answer mine."

The vitriol in his voice had me reflexively curling my hand against my chest, and I had to consciously relax it. He hadn't *technically* answered all of my questions, but I was willing to let it slide... for now. "I knew to be here after overhearing a pair of cops in the woods by where Katie died."

Suspicion instantly replaced his anger. "What were you doing there?"

"Honestly? I don't even know. Mostly grasping at straws." I debated sharing my conclusions about Katie knowing that she was being hunted, but decided against it. That was the *last* thing he needed right now.

He stepped closer again, though he didn't seem to be aware of it. "And what straws did you find?"

I calmly met his fiery, and what I now realized was hurt, gaze and placed my hands on his heaving chest. I sent up a silent prayer that he wouldn't recognize my resulting shiver for what it was and said softly, "I didn't kill them. I'm not your enemy."

He studied my face for a few tortured seconds that had my heart beating double time for reasons it *absolutely should not*. Finally, his intense gaze lost its edge of animosity and the tension bled out of him. I offered him a small smile, aiming for reassurance. His gaze flicked down to my mouth and back up to my eyes.

I was suddenly acutely aware that my heart wasn't the only one doing double time. The meager distance between us shrank, though I wasn't aware of either of us actually moving. Then his breath ghosted over my lips. I swallowed hard, captivated by his unblinking gaze, so much softer now than it had been minutes before, and the sense of *promise* radiating off of him.

When our lips pressed together, it felt more like an inevitability than a surprise. As if every time we'd run into each other had been leading up to this one impossible moment that shouldn't have happened. I struggled to dredge up some give-a-damn and came up empty. The gentle movement of his mouth against mine was sweet, almost tentative, and not nearly enough. Then he pulled away just enough, so that we were no longer touching.

Not nearly satisfied, I flicked my tongue out to taste my lips. He mirrored the motion, his gaze becoming increasingly intense as he tracked my movement in the dying light. Unmitigated want flared to life inside me. Before I could think to do anything—or nothing—about it, Xander's mouth was back on mine and he was pushing me back against the cool concrete of the dugout. The hard, determined press of his mouth ignited something within me and I kissed him back just as fiercely. I wasn't just hungry; I was *starving*.

My hands, which had miraculously remained on his chest, drifted higher, revealing that he was every bit as solid as I'd imagined. At last, I got my fingers to his hair, tangling them into the silky strands, then nearly pulling a chunk out when he nipped at my bottom lip, forcing a groan out of me.

Abruptly, everything was gone—his mouth, his body, his hands. I suddenly had a much better understanding of the phrase "have the rug pulled out from under you." To say I felt off kilter after the heated exchange would be putting it mildly. I pulled my gaze up in time to see him run his hands over his face and then through his hair.

"Shit. I'm sorry. I shouldn't have done that. You've made it very clear where you stand." He shook his head as if trying to shake free the unbridled lust I'd just tasted and, for one insane second, I was tempted to correct him. "I should get back to the dorm. Let the others know what I found."

"That sounds like a good idea," I said, beyond relieved I didn't sound as breathless as I felt.

"I'll talk to you later?" The hint of question had my stomach doing a ridiculous flip.

I gave him a soft but genuine smile. "Of course."

"You, um, going to be okay getting home?"

"Don't worry about me. I can handle myself," I said with a wink. Understatement of the century.

He nodded, then turned on his heel and walked off into the twilight that now encompassed us. I waited for him to become nothing more than a blur of shadow in the nearby streetlight before slumping against the wall of the dugout.

"Whoa," I sighed into the evening. While it wasn't the *best* kiss I'd ever had, what it lacked in skill, it more than made up for in intensity. I recognized potential when I saw it and Alexander Wolfsbane was walking potential. It was almost a shame it would never happen again.

9

◀◆▶

SHARP SHOOTERS

"WELL, WELL, WELL. WHAT do we have here?"

At the sound of Hyacinth's voice, I spun around to find her in my most definitely locked apartment. "Hye! When did you get here? More importantly, *how* did you get in and why didn't you bother to call first?"

She waved a dismissive hand, then stepped over the threshold into my bedroom. "Picked the lock. Your apartment complex has shit all for security, by the way."

I snorted. "They're not exactly planning for a hostile takeover. Now when you say 'picked the lock', please tell me you don't really mean 'broke the lock.'" I scowled in response to her malicious grin. Finally, she released an exasperated breath.

"You can stop clutching your pearls. I mean, actually picked." To emphasize her point, she held up a discreet lock pick set before vanishing it back into her leather jacket. Hyacinth was typically the definition of badass and today was no exception. Between the black leather jacket, ripped jeans, and military boots, she could have just as easily been a rock-

93

star slumming it in Blackwell Hollow as a prodigious vampire hunter.

I crossed my arms, noting absently that she was wearing the ironic "I turn into bats to avoid people" shirt I'd gotten her. "A call would have sufficed... or a knock. You didn't need to break in to give me whatever intel you found."

She flipped my textbook shut with a pointed nail lacquered a glossy black. As if she needed one more thing to set her apart from the "plebeians" as she put it. "But then I wouldn't have the joy of requesting your company on a little outing I set up for us."

"Request or demand?" I asked tentatively. If she still had traces of her "upgrade" in her system, she could theoretically make me do whatever she wanted. Hye obstinately held that juicing didn't give her the ability to glamour, but I trusted that about as far as I could throw her.

The bed released a massive puff of air as she flopped on it. "You're always so hella extra." She narrowed a look at me before I could make a pot-kettle comment. "Today, it's a request. Though I'll be thoroughly put out if you turn me down. We never hang out, just the two of us anymore." She scratched one of her talons on the duvet. "Believe it or not, I didn't *just* come here to keep an eye on you. There's not exactly a lot of people who do what we do that I can talk with and certainly none our age."

I resisted the urge to correct her for the thousandth time that I didn't *do* that stuff anymore, had moved clear across the country to get away from it. Caving a little, I admitted, "I miss you too."

She scoffed. Feelings in her eyes were weakness, and she'd die before admitting she had them like the rest of us. Abruptly, she popped off the bed. "That sounded like agreement to me. In which case, you'll need to change."

"Into what?" I plucked at my sweater. "Something more hunter?"

She snickered. "I was going to go with something less preppy, but that works too." Before I could dig into where exactly we were going, she meandered out of the room. "And hurry up," she called back. "Daylight's a wasting."

Hyacinth continued to dodge my questions throughout the drive about where she was taking us, leaving me to fret in silence about what trouble awaited me. Because with Hye, there was always trouble. Once it had been fun getting up to no good, then our respective families had pushed us to live up to our legacies. I'd rebelled. She hadn't.

Finally, she pulled into a parking lot for a place called "Sharp Shooter" that I didn't know even existed. She gave me a wide grin as she slammed the car into park and, for a miniscule second, we were teenagers again, going on another misguided adventure.

"Come on, slowpoke. I've hunted corpses faster than you."

I rolled my eyes and got out of the car. Considering most of the "corpses" she hunted were, in fact, ridiculously fast, the reprimand didn't really hold water. "Hye..." I began as I eyed the entrance.

"Nope," she cut me off. "None of that. I've already reserved an outdoor range for us and I refuse to let you be a wet rag." She hooked her arm in mine and I couldn't help but chuckle as she half steered-half dragged me into the establishment. She spared the man behind the front desk a wave and he buzzed the door to let us out back. That he neither asked for our IDs nor followed to give us the standard safety brief was a true testament to how much money talked.

Behind the building, I was surprised to find a well-equipped range with lanes cordoned off by thick rope. Few shooting ranges had an outdoor area equipped for archery *and* firearms. I glanced at the large red sign listing proper safety protocols, namely not leaving the designated areas with a loaded weapon and to keep ear muffs on at all times. "Um, Hye, not to rain all over your parade, but you know I don't work with firearms."

"Then I guess it's a good thing I didn't bring any. I did, however, bring you a present."

I ripped my gaze away from the sign at the unexpected lilt in her voice. "What?"

She pulled a long, narrow box from beneath a bench and placed it on top. "Go ahead." She gestured grandly and stepped back.

With increasing trepidation, I approached the nondescript box. I'd barely cracked the lid to peer inside when the sun glinted off the metal detailing and I slammed it back down. "Are you out of your fucking mind?" I hissed, looking around at the back lot for witnesses. Suddenly, the open-air range didn't seem so appealing.

"Pft, again with the theatrics." She shrugged out of her jacket, revealing gorgeously toned arms, and began to stretch. "You can dial back the panic. I rented the whole back lot. The space is all ours until they close." She whipped her box braids into a bun high atop her head before stepping back up to the box and flipping the lid up to bounce against the concrete wall of the building. "How about some gratitude?"

"Hyacinth," I groaned, returning my gaze to the unstrung recurve bow. I was still trying to find words to explain to her how truly terrible an idea this "gift" was when my focus caught on a small detail on the bow—an engraved crest. More specifically, the *Harker* crest. "Motherfucker. This is *my* bow."

Hye smirked. "Damn right it is. And it wasn't easy to get."

I scowled at her. No shit, considering it was supposed to be hanging in my bedroom within the Harker family mansion, which was virtually impenetrable on a *bad* day.

"You can cut the 'tude. I got the intel you needed as well. Just thought I'd bring you a little piece of home."

"What? Couldn't find my teddy from when I was five? Or my compound bow, for that matter?"

She crossed her arms. "I'm considerate, not stupid. Besides, the longbow was more of a challenge to get and we both know you had a rabbit, not a teddy."

"Which you set on fire, if memory serves."

Her trademark malicious grin returned. "It was haunted."

"Was not," I grumbled under my breath. Although I hadn't used the bow in at least five years, the wood was still perfectly maintained, polished to a sheen, and she'd even packed fresh string and a quiver of arrows.

"Yeah, yeah," she quipped.

I paused mid-string to look at her. "Hye..."

She released an exasperated breath as she pulled out a significantly smaller box. "Fine, I was late because the infusion took a little longer than usual to subside. There might still be a few traces in my system." She said it casually enough, but I recognized the tightness in her shoulders and I now understood this sudden outing a lot better. She glanced warily at me out of the corner of her eye as she opened her box to reveal razor sharp throwing knives.

Rather than lecture her again about the dangers of the path she was on, I finished stringing my bow and swung the quiver over my shoulder. "Tell me about the hunt? Then you can fill me in on what you found for me."

She noticeably relaxed and even graced me with a smile. Then she launched into a horrific tale of blood and violence, her knives punctuating the story with hard thuds as they met the distant target. I listened intently, though my heart hurt more with each word. No matter what justification she used, I couldn't reconcile myself to her methods... or the fact that she'd likely die sooner rather than later because of those methods. She finished retrieving the last of her knives and gestured for me to step up.

I pulled the fletching back far enough to tickle my ear and released a breath. To my surprise, the arrow flew true and hit inches from the bullseye.

Hyacinth snorted. "Someone's rusty."

"Shut your face." I rolled my shoulders and gave myself a good shake, then fired two shots in rapid succession. The first hit the mark dead center and the second split it. I gave her a cocky smile. "You were saying?" She held up her hands in surrender and I shifted my focus to the next farthest target. "So, I take it rather than just ask, you took it upon yourself to snoop around my house?"

"Naturally. For the record, I did find your compound bow in the armory, but didn't have time to deal with the safeguards there." She smirked, and I rolled my eyes. "As for the intel, that was a little harder to get to than I expected." I shot her a look, and she quickly deflected. "I still got it, just saying you Harkers are paranoid."

"Because the Van Helsings are the epitome of laid back?" I bypassed the other targets, aiming for the farthest available. By my estimate, it was several yards closer than the shot that killed Katie. I released my arrow on an exhale and a split second later, the shot landed true.

"Anyway, according to Harker records, the last known pack in the North Carolina area was located closer to the western border of the state."

I let the bow slip through my fingers until the base rested lightly against the ground. "When was that?'

"About two hundred years ago."

"Shit," I hissed. "Anything more recent?"

She shook her head. "Notes in the margins speculate that they either moved on or died out, but no account of when that might have happened."

"Fucking useless."

"Pretty much." Hyacinth stepped up beside me and tossed several knives to create a circle around my initial shot. "Also, while I'm pretty sure you already looked it up, I checked any native wolf migrations that might have overlapped the area."

"And?"

"Nothing. A couple rumors out west where the original pack might have been, but nothing concrete. Likely oldwives' tales holding over from the past." She threw her last knife, completing a rather ridiculous smiley face, and looked at me. "How are things going on this front?"

I sighed and slogged over to slump onto the bench. "Not great. We're up to three bodies now and I'm officially under 'advisement'," I said in air quotes, "not to leave town. I should get a call from the detective any day now to schedule a follow up interview."

"Fuck. Three bodies? That's not good. And no leads?"

"Nope," I said, popping the P.

"And you're still thinking werewolf?"

I shook my head. "I'm not so sure anymore. My instincts are saying werewolves are definitely involved, but it doesn't fit with the crime scenes. All the victims have died by arrow and at least two by an exceptionally talented archer." I met Hyacinth's dark eyes. "Like Harker good."

She sucked air through her teeth, and I echoed the sentiment. "That's really not good."

"No kidding. And my super helpful childhood friend just brought me a fucking bow."

She scoffed. "A recurve bow and a compound bow are miles apart from each other."

"I know that. And *you* know that. But I doubt these dumb-asses could tell the difference if I shot them."

"Now there's a thought." She gave me a wink, then walked off to retrieve her knives and hopefully my arrows.

10

TENACIOUS TAKASHI

I TRIED TO CATCH up with Jennifer after class, but short of shouting or physically pushing people out of my way, my odds weren't looking good. By the time I made it out of the College of Liberal Arts, there wasn't any trace of her. Frustrated more with myself than her, I fished out my phone to ping her before she got too far. I didn't even pull up her contact information before a familiar voice had me frozen.

"Miss Harker, such a pleasure to see you," Detective Takashi's gaze drifted behind me to the building, briefly landed on my backpack, then returned to me, "here."

The hair on the back of my neck stood on end. Perhaps the average student wouldn't find anything untoward or sinister about his statement, but I was a far cry from average.

"Detective," I replied, with all the nonchalance I could manage without sounding suspicious. I held up my phone. "I've been expecting your call. You needn't have come to campus, but I appreciate your consideration of my busy schedule. Were you wanting to talk now?"

Takashi blinked, clearly taken aback at how I interpreted his presence. After a moment, he cleared his throat and straightened to his full height. "Actually, I was in the area on some other business. But now that you mention it, now would be a convenient time for our follow up. Though I'd prefer to have it at the station, away from..." he trailed off as he clocked a student walking by us a hair too slow.

"I believe I understand your meaning. My next class isn't until four. That gives me about two hours to meet you at the station and have our discussion, then walk back to campus."

"There's no need to do all of that walking. I'd be happy to put more time back in your day by driving you to the station and then back to campus. Please, allow me." He shifted enough for me to glimpse the squad car parked in a blatantly marked "No Parking" zone. Oh yeah, *total* coincidence that it just so happened to be outside of my class at this exact time.

"I'd rather not," I said, perhaps *too* bluntly.

His eyebrows shot up and suspicion sparked in his eyes. "And why would that be?"

I hiked my backpack higher on my shoulders. "My family has very firm ideas about getting in a police car unless it is absolutely unavoidable."

"That's an interesting tenet to live by. I suppose it's a good thing your family's not here then." He angled his body less subtly toward the vehicle.

I gave him my most saccharine smile. "And yet, I remain a Harker. The station's not too far from here. A brisk walk will see me there in ten or fifteen minutes."

It didn't take a genius or even seeing his clenched jaw to know Takashi didn't like that one bit. To his credit, he recovered quickly enough. He held two fingers up and signaled the car to go. "In that case, I insist on escorting you. Given these troubling times and your own harrowed experience."

I was sorely tempted to point out that it was broad daylight and there were literally witnesses everywhere, but that wasn't what he was getting at. He wanted to make sure I didn't "conveniently" disappear between here and the station. I fluttered my lashes and gave him a simpering smile that made me want to claw my face off.

"An escort would be quite gallant of you and I'd appreciate the company." Thank the goddess I could lie through my teeth and keep a straight face. Part of me was tempted to break into a run just to see what he would do. Given I'd taken back up my early morning runs, I was definitely in a position to easily outstrip him, even with my backpack. But there was a chance he'd simply shoot, and I wasn't willing to risk a bullet wound at this stage in our relationship.

With an equally unsettling smile, Takashi gestured for me to walk. The strained silence that dogged our heels was rife with anticipation. Luckily, I didn't have to suffer for long. Takashi slid me a look as we passed a group of students energetically discussing the next football game. "Tell me more about your family. Do they visit often?"

"Not really." And by that, I meant not at all.

He nodded as if he understood. "I take it you're not close."

"Quite the contrary. I'm very close with my mother, though she disapproves of my choice in university. Besides which, being close is not a prerequisite for keeping tabs on me."

Takashi missed a step. That's right, asshole. My family might not be in a neighboring town and visiting every weekend, but that didn't stop them from inserting themselves into my life. "Why *did* you choose to attend Blackwell Hollow University? Surely, with your connections, you could have gone anywhere."

"I like it here," I replied without elaborating. No way in hell was I about to tell him I'd all but sprinted across the nation to get away from said meddling family.

He was clearly about to push when a student skidded in front of us. A student I recognized.

"Hey, Diana!" Xander spared a glance at Takashi, then stepped closer. "I realized I never gave you my number so we could coordinate on that project."

"Oh my God, you're right!" I said way too emphatically. Dialing it back, I pulled out my phone. "Can't believe I spaced." He rattled off his number, and I put it into my contacts, then texted him so he'd have mine. I half hoped he'd find a plausible reason to pull me away from Takashi. No such luck.

"Got it. Thanks! I'll review my schedule and let you know when I'm available." He beamed brightly and for a small moment, I forgot all about Takashi. Xander was truly beautiful. You couldn't really say that about a lot of men. Rugged, handsome, pretty maybe. But beautiful? Not so much. Xander however, had those shimmering brown eyes and hair like a raven's wing. And let's not forget the lean muscles. Definitely can't forget about those. I mentally shook my head to clear the renegade lustful thoughts. He was young. *Too* young. Four years might not seem like a lot to some, but given how fast I'd had to grow up—the things I knew—it might as well have been an eternity.

He bounded—literally fucking bounded—away and much to my chagrin, my heart sank slightly. Then my phone vibrated lightly in my hand. I glanced down to find he'd already replied.

Xander: Let me know when you're done & we'll meet up

Aside from the ampersand, I was impressed at how everything was not only spelled correctly, but the text was also grammatically correct. Then again, it wasn't exactly a complex text. I sent back a quick "K" before pocketing the device and looking back at the detective.

"Boyfriend?" he asked with an arched brow.

"Lab partner," I corrected.

"Wasn't aware that a degree in business administration had 'labs.'" He gazed off in the direction Xander had disappeared.

I checked an eye roll. "It's for the biology requirement."

"Hmm." His suspicious humming once again put my hackles up.

A less than companionable silence shrouded us as we wove our way across campus. I kept waiting for him to delve deeper into the blatant lie about being in biology with Xander, but his mouth remained pressed in a grim line for the entire awkward ass walk. It was a blessing, really. The last thing I needed was for him to dig into my best lead for these murders. Thankfully, the station came into view, effectively distracting the detective.

"Miss Harker," Takashi said, waving me inside as he opened the door.

I gave him a smile I hoped he'd read as sincere instead of strained. My skin prickled as I stepped inside, though I couldn't determine if it was because of where I was or the sensation of being watched. Much like the last time I was here, Takashi led the way to an interrogation room—not that he called it that. Once inside, he folded his hands on the metal desk, then seemed to rethink his posture and leaned back in his chair that was hopefully every bit as uncomfortable as mine.

"You mentioned the other day that you had some additional questions for me?" I asked when the silence stretched into uncomfortable territory.

"I do. I was wondering if you'd remembered anything else about the murders." To my surprise, he didn't pull out a folio filled with more grisly pictures curated to get a rise out of me.

Playing dumb, I asked, "Murders? I know you showed me the picture of that poor girl in the woods, but I was only present—if you could say that—for the one on campus." I feigned a lightbulb moment and leaned forward. "Were you able to learn the girl's name?"

"We were." Takashi gave me a speculative expression. "We're planning to release that information to the press in the next day or so."

I didn't need supernatural senses to pick up on the blatant lie, but I wasn't about to point out to the detective that I was onto him. "I imagine the families will be incredibly appreciative. Please let me know if there's anything I can do for them." And I meant it. These deaths were a tragedy and I couldn't begin to imagine what their families were going through.

"That's very generous of you," he replied without emotion, causing my skin to crawl. "It's unfortunate you haven't remembered anything else about that night. Perhaps your memory is clearer around the afternoon of October the fourth, say between one and five p.m."

The day Dimitri died. Had he seen me there? Had Xander told him, after all? Maybe I hadn't been as careful as I'd thought with the officers in the woods. "Um, the fourth?" I feigned thinking hard. "That would have been a Wednesday, right? I would have been in statistics. After that, I either head to the library with some of my friends to study or go straight back to my dorm to get a jump on assignments."

"And I'm sure these friends can corroborate your story."

"Of course," I said as glibly as I could. Was I sweating?

Takashi continued to stare awkwardly at me. Finally, he leaned on his forearms, and I fought the impulse to lean away. "At your initial interview, you provided quite an education about different types of bows." I obstinately ignored the sinking feeling in my stomach and kept my mouth shut, lest I inadvertently give him more ammunition for this "interview"... again. Abruptly he stood, pushing back his chair with a skin-crawling screech, and walked toward the door. It cracked open and someone on the other side passed him a folder before closing it again. "I was hoping you could lend me some more of your expertise."

"Like I said before, my family are hunters. I know a few things." The urge to shift beneath Takashi's stare slithered relentlessly up and down my spine.

He nodded, like it was the answer he expected, then pulled a photo from the folder. To my relief, it *wasn't* the corpse of Dimitri, though my investigation could have benefitted from seeing it. Rather, it was an image of a perfectly nondescript compound bow, matte green, with a mounted scope. "Would you say this is the type of bow responsible for the deaths of Joseph Mannis, Katie Long, and Dimitri Sokov?"

I flicked what I hoped was a surprised gaze up at Takashi. "That's three names. Was there another murder?" I asked, infusing my voice with as much horror as I could manage. To be fair, it wasn't all that hard. This man was sitting on three murders and, to my knowledge, had yet to inform the university or the town.

His face remained impassive as he tapped the image. "Answer the question, please."

"I suppose it could be. Even then, they'd have to be one hell of a shot."

The detective's eyes glittered with triumph as he removed yet another picture from his folder. "I'm so glad you agree." He laid the image on the table with an understated flourish as he resumed his seat. I blanched at the printed image of *me* at an archery contest and forced myself to continue taking slow, steady breaths.

"You see, I know how to do my homework too, Miss Harker." He squinted down at the image I now realized was a printout from an online magazine. "Top marks. Looks like you might have even set a few records. I don't know about you, but from where I'm sitting, I think that makes you an expert. And one hell of a shot."

My palms were officially sweating. I attempted to surreptitiously slide my hands along my thighs to remove the damning moisture, but dared not do more. "That was a long time ago."

"Perhaps five years is a while back. But, funny thing," he wagged his finger and chuckled, though I didn't find any aspect of this meeting remotely humorous, "I could swear that you're shooting with this exact bow." His wiggling finger stabbed down onto the image of the compound bow once again and his eyes narrowed. "Tell me, Diana, done any shooting lately?"

Fear shot icy cold down my back. If he'd found this, he'd found other competitions. And if he looked, he'd no doubt find a record of my untimely visit to Sharp Shooters. Damn Hyacinth. But I couldn't wholly blame her. I could have walked away when I realized where she'd brought me. But I'd stayed. I'd shot. I'd even had fun.

"Miss Harker?" Detective Takashi pressed.

"I haven't shot a compound bow since that picture was taken."

He tilted his head and studied me like I was a slide beneath a microscope. "Seems like quite the waste of talent." He released a low whistle that made goosebumps ripple across my arms. "Four national titles, never lower than third. I can't even count how many regional championships. Then to give it all up... Then again, maybe you didn't. You just moved on to more challenging targets."

I was fairly positive there wasn't a drop of blood left in my face, which wasn't helping my case in the least. Still, I had to say *something*. I couldn't very well let an insinuation like that go unanswered. "To go from static targets or even deer to...

people," I said with all the disgust it deserved and a shudder, "is quite the stretch."

He shrugged. "Maybe. But then it's not every day that we find three students shot to death by an arrow." Without warning, he gathered up the photos, smacking the folder on the desk to order them, and stood.

Floundering, I followed suit. "Sir?"

"Officer Carter will see you out. Oh, and, Miss Harker?"

"Yes?" I asked, unable to keep the slight quaver from my voice.

"What I said before still stands. Don't leave town." He brushed past me and continued out the door, leaving me to wait for Officer Carter and do my damnedest not to freak out.

11

THE SILVER BULLET

I LOOKED UP AT the sign above the bar and snickered to myself. "The Silver Bullet" glowed in blue neon and didn't look any more familiar in person as it had when I'd read the name in the text Xander had sent asking me to meet him here. I stepped inside out of the chill evening and looked around. The few patrons within all turned to see who'd entered. I shrugged off their curious gazes and made my way toward the bar. As far as bars were concerned, The Silver Bullet was about as low key as one could get, resembling a café lounge more than a college bar. That was at least one plus in what already felt like a terrible idea.

It was bad enough I'd given into the impulse to kiss Xander the other night. The last thing I needed was the incentive of alcohol to encourage me to do it again. But after that epic disaster of an interview with Takashi, I needed a drink more than I needed to keep control of my errant hormones. No sooner did I slide onto a bar stool than the bartender walked up.

"What can I get you?" His low rumbly voice had an intrigu- ing lightness to it that paired with his equally contradictory appearance. The man was at most a few years older than me with light brown hair a shade or two darker than his skin. He was built a lot like Xander, his tight bar shirt clinging to ripcord muscles that conveyed strength without bulk.

"Uh, I'll take whatever lager you have on draft." I slid my card and ID across the bar top.

He gave the ID a disinterested glance and took the card. "Did you wanna open a tab?"

"Yes, please." I watched as he keyed in my information on the order screen and ran my card. Either his eyesight was superhuman or this bar was disturbingly relaxed.

He returned the plastic and whipped out a fresh glass, letting it twirl in the air before catching it at just the right height to slide it under the tap. I couldn't help but be impressed, not least of which because it didn't seem like he'd done the fancy move for my benefit. "Haven't seen you here before," he commented as he deposited the frosty glass with the perfect amount of head in front of me.

"That obvious?" I asked with a wry smirk.

He shrugged, causing the muscles beneath his shirt to contract in an exceptionally distracting way. "Most of our clientele are regulars."

"Guess that explains the funny looks."

His gaze slid over my shoulder and the shift in the room was palpable enough that the hairs on the back of my neck stood on end. "Suppose it would. So, what brings you to our fine establishment? Meeting someone?"

I took a sip of the lager, surprised to find it wasn't a common domestic and packed a heck of a punch. "Um, yeah. I guess since he suggested this place, maybe he's a regular too." Though I doubted he was drinking alcohol since he was technically underage.

The handsome bartender rested his forearms on the counter and leaned forward with a smile. "Maybe. What's his name?"

Before I could respond, a rush of cold air flooded the room. The bartender and I turned to see who had entered. The man standing in the entry had become all too familiar a figure. My traitorous pulse picked up as I took in how nicely his jeans fit his well-muscled legs and the flash of happy trail that appeared as he reached up to shake something out of his hair. It wasn't until he walked closer, wearing the same smile he always had when he saw me, that I realized he was covered in fine, misted droplets and his shirt was clinging to him. I swallowed thickly and darted a wary glance at my half-empty glass. No way the drink was *that* strong.

"Xander!" the bartender exclaimed, straightening up. The two slapped hands and Xander dropped onto the stool beside me.

"Hey, Luca. How're things?"

The bartender—Luca—shrugged. "Steady enough. The usual?"

Xander shook his head. "Nah, just beer tonight. Need to keep my wits about me."

"One beer coming up." Luca once again spun out a glass without really looking at it. When he placed it in front of Xander, he squinted at him, his gaze darting between the two of us before he let out a muffled guffaw and slapped the counter. "Why didn't you tell me you were here to meet Xander? You're money's no good here." He waved a hand to dismiss my protests as he spun around to delete my information from the computer.

I leaned closer to a smirking Xander. "What's that about?"

"My dad owns the bar."

"Oh." I shifted away and took another sip. Well that certainly explained the lack of ID-checking. Was Xander somehow loaded and I'd missed it? He certainly didn't act like any of the entitled pricks I'd been forced to rub elbows with growing up.

He glanced at me. "Give me a quick sec? I need to touch base with Luca about a couple things." Before I could respond, he'd already taken a small step to the side. Luca returned, replacing my now empty glass with a fresh one and Xander tilted his head for him to come closer. "Any trouble from the recent events?" he asked quietly, but not quiet enough for me not to hear. I pretended to be completely engrossed in my new drink as I listened attentively to the semi-private conversation.

"Not too much. What about at the House? Things settle down there yet?"

"For the most part. That disaster over summer still seems to be hanging over everyone's head, though," Xander responded with a shake of his own.

"They won't really settle down until your pa officially steps down. How is the old man anyway?"

"He's holding up. But he's tired. What happened at Solstice really took a toll on him. I don't think he ever saw it coming." Xander released a heavy sigh. "Maybe it was a mistake to come back. I'm still needed there."

Luca reached out to clasp Xander on the shoulder. "If you weren't here, things would be worse."

"Would they? Maybe this is all my fault."

I tightened my grip on the cold glass to prevent myself from offering similar comfort. It had been a while since I'd considered Xander a possible suspect. Now I just felt for the guy. He'd lost so much and still somehow managed to approach each day with a smile.

"Don't think like that." Luca gave Xander's shoulder a reassuring squeeze before letting go. "Now enough talk about all that. What can I do to help?"

"Nothing, really. Keep your eyes peeled and your nose to the ground. Something will turn up eventually." Xander smiled at me. "Diana, here, is actually helping out."

Luca's eyebrows lifted. "That so? Well, it's a pleasure to meet you, Diana. Any friend of Xander's is a friend of mine."

I accepted Luca's outstretched hand, shocked to find it every bit as over-warm as Xander's tended to be. "Nice to meet you, too."

Xander continued to beam at me another moment, then turned his focus back to Luca. "We could actually use some privacy, but feel free to keep the drinks coming." He lifted his glass and tilted it for emphasis.

Luca nodded. "Sure thing, boss." He tossed a bar towel over his shoulder and moved to the far end of the bar.

"Well, that's... something," I said from behind my glass.

Xander hiked a shoulder. "Eh, I just know the right people."

So did I, but I was getting the distinct impression that it paled in comparison to the way Xander knew people. "Speaking of knowing people, I bet you know everyone here, don't you?" I asked, squinting at him.

He ducked his head, but not before glancing over his shoulder into the room. "Guilty."

"Is that why you wanted to meet here?"

"In a sense. I knew we'd have privacy, but it's also public. Mostly, I just wanted to make sure you were okay." His hand settled over mine, infusing it with warmth that spread from the tips of my fingers to burn on my cheeks.

I quickly grabbed my drink with my free hand and took several swallows of the bitterly cold liquid. "Why would you think I wasn't?"

"When I spotted you earlier, you seemed anxious. Then when I realized the detective was there, I assumed it was related and you might need an out."

The sentiment was one of the sweetest I'd encountered in a long time. I'd been expected to be completely self-sufficient at such an early age. I still struggled to ask for help... or accept it. He rubbed his thumb in slow circles on my hand and the encroaching fuzziness in my brain intensified. "Thanks," I managed to croak out. Okay, maybe these drinks really *were* that strong.

"I take it he brought you in for more questions. How'd that go?"

I groaned, pulling my hand free of his warm touch in order to cover my face. "Not great." I peered through my fingers to see his face scrunched with concern.

"Anything I should be worried about?"

I let out a heavy sigh and dropped my hands. "If you're asking if he's made the connection that all the victims lived in the same dormitory, he didn't say. It's possible, but I doubt it. Though I'm not sure how he's missed it."

Xander released what sounded suspiciously like a relieved breath. Maybe I'd been too quick to dismiss him as a suspect. Murderous psychopaths could pass as bouncing rays of sunshine if they had to. I mentally snorted. They could, but it was incredibly unlikely they'd bother. But then, it also wasn't uncommon for murderers to insert themselves into an ongoing investigation. I pushed the intrusive thoughts to the side... for now.

I cleared my throat and finished the last of my second beer. "He did say the department was planning to release the victims' names at an upcoming press conference," I said, discreetly watching for his reaction. His face remained unhelpfully neutral.

"Do you think he really will?" Xander's hoarse voice could have been worry for exposure or an expression of grief. What-ever the reason for it, chills ran over me while heat swirled low in my belly.

I reached for my drink again, forgetting that it was empty, only to find it full again. I blinked in surprise and took a healthy swallow. Luca might have erased my card details, but I'd be leaving him whatever cash I had on me. When I finally set the glass back down and met Xander's gaze, it didn't seem like he'd blinked. "Honestly? No. I think he said that to try to provoke me into revealing something." Exactly what I'd just done to Xander with an almost identical result.

"Don't suppose *he* has any leads?" he asked derisively, then downed the last of his beer. This time, I noticed when Luca surreptitiously replaced it with a full glass.

"You mean besides me?" I arched an eyebrow.

"That's not... You already told me, more than once, that you didn't kill them."

"And you believe me?" While it was refreshing not to have to constantly prove myself, I found his easy acceptance of my word disconcerting.

"You haven't given me any reason not to. Besides, I'm a pretty good judge of character," he added with a smirk.

I leaned closer, invading his personal bubble. "Is that so?" I asked softly, my gaze falling to his plush mouth as the tip of his tongue flicked out. It took an alarming amount of willpower to force myself to straighten back up. Without thinking, I drank more of my beer, though it did nothing to steady the room which had begun to teeter. Or maybe that was me. I glanced down, and sure enough, my swinging legs were causing the bar stool to rock. Mystery solved; I polished off the drink.

"At any rate, the good detective doesn't share your con-viction." For a split second, I nearly let slip what Takashi had found out about my past. Shaking my head—which proved to be a massive lapse in judgment—I turned the tables. "What about you? Find anything helpful in your own sleuthing?"

He gestured at Luca for something before answering. "Not really. I've spent most of my time working to keep everyone at the dorm calm. No one is keen on the curfew, but at least they're taking it seriously now." He glanced over his shoulder again, but as much as I wanted to see what he was looking at, I was more enraptured with the way his mouth was moving.

I ripped my gaze away from his mouth yet again. Clearly, I needed to get intimately reacquainted with my vibrator if I was lusting this hard after someone. But was it just lust? Xander was *nice*. I... *liked* him, though hell if I knew why. I squinted at him sideways.

"Uh, Diana, are you okay?"

"I'm fine." I flapped a hand at him to emphasize my point, but only managed to unbalance myself. The stool teetered precariously, and I lurched to steady myself on the counter at the same time Xander grabbed the rebellious seat. Oh no. This was bad. And it was too late to do a damn thing about it. Normally I held my liquor just fine, maybe not at the level of a frat boy, but I wasn't a lightweight. Except I'd bypassed philosophical drunk and even happy drunk, and was currently on a bullet train to sorority-girl drunk. Fuck my life. I groaned in dismay at the inevitability of turning into a giggly disaster at any minute.

"Easy there. Here, have some water." He nudged forward a glass I hadn't noticed, that apparently had replaced my latest empty beer.

"Just how high was the ABV on that beer?"

"Um..." Xander trailed off, peering at the liquor wall. "Well, they're all home brews, so more than the standard four-point-five, or whatever it typically is."

I narrowed my eyes at him. "How much more?"

He grimaced. "A lot?"

"Jesus." I flopped my head onto my arms resting on the counter, nearly toppling the water and threatening my precarious perch atop the stool.

"Sorry, I probably should have warned you. Drink up your water and I'll get you home." He rubbed his hand up and down my back in soothing strokes.

I let out a contented hum. "Mmm, that's nice."

His low chuckle instantly had tingles radiating through me. Or maybe that was the ridiculously strong beer. "Glad you think so. Now, water. Please." He gently coaxed me up enough to get the straw in my mouth. My reward for hydrating was that he kept rubbing my back.

When the last of the liquid spluttered up, I released the straw with a satisfied "Ahh." I rolled my head to smile cheesily at him. "Ta-da."

"Quite the magic trick." He slid from his chair, still smiling at me, and I followed suit, if only to keep close to him, like a moth drawn to a flame. Shame I'd apparently grown two left feet and my legs had turned to uncooked noodles as we sat.

I flopped into him, my embarrassment almost immediately eclipsed by how insanely snuggly he was. "Oooh," I trilled happily, burrowing deeper into his embrace. This time when he laughed, I could feel his chest vibrating beneath my cheek.

"I'll see you around, Luca," Xander said over my head.

"Be careful out there." Luca's rumbly reply sparked a connection that I'd somehow missed when I'd been significantly more sober—he knew about the murders.

I popped my head up to ask Xander if he'd told him, but lost my train of thought when I realized that everyone else in the bar had already left. Frowning, I turned to Luca to ask him if we'd really shut the place down, but Xander's arm tightened around my waist and I lost my trail of thought again.

"It was nice meeting you, Diana," Luca said with an easy smile that instantly had me grinning like a fool back at him. "Don't be a stranger." He winked and I giggled, nearly missing the low rumble coming from Xander's chest that sounded oddly like a growl. Oh yeah, I was *totally* drunk.

Xander began guiding me toward the door and I dug my heels in. "Wait!" I floundered at my pockets for my wallet and had scarcely located it when Luca intervened.

"I already told you—your money's no good here. Now off with you two, before it gets much later."

"You heard the man," Xander said, shifting his grip to take on more of my weight. Whatever strength I'd assumed he had, I clearly hadn't done him justice as he all but carried me out of the bar.

No sooner did we step outside, than a light mist blanketed my face. "Oh."

"Yeah, smells like another storm. We better get you home before it breaks."

"Yep," I replied, popping the "p" with a giggle.

"You are adorable," he said, booping me on the nose.

I returned the boop in kind. "So are you." His resulting smile put the neon glowing above us to shame. My stomach did a funny loop and I found myself once more entranced by his full lips. Suddenly desperate to feel them again, I leaned forward and captured his mouth.

He released a muffled squeak of surprise before succumbing to my insistence with a sharp intake of air. I moaned into his mouth and looped my arms around his neck. His hands splayed across my back and I shuddered. But just as quickly as he'd given in he pulled back with a gasp. "Diana," he said softly, his breath caressing my cheek. For all the times I'd demanded people not call me by my proper name, I *adored* it when Xander said it.

I hummed in response, already tilting my head in anticipation of another core-melting kiss.

He gently removed my arms from his neck. "As much as I want this, and trust me, I really *really* want this," he paused to brush damp strands of hair out of my face. "I don't want it like this." He replaced his arm around my waist and I instantly leaned into him. "Come on, let's get you home before we both end up waterlogged."

I grumbled something that might have been an agreement while internally snickering to myself. It was going to be hilarious watching him try to get me home when I hadn't told him where it was.

12

UNWITTING CONFESSION

I JOLTED AWAKE AND nearly deposited myself on the floor for my efforts. Only a frantic clutch of the armrest that threatened to pull my arm out of its socket kept me on the couch. I pushed back the throbbing in my head to take stock of my precarious situation. Most importantly, why the fuck was I not in my bed?

"Good. You're awake."

The oddly emotionless statement injected straight adrenaline into my already struggling heart. I whipped my head around to look at the table sandwiched against the wall behind the couch. For an embarrassing second, joy fizzled like soda in my chest at discovering Xander sitting there. Then my gaze fell to the long box propped open on the table and an entire package of mentos plummeted into my metaphorical soda.

"Care to explain this?" For all of his monotone, his eyes were hard and there was an undeniably sinister undercurrent.

I used shifting to a more upright position to buy myself time to think. Still coming up blank for anything resembling a plausible explanation, I stalled. "How did you know where I lived?" It seemed safe to assume he'd escorted me home after I'd had *way* too much to drink.

"You told me. Now, the bow, Diana." The hardness bled from his eyes to tighten his mouth, causing a muscle in his cheek to twitch.

"It's not what it looks like." I grimaced the second the words left my mouth. Really? All the things I could say and I went with the most cliche option possible? At last, my hungover brain finished clicking into gear and I remembered one very important detail: that box had *not* been out. "Did you go through my things?" I asked, anger clipping the accusation.

"Why? Any other murder weapons you're afraid I'll find?" he snarled.

Completely over his high-handed questioning, especially when I had all seven fucking dwarves going to town inside my skull, I stood and stomped over to stand across from him, the bow containing the damning equipment between us. A move no part of my body appreciated, least of all my head. "It's not a murder weapon. It's not even a compound bow. And it definitely wasn't sitting out on the table when I left yesterday." I reached out and flipped the lid shut. The resulting crack as it closed filled the room and felt like a dagger to my pounding head. I pushed past the haze of pain and crossed my arms.

Defying physics, Xander's glare intensified. "I know what a bow looks like. I also know that it's just as capable of the damage I've seen."

I released an exasperated huff. "Except a compound bow was used to kill those kids."

"And you expect me to believe you?" He lurched off the bench seat, anger radiating off of him so intensely I almost stepped back to put distance between myself and an obvious threat. "All the information I have about the weapon used to kill my friends—my family—came from you. And now I find..." He gestured wildly at the innocuous box while his mouth struggled to form the right words. "This!" he finished at last.

I involuntarily tightened my arms like they could smother the unexpected hurt. "You knew I was an archer."

He took an aggressive step toward me and it took everything I had to stand my ground. "No, I knew you were knowledgeable about archery. You never said *anything* about actually being able to shoot one of these things."

"Gee, I wonder why," I snapped before I could rethink the wisdom of the statement.

His shoulders tensed and his very presence seemed to swell as if he'd somehow gotten bigger. "The truth. All of it."

"I'm a hunter," I blurted without my usual finesse. "Animals. Only animals. Never people!" I scrambled to add as first shock then unrefined rage twisted his features.

Xander narrowed his eyes, as if sensing that I was holding something back. I mentally crossed my fingers that he wasn't one of those people who could always seem to tell when you were lying. Not that I was. Werewolves *weren't* people, they were aberrations of nature. "What else?" he pressed.

"I'm maybe a national archery champion," I confessed with a wince.

He advanced toward me, and I quickly held up my hands.

"But I haven't competed in years. Hell, I chose to go to Blackwell because I didn't want to pursue my family's hunting business. For the record, they *weren't* happy about it." Braving his wrath, I reached for him. My fingers hovered just over his stone-like arm for a moment before I eliminated the minuscule distance.

He subtly shuddered when I made contact, and I chose to see it as a sign to keep going. Slowly, but without showing fear or hesitation, I extended the touch from just my fingers to my whole hand and stepped closer. His nostrils flared, but otherwise he remained a statue.

"I didn't kill your friends, Xander. I swear. And if you'll let me, I'd still like to help you find who did." I rubbed my thumb in slow arcs along his tense forearm and maintained eye contact. Xander might be a human instead of a hostile animal, but many of the methods to deal with one sufficed for the other.

His hard gaze softened ever so slightly, buoying my hope. "Why do you have this and why was it hidden?" He tilted his head toward the table.

"So you *did* go through my things," I said with a smirk.

To my surprise, his lips actually twitched like he wanted to mirror it. "Your vent was making a funny noise. When I investigated the cause, I found it. No more stalling."

"My asshole friend brought it from home for me." Just the mere thought of Hyacinth caused my head to throb. I removed my hand from Xander's arm to rub my pounding temple. "Ugh, do you mind if I get some water while I explain?"

Rather than respond, he simply held a hand out toward the kitchen. Taking him up on the passive agreement, I made my way over. Only after chugging two glasses and popping some ibuprofen did I continue my sordid explanation.

"Between you and me," I said, sitting the empty glass on the counter, "I think my friend is lonely. She manages to get along with most people, but doesn't actually have many friends. Growing up we used to shoot together—she does knives and I do archery." I plucked absently at the price sticker on the jar of honey beside me. "She, uh... followed me here to Blackwell."

"That's... weird," Xander said from the other side of the peninsula. Oddly I was both relieved and sad about the distance.

"You don't know the half of it."

His face took on a curious expression I couldn't quite define. "Is it possible she has a thing for you? Wouldn't be the strangest thing someone in love has ever done," he finished wryly.

I snorted and he stiffened. "She definitely didn't follow me here out of romantic interest. Trust me." His face clearly said the jury was still out on that front. I sighed heavily and admitted a truth I'd kept almost as buried as what I was trained to hunt. "Once upon a time, I had a massive crush on her. We were inseparable growing up. When I finally got brave enough to ask if she felt the same, I was informed in no uncertain terms that she did *not* return those feelings."

Xander frowned. "Then why follow you to college? Doesn't she have other plans for her life?"

"That she does. Like I said before, I think she's lonely. She masks it well, but she's never been good with trusting people. She knows me. I'm safe." Her literal human security blanket to ward off all the terrible things that eat at her humanity. "Anyway, no one's ever been able to control Hye. She went back home recently for a... medical treatment. When she returned, she surprised me with that." I gestured behind him toward the box. "Psycho broke into my house and everything."

Xander's eyebrows threatened to disappear into his hairline. "Seriously? With the murders and everything? I mean, I know they're not public knowledge, but still."

"That's Hye for you. And I am sorry I wasn't more upfront with you about being an archer. I'm just so used to keeping those sorts of things to myself. People tend to look at you funny." I wrapped my arms around myself as I stepped around the peninsula to stand in front of him, suddenly feeling extremely self-conscious.

He slipped a finger under my chin, causing heat to immediately pool beneath his fingertip, and gently tilted my head up. My damnable heart raced as I peered into his stunning mahogany eyes. "I get it. We all have our secrets."

"Yeah? You telling me you've got secrets too?" I quipped.

This time he did mirror my small grin. "You could say that." His obscenely long lashes fluttered as his gaze dropped briefly to my lips.

"Oh?" I asked, breathless.

"Mmhmm," he hummed as he trailed the same fingertip lightly along my jaw and made my heart skip. "I'm sorry I went through your things." He let out a wistful sigh that ghosted lightly over my face. "And for jumping to conclusions and ambushing you."

I swallowed thickly, painfully aware that in my constant battle with my libido around this man, I was losing, and scrambled for a way to change the topic. "Um, thanks for getting me home last night, even after I made a total fool of myself."

His gaze flicked back to mine, and my breath caught. "I don't think you made a fool of yourself."

"So I just imagined drunkenly kissing you?" I asked with a raised brow.

A smile twitched his lips. "Do you often imagine kissing me?"

Short answer? Yes. Hell yes. Oh my gods, I could live in that mouth. Long answer? All that, except I didn't want to. But explaining that took way more brain power than I currently had at my disposal. Not to mention I could scarcely hear myself think over how loudly my heart was hammering. "Do you often answer a question with a question?"

"Depends on the question. I, for one, have zero shame admitting that I've imagined kissing you a thousand times over."

If I'd thought my heart was racing before, it was bordering on cardiac arrest now. And my mouth had gone so dry, it was as if I'd never drank water in the first place. "But not while I was drunk," I supplied thinly.

He blinked slowly as his thumb passed a hair's breadth away from my bottom lip. "Definitely not," he whispered. "Diana?"

"Yeah?" I asked just as quietly, the air all but squeezed out of me by the vise-like grip of overwhelming *want*.

"I'm really gonna need you to decide if you want to pursue what's between us. The mixed signals are killing me."

My breath hitched. I had a million and one reasons why pursuing anything with Xander was a terrible idea. He was too young for me. He was my friend's cousin. He was every bit as entrenched in this murder investigation as I was. He all but accused me of murder. And outright accused me of lying to him.

Okay, so they weren't really all that many reasons. I *had* lied to him... technically still was. I'd also implicated him in the murders. There was no getting around both of our suspect involvement in the investigation. And as for age... That was really more a point of arbitrary preference. He might have been a few years younger, but he was a far cry from immature. As an added bonus, while he could be ridiculously sexy when he was angry, he might actually have been the best person I knew. Stacked against all of that, my opposition was quite trivial. And I was *not* a trivial person.

I gave myself another pained heartbeat to give my mind a chance to come up with any other reservations. When none appeared, I wrapped a hand around the back of his neck and brought his mouth down to mine. Like all the other times we'd kissed, heat blossomed inside my chest, bringing with it a sense of inevitability.

His warm hands splayed across my lower back, pulling me closer. I groaned into him, eager for the contact and still craving more. He licked along the seam of my lips and I opened. His tongue teased and played until I couldn't take it anymore. I snagged his bottom lip between my teeth, then dove into his mouth to take what I wanted. His resulting groan bordered on a growl and I mentally patted myself on the back.

He pulled back with a gasp and I couldn't help but notice how blown his eyes were... or the hard-on pressed into my belly. "What would you say to stepping this up a bit?" he asked, his voice raw and husky and panty-wettingly sexy.

"Fuck yes." I grabbed his exceedingly warm hand, and all but dragged him toward the bedroom. While I wasn't exactly sure what he had in mind, at this point, I was so inundated with denied want that I was pretty much down for whatever. Plus, I trusted him to stop if I hit the breaks. And, if for some reason, I was horribly wrong about that, I was more than capable of making him.

We'd barely made it to the edge of the bed when he re-captured my mouth, his fingers burying themselves in my hair to cradle my head. I all but melted into the caress while the fevered kiss threatened to consume me. I tugged at the hem of his shirt and he broke away long enough for me to yank it over his head before returning with a vengeance. He tilted my head back and continued his voracious quest along my jaw and neck, spreading delicious heat along the increasingly sensitive skin. I shuddered beneath the combined assault of nips, licks, and press of lips.

Determined to give as good as I got, I fisted his hair and brought his mouth back to mine. With my free hand, I explored the incredible definition of his abs and chest. He wasn't gym-chiseled by any means, but he was undeniably fit and fucking edible. I involuntarily dug my nails into his pec when he sucked on my tongue, then adjusted my hand to tweak his nipple. He released a muffled yelp, but didn't move away. If anything, he kissed me harder.

By the time we pulled apart, I'd nearly forgotten that oxygen was necessary for living. "Now what?" I panted, both my hands roving mindlessly over his bare chest and stroking the small thatch of soft hair over his sternum.

"I want to taste you," he said huskily, combing his fingers through my short hair.

I couldn't help but snicker. "I'd say you have been."

His dark eyes took on a wicked cast that had the best kind of goosebumps erupting all over my body. "Oh, I can do much, much better."

"Someone has a high opinion of their prowess."

He shrugged. "Is it over confident if it's true?"

I snorted. "I'll be the judge of that."

His grin broadened until it resembled the same enthusiastic golden retriever one from when we'd first met. "I look forward to your verdict." Without warning, he picked me up like I was nothing and promptly tossed me onto the bed.

A laugh burst out of me as I bounced. The flash of humor, however, dissolved when he crawled up my body to seal our mouths together once more. I dug my fingers into his shoulders and arched into him as I continued to devour his mouth. Finally, he pulled away with yet another playful nip at my swollen lips.

He hooked his fingers on my pants. "This okay?" he asked, the question ghosting tantalizingly over my lips. Even that barely there touch emanated heat.

"Yes," I replied so huskily I barely even recognized my own voice. Shit, was I really that hard up or was it just something about Xander?

He took his sweet ass time shimmying me out of the tight denim. Finally, my legs were bare and the only thing between him and my throbbing sex was a thin strip of soaked cotton. He hissed a breath and I looked down at him just in time to see his nostrils flare and his eyes dilate. "Stars, Diana, you have no idea..." He trailed off, but before I could ask, he buried his face in my mons.

I bit back a moan at the unexpected pressure of his tongue teasing along the seam. To my surprise, the fabric still between us did little to reduce the incredible sensation. And fuck he was hot, bordering on feverish. I writhed beneath him, aching for more but not wanting him to stop. Except he did.

Xander shifted his focus to tease the waistband with his teeth along with my quivering abdomen. He rucked my shirt higher to expose more of my stomach, which he licked and teased like he had every other part of me he'd gotten his mouth on. I couldn't decide if I was disappointed or impressed that he didn't venture higher to my breasts. Then his finger curled around the wettest part of my panties and I gasped at the electrifying brush of fingers on bare flesh. He continued to kiss along my lower abdomen as he used his hold to pull the interfering fabric down my legs. Once they were free, he gently coaxed my thighs wider, both of us now breathing just as hard as the other.

I about near came off the bed when his tongue ran over my swollen lips and flicked at my clit. I wasn't any more prepared for him to do it a second time or for the way his low groan vibrated against the increasingly sensitive sex. Each flick of his tongue was a flash of heat ratcheting up my pleasure to dizzying heights. He continued to lap hungrily until I had to put my fist in my mouth to keep from crying out.

"None of that," he purred, sending another wave of sensation pulsing through my aching core. He placed a soft kiss on my pelvis as he gently but firmly pulled my hand away. "I want to hear you." There was something about the growly statement that almost made it sound like he was also saying he wanted everyone else to hear too.

Not entirely sure how I felt about the whole damn complex hearing me come completely undone but also not interested in the least in telling him to stop, I simply nodded and let my hand fall to the side.

A smile that was more of a smirk flashed across his face before he lowered his head and sucked ruthlessly on my clit.

"Holy fuck!" I reflexively buried both my hands in his insanely soft hair and fought like hell not to buck against his mouth. Right when I didn't think I could possibly take much more stimulation, he backed off, lazily trailing his tongue along my slick folds. I released a shuddering breath and glanced down to see him, only to throw my head back with another garbled shout as he plunged his tongue inside.

From there, he alternated between driving me wild by fucking me with his tongue and torturing my clit with expert swirls. I was coming to the very real conclusion that his statement of prowess was *not* an empty boast. He brought me to the brink again and again, only to back off right as I hovered over the precipice. Then he plunged a finger into my wet center and I made a keening noise I'd never made before in my life.

The sound seemed to spur him into a fever pitch as he redoubled his efforts to disintegrate me with pleasure. I was already bracing myself for him to ease off yet again when he added another finger and made a come-hither motion while he sucked on my overly sensitive clit. My hold on his hair tightened, and I bowed off the bed. He made the gesture again and again, punctuating it with sharp flicks of his tongue.

I barely had a chance to register that he wasn't going to back off this time when my orgasm ripped through me like a damned force of nature. I clamped down around his fingers and cried out my release, which didn't seem to have an end in sight. When the flood of sensation finally ebbed, I sagged boneless back into the mattress, feeling sated and a little drunk.

Soft, fluttering kisses decorated my abdomen as Xander worked his way leisurely up my body. I fluttered my eyes open, expecting to find him grinning smugly above me. While he was smiling, it was gentle instead of self-satisfied. And there was something in his eyes, an almost kind of wonder I couldn't quite place. When he leaned down, I was more than ready to greet him with a kiss when he altered course to nuzzle into my neck. I got that some women were weirded out about tasting themselves, but I wasn't one of those women.

"Come here," I whispered, tugging lightly on his hair, which I'd apparently never released. He did so, hesitating as I brushed first one kiss, then another over his lips, until he relaxed into the deeper kiss I was after. "Angle your hips up," I said softly into the space between us. A frown creased his brow, but he did as I asked, giving me just enough room to wiggle a hand between us.

His eyes widened as I flicked open his jeans one-handed and maneuvered his cock free. The heat and weight of him had me wishing I could get a better look, but I had a sneaking suspicion that if I released my hold on his hair, he'd spout some line about my not needing to reciprocate and retreat. He'd learn. I didn't do anything I didn't want to.

I gave his length a firm squeeze and his eyes fluttered shut. I captured his mouth once more to distract him as I let go and dipped my fingers between my folds to capture the moisture there. Fingers now properly slick, I re-wrapped them around his cock.

He groaned into my mouth, breaking the kiss. "Fuck, Diana," he hissed between clenched teeth as I stroked him with increasing speed. I tightened my grip and twisted slightly when I got to the head, then did it again. "Oh...*fuck*," he moaned, meeting my strokes with his own thrusts. "Mother of the moon. Please don't stop. Oh, Goddess, please..."

From my vantage, I could see what every pass, twist, and tighten did to him and let it fuel my high. I increased my speed until the muscles in his neck were taught and his arms were shaking with the effort of holding himself up. "Come for me, Xander," I said, not relenting.

He made a low whimper, then went rigid, before grunting through his release. Hot ribbons decorated my stomach and I couldn't have cared less about the mess we'd made. With a defeated sigh, he slumped down to lie half on top of me. "You're going to be the end of me," he mumbled against my neck.

I barked a laugh and cuddled him close. We'd both earned a respite after that. Before long, we'd clean up and say goodbye for the night, but it could wait a little longer. Who knew, maybe if I was lucky, I'd get another round before then.

13

—◆◇◆—

MORE BAD NEWS

I FELT BETTER THAN I had in weeks. And it wasn't the sex. Okay, it wasn't *just* the sex. Xander had absolutely earned his boast of being freaking amazing with his mouth. Shame I couldn't keep riding that high. Thanks to Takashi unearthing my past as a champion archer, I was now officially his number one suspect in a murder investigation the rest of the campus was oblivious about. Which meant the ominously vague voicemail from my mother demanding that I come home for a visit soon "or else", would be that much harder to fulfill. But right now, my most pressing problem was how the fuck I was going to tell my friend I'd had sex with her cousin and had every intention of doing it again.

I caught sight of Jennifer and took a bracing breath before walking up to join her at a picnic table. It would have been easy to assume that she'd braved the chill because the inside of the student union was packed to the rafters. But even though that was likely true, the real reason was because it was a beautiful day. Any time the weather was nice, Jennifer opted to be outside. Not that I blamed her. Being surrounded by so many voices and bodies pressing in on you could be... stifling.

She glanced up from her lunch, flashing me a smile. I did my best to return it, though I couldn't help but wonder how long hers would last once I broke the news. "There you are!" A sudden frown creased her brow as I slid onto the bench across from her. "Where's your lunch?"

"Oh, uh, I wasn't hungry." The thought of eating anything while this weighed on my mind instantly had my stomach rolling.

"Uh-huh." She pointed a french fry at me. "Alright, spill. What's got you twisted?"

One of these days I was going to have to ask her how she did that with such unerring accuracy. "What makes you think I'm twisted up about something?" I stalled.

She narrowed her eyes, her frown deepening.

I let out a huff and glanced off to the side as I struggled to find the right words. Suddenly my gaze caught on a large canine being walked not too far away and I did a double take.

"What? What is it?" Jennifer leaned across the table to try and get a look at what had caught my attention.

"Nothing. For a second, I thought that was the dog that's been turning up at my place the last several weeks. Though come to think of it, he hasn't been by in a while," I mused aloud. Ever since I'd officially teamed up with Xander as a matter of fact. Perhaps the foreign scent had thrown him. He hadn't seemed too keen on Leena when she'd been at the apartment. I was so lost in my speculations that it took me a second to realize Jennifer had gone stock still. "What's up?" I asked, glancing around to determine the cause.

"You said a... dog has been visiting your place?"

I shrugged, still not sure what the big deal was.

"And why am I just now hearing about this?" The way her voice rose had me shifting uncomfortably on the bench.

"I thought I'd already told you?" I offered sheepishly. "Plus, it's not like it was a big deal. He was wet and scared. I just gave him a warm place to stay and fed him. A few times," I tacked on in a mumble.

"Diana!" she hissed. "You cannot just let wild animals into your apartment."

I rolled my eyes. "Please. I'm a big girl and can take care of myself. Besides, he was far from feral. He was sweet and even did tricks."

"I'll bet he did," she growled so low I almost didn't catch it. Given her alarming reaction to learning about my canine companion, I was seriously second-guessing the wisdom of telling her about me and Xander.

As if the universe hadn't shit on me enough lately, the man himself appeared at the end of our table. "Hey, Diana. Jenny, I need a word."

Thunderclouds rolled across Jennifer's face as she vacated her seat. "A word. I'll give you a fucking word. What the fuck were you thinking?" she hissed, though not quietly enough for me not to overhear since she was only standing a foot away from the table, and there was no missing the way she flung her hand out toward me.

"Look, you can lay into me later. Right now, we have bigger concerns."

Jennifer crossed her arms and scowled at him, though I was a bit at a loss for why she was so mad at him, given I'd yet to tell her what had happened between us. "Well, what is it?"

"Tor has been shot."

The blood drained from Jennifer's face and I scrambled out of my seat. "When?" she squeaked.

"Who's Tor?" I asked on top of her.

"Tor's one of our dormmates." He shook his head. "I'm not sure when he was shot, but he was still bleeding when he got to the dorm."

"Shot with an arrow? Do you still have the shaft?" I interjected, unable to take another second of the agonized silence.

Xander released a shaky breath and darted a glance at me. "The arrow was missing when he arrived. We should hurry. I've been rounding up everyone back at the dorm. You were the only one who didn't answer their phone."

"Shit," Jennifer hissed through her teeth. "It's still on silent from class."

"I get it, but we really need to go. Now. He... wasn't looking too good." The sorrow on Xander's face tore at my heart.

"Maybe I should go with you. Even without the arrow, I might be able to deduce something," I volunteered.

He and Jennifer shared a look before he stepped closer to me. "Helpful as that might be, I think it would be better if you didn't. This is something we need to handle as a community."

"But—"

He grabbed my hand, cutting off my argument. "I'll fill you in later. Promise." He gave my fingers a gentle squeeze then placed an equally soft kiss on my lips. The intimate gesture definitely didn't go unnoticed by Jennifer. It also didn't erase the sorrow hanging on him like a thousand-pound cloak.

"Okay," I replied softly, reluctantly letting him go. It didn't take long for the pair to walk beyond my field of vision. Once they were gone—and obviously not coming back—I glanced around at a loss. Now what? Sighing to myself, I swung my backpack onto my shoulder and headed in the direction of my next class.

Hours later, I was back in my apartment and still hadn't heard so much as a peep from Xander or Jennifer. I caught myself pacing and vented a frustrated growl. What was going on? Would they take pictures? And why had Xander thought it best for me to sit this out? Sure, part of me got that they were a tight community and had already been through *a lot*, but what if I could have helped?

I checked my phone for any notifications I might have missed since I'd last checked it a minute ago. Nothing. On the verge of chunking it into the sofa cushions, another thought struck me. I'd already planned to have one difficult conversation today. Since the one with Jennifer hadn't exactly occurred, there was no reason I couldn't channel that energy into another. Taking a deep breath, I dialed my mother.

Exactly three rings later, she picked up. "Diana, how good of you to call."

I winced at her dry tone. Okay, maybe I could have been a *little* better about staying in touch or at least sending regular updates. "How are... things?" I nearly smacked myself in the head. My mother and I hadn't used to have such a strained relationship. Not until I walked away from everything our family stood for.

She let out an exasperated breath and I could practically see her sliding into her sitting chair. A wistful smile crossed my face as I imagined the stack of books piled up beside her, and whichever one she was currently reading resting on the arm.

"Your father is... well, your father is your father," she said, bringing me back to the conversation. "You know he still disagrees with your decision."

I gave a derisive snort. "'Disagrees' is a mild way to put it. Quite frankly, I'm surprised he didn't demand Hyacinth drag me back home when she was in town for a visit."

"When was Hye in town?" she asked, her voice lifting in curiosity.

I bit the inside of my cheek at the slip. Well, one thing was disturbingly clear: Hye could get in and *out* of anywhere undetected. I couldn't decide if I should be impressed or incredibly concerned. "Um, yeah, she'd mentioned a few weeks back that she was going for another transfusion."

My mother's irritated snarl was just loud enough for me to make out, reminding me that while she toed the familial obligation line with the best of them, Vanessa Harker hadn't always been part of this world. Once upon a time she'd been a true debutante well on her way to ending world hunger and establishing world peace, or so I liked to believe. "I still don't see how *they* could subject their child to such treatment," she sniffed.

"She's far from a child, mom. Trust me, Hye makes her own decisions." That was putting it mildly.

"Perhaps she does now. But I refuse to accept that a twelve-year-old had any true understanding of what was being asked of her at the time. It's unconscionable. Those magical transfusions are abhorrent. They all but signed their own daughter's death warrant." It was tempting to point out that she hadn't exactly been asked as much as expected. And on that front our families were unerringly similar.

"There's no undoing it now," I gently reminded her. "Now, about that message you left..."

"No, I suppose not," she mused softly before pulling herself back together. "Yes, the message. It would seem your uncle has yet another ridiculous scheme."

"Uncle Nemo? He's always going off about something. I hardly think that's grounds to demand a visit on pain of an unnamed threat."

"What? Visiting your mother isn't enough of a reason?"

"Mom..."

"I'm teasing, Di. I understand your desire to be on your own, away from... everything. I may not agree with it, but I understand. As far as your uncle is concerned, while most of his schemes don't amount to much, he seems to have actually struck upon something this time. Something... concerning."

"And whatever this 'concerning' thing is, you're not going to tell me over the phone." It wasn't a question. It wasn't that my mother distrusted technology–far from it. She used it extensively on a daily basis in her job as a programmer. Which left me wondering the true cause for her caution.

"This isn't something that should be discussed outside the *home*," she said, emphasizing the last word. And I had my answer. Whatever my uncle had found involved family secrets. The kind of secrets no one with the Harker name would dare utter beyond the security of wards.

I rubbed the back of my neck, tugging restlessly at the short hairs there. "It, uh, might be difficult for me to get away. Exams and what not. You know."

"Diana Allison Harker, I have been more than respectful of your decision to forsake all of us—"

"Mom," I tried to interject.

"No. I have given you your space. But you *will* get your wayward self up here within the next fortnight or you'll *wish* I'd had Hyacinth bring you back."

I blanched. My mother may be decidedly more empathetic than my father, but she wasn't one to make idle threats. "Okay, mom, I'll do my best and let you know when I'm able to get away." A task I had no idea how I would accomplish with the tenacious detective sniffing around.

"That's better." The line was quiet for a few moments. "I do miss you, sweetie," she said softly.

The tenderness in her voice had me transported back to a time when I'd be sitting on her lap, reading along with her as best I could. "I miss you too, mom. I'll try to be less of a stranger."

We finished saying our goodbyes and hung up. I stood for a minute just staring at the blank screen of my phone. It hadn't been a lie; I did miss my mom. We'd always had so much in common, unlike me and my father.

A banging on the door lurched me out of my reminiscing. I narrowed my gaze at the locked door and toyed with pretending not to have heard, or even better, not to be home.

"Diana?" Xander's voice cracked on my name, and I doubt I'd ever moved so fast.

I frantically undid the locks and ripped open the door. Xander stood braced against frame, his face a twisted expression of agony. "Oh gods, what happened?"

"Tor's dead."

14

ONE DEAD, ONE MISSING

I STAGGERED BACK FROM the door, temporarily overcome with shock, allowing Xander to step inside. He raked his fingers through his hair as he waited for me to close the door behind him. To say he looked wrecked fell short of encompassing the level of distress rolling off of him.

"I don't understand. I thought you said it wasn't a fatal wound." I stepped closer, not sure if I should reach out to him or give him space. All I knew was that I hated seeing him like this. Xander was the embodiment of the perfect summer day, but the man in front of me looked like he'd been tossed into the storm of the century without a windbreaker.

He shook his head, his eyes tight. "It wasn't. It *shouldn't* have been."

Unable to take it anymore, I led him to the couch. Once he was seated, I grabbed him some water along with the bottle of bourbon I kept in the pantry. I set both within easy reach, giving him the freedom to choose what he needed.

"How about you start at the beginning? I know I caught snippets earlier, but maybe there's something that will stand out." He took a deep breath and let it out shakily. I placed a hand on his arm. "Only if you're up for it. We can just sit here, if that's what you need."

He groaned and dropped his head into his hands. "I don't even know why I'm here. I shouldn't be dragging you into this."

"First of all, let me worry about myself. I'm a hell of a lot tougher than I look." His lips twitched in an almost smile and he looked at me through wet lashes. The undeniable affection shining in his eyes hit me in the chest and for a small second, I forgot to breathe. I quickly shook off the unexpected reaction and continued. "And secondly, like it or not, I'm already in this."

"You're right. I just..." Doubt clouded his warm brown eyes and he looked away. Then he cleared his throat. "The last week or so had been fairly quiet. We were beginning to think we might be able to hold our usual full moon event. He was out with Kai scouting out possible places to... party."

I bit the inside of my cheek to keep from interjecting. I couldn't imagine what kind of party would be worth being out at night given there was a murderer on the loose.

"Something happened. I'm not sure what. But they got split up. That's when Tor was shot."

"Where was he shot?" I asked as gently as I could.

"Near as we can tell, in the right arm." He gestured to his bicep. "Aside from the fact that the arrow had been torn out of him, there wasn't anything unusual about the wound and we haven't found another."

I sucked in a breath. "Did Tor remove it or..."

Xander's sharp gaze killed the rest of my question.

"Did he get a look at them, at least?" I asked softly, barely above a whisper.

He shook his head. "Like the others, he was shot from behind." I flashed to an image of a deer sprinting through the woods, running for its life.

"What about Kai? You said they got split up. Is it possible he saw something?"

"Maybe."

I frowned at the unusual response. "Couldn't you just ask him?"

Xander sank in on himself. "Kai didn't come back. He could be dead out there for all we know and I can't in good conscience send anyone to go look for him." Oh fuck, that was bad. What was worse was that Xander seemed to be shouldering the entirety of the awful situation. Like he was personally responsible for keeping everyone safe. "I keep hoping I'm wrong, that he'll turn up unharmed. But I can't shake the feeling that he's out there somewhere with yet another arrow sticking out of his dead body." Xander's whole body trembled as if struggling to contain all of his anguish.

"Let's go back to the arrow," I said, stroking his back. "Any insight at all around that? Like how did the shooter manage to retrieve it if Tor was actively running?"

"Best guess is that either the force of it made him fall or he tripped and hit his head. But if he was down, why not finish Tor there? Why just take the arrow and let him go?" Xander gave me a pleading look like I could somehow provide an answer.

"I don't know. It doesn't make sense. Taking the arrow, I get. That's evidence. But you're right, letting Tor go was... cruel." I was tempted to add that it also smarted of sending a message, but that led down a path I wasn't ready to entertain at the moment and certainly wasn't something Xander needed to be agonizing over.

"We all thought he was so lucky to get away and then..." Xander balled his fists on his knees. "He didn't get better. He kept getting worse."

It seemed a safe bet that Xander and his whole dorm were doing their damnedest to stay out of police scrutiny, but the question bore asking. "Why not call an ambulance? Surely a hospital could have helped."

He released a derisive laugh. "The injury wasn't even serious. By the time any of us thought to call, it was too late." While I was pretty sure *most* people would consider getting shot with an arrow a serious injury no matter where they were hit, saying so wouldn't help matters now.

"Could the arrow have been poisoned? Or maybe he'd been fed it when he went down."

Xander was shaking his head before I could finish. "Not possible."

"Okay, maybe force-feeding poison is out of the question, but what about an injection? Depending on where it was administered, it could go undetected."

"It wasn't poison."

I huffed and leaned back against the couch with a scowl. "You seem awful sure of that."

"Because I am. Just trust me, poison didn't kill Tor."

"Then what did? Because, unless that arrow nicked an artery, that's not a fatal shot."

Xander launched up from the couch. "Don't you think I know that!" Almost immediately, he groaned and dropped his head in his hands. "I'm sorry, I shouldn't have shouted. You're just trying to help."

"No, I'm sorry," I said, joining him. I rubbed his arms, which I just realized were bare despite the very noticeable chill outside. Not that Xander was anything but his usual overly-warm self. Finally, he lifted his head to look at me. "You're hurting. You didn't come here so that I could interrogate you about how your friend died. How about some tea to relax instead of the hard stuff?"

He gave me a sad smile. "Chamomile would be nice."

I felt a flash of surprise. How did he know I had chamomile? I quickly shook myself out of it. Even people who didn't like tea had chamomile in their cabinets. I was about to get up when his shoulders caved inward.

"Sorry, I don't mean to be an imposition. Honestly, I don't even know why I came here. I just needed—wanted to see you." His raw confession made my chest flutter.

I stamped down the renegade reaction and cupped his face. "I'm here. And you're *not* an imposition." He let out a stuttering breath that almost relaxed the tension knotting his shoulders. Suddenly, a thought struck me. "Come on." I grabbed his hand and led him toward the bedroom.

"Diana, that's not... I'm not expecting anything."

I threw him a cheeky grin over my shoulder as we approached the bed. "Good, because you're not getting anything. Now, shoes off and get under the covers."

He clearly tried to fight it, but a genuine chuckle escaped. "Would it be too presumptuous of me to take off my shirt?"

"You won't hear me complaining," I replied, my grin decidedly saucier. I waited long enough to appreciate the revealing of his gorgeous chest and to make sure he was actually getting in the bed before zipping back out into the living room to snag my laptop and the requested chamomile tea. "Any favorite shows we might be able to look up?" I asked upon returning.

He shrugged, bunching the duvet. "Not really. Though I've found cooking shows to be oddly relaxing."

"That, I can work with." I plopped on the bed beside him and immediately began browsing for something. By the time I landed on one with plenty of episodes, Xander had scooted closer and was resting his head on my shoulder. I fired up the first episode, when he didn't comment on the selection and shimmied down into a more comfortable position.

The show had been running for about ten minutes when Xander's hand wrapped around mine. My stupid, traitorous heart gave a little skip when he rubbed his thumb along the back. "Thank you," he whispered so softly that I wouldn't have heard at all if his lips hadn't been so close to my ear already.

I glanced down at him to find his expressive eyes gazing back at me. Without even thinking, I stroked his cheek with my freehand then gently pressed my lips against his. I'd had a lot of kisses over the years, but I doubted I'd ever had one so sweet. The fluttering returned with a vengeance and I pulled away. "Anytime."

As one episode bled into another, peppered with the inevitable commercials, I wanted to mull over everything he'd told me. Instead, I kept coming back to that at his lowest Xander had sought me out. For comfort. Not to solve all of his problems or bounce ideas off of, but because he found my presence soothing. And I didn't have a damn clue what to do with that information.

We hadn't actually known each other that long. How was it that he could trust me so much already? How was it that I trusted him? Which I did, though it didn't make a lick of sense. But then, neither did the way I reacted whenever he was around.

I absently combed my fingers through his silky hair. His warm breath ghosted over my collar and he nuzzled my neck before settling back down. A different warmth spread through my chest at how easy and comfortable it was to be together. No expectations, no pressure to do more, just quiet companionship. My heart of hearts swelled with its secret truth. I didn't just like Xander, I was falling for him.

15

—◆○◆—

SHOT IN THE DARK

ALERTNESS CAME IN SLUGGISH waves until the urgent need to stretch finished waking me up. I glanced to my side, where Xander was now stirring as well. The warmth he'd been cocooning me with vanished as he rolled onto his back with a groan.

"Sorry, I didn't mean to fall asleep," he mumbled, still sounding completely exhausted.

I shifted to face him and brushed a chaste kiss over his lips. "You have nothing to be sorry for."

His eyes shimmered with a smile as we continued to gaze at each other. I was on the cusp of leaning down to snare him with a more in-depth kiss, morning breath be damned, when his phone pinged. He shut his eyes and I could *see* him don his composure like armor.

"I take it, you need to get that?"

"Yeah," he sighed. "I'm almost too afraid to look."

My heart sank at the revelation that it could be yet more bad news. But I refused to voice that, aiming for an optimistic approach I didn't fully believe. "Maybe Kai has returned and he can shed some light on what happened."

151

"Maybe. Or everyone is clamoring to know where I am and what I'm doing about the situation." He unlocked his phone only to immediately darken the screen. "Yep. They're all freaking out." He ran his hands over his face. "I should really get going."

He swung his legs over the side of the bed and I couldn't help but admire the sculpted lines of his back as he reached high overhead for a long stretch. His arms fell back to the mattress, and he shook out his hair, which somehow had escaped the disaster of bedhead. I had no delusions about how likely it was that my hair was sticking up at several weird angles.

We proceeded to put ourselves together for the day in relative silence. Sadly, no amount of dragging my feet could put off our inevitable parting. Hell if I knew why I was so reluctant to see him go, but there it was. He was comfortable in my space. More importantly, *I* was comfortable with him in my space, not something I'd encountered, well, ever.

"Good luck," I said when we stood before the door. "Keep me in the loop?"

He gave my hand a quick squeeze, though I wasn't sure when he'd taken it. "As much as I can." Rather than dwell on the vague response, I squeezed his hand back before letting it go.

"While you're dealing with things at the dorm, I'll see what I can find on my own."

He nodded absently, his mind clearly already somewhere else as he turned to go. He made it halfway out the door when he spun back around, capturing my face with his warm hands and kissing me within an inch of my life.

I squeaked in surprise, but that didn't stop me from tangling my fingers in his shirt and clinging to him for all I was worth. If I didn't know better, I'd assume he was secretly a witch and had cast some sort of spell on me. Completely impossible given the anti-hex ring I wore on my pinky at all times, but it didn't diminish the intensity of the pull I felt toward him.

He finally pulled away with a shuddering breath and I got lost in his eyes. As dark as they were, I could still make out thin bands of lighter and darker shades, much like the rings of a tree. "I know it's pointless to ask you not to venture out by yourself, so I won't. Just... be careful. Okay? And if you run into trouble, any at all, call me."

I nodded and gave him a small smile. It was both adorable and heartwarming that he was worried about me, especially given all the things he was already worrying about. It also meant the world that he didn't question whether or not I could handle myself.

"I mean it, Diana. I don't care how trivial it may seem or if you think I'm ears deep in dorm drama, you call. Promise?"

How could I not after that? "I promise." On cue, his phone dinged three times in rapid succession. I chuckled and gave him a gentle shove. "You better get going before they send out a search party."

Panic briefly flared in his eyes at the prospect before he wiped the expression from his face. "I'll be in touch. And, you, be careful." He swiped his lips against mine a final time, then turned to leave.

I continued to stand in the open doorway while I watched him go completely entranced by his perfectly tight ass. To my surprise, he didn't walk toward the front office and the transit or even the parking lot, but toward the woods. He glanced over his shoulder before he crossed the tree line and I returned his wave.

Once he was completely out of sight, I shut and locked the door, then took a quick shower and settled down with some coffee to survey a map of Blackwell Hollow. I added colored dots to the downloaded image where all the bodies had been found. While I was at it, I marked my apartment and Luxom Hall.

I blinked a few times as I realized there was almost a straight shot of woods between my place and Xander's dorm. Granted, it was a relatively wide expanse to traverse, especially on foot. Even so, what were the odds? I shook my head and made a few notes on possible routes Tor and Kai could have taken on their misguided quest. Then I packed my things and headed out.

As I meandered along the outer rim of campus, I wondered again what would possess Xander's dorm to try and hold a party at a time like this. What's more, Xander didn't even mention canceling it despite what had happened to Tor and Kai. I shook my head. He'd likely not thought to mention it. Standing tradition or not, no way were they going forward with something as trivial as a party.

At least knowing what the two had been doing when they got split helped me retrace their steps. Or I thought it would. By the time I walked out of the sixth bar/café/restaurant/event space, I was seriously doubting if they'd *ever* booked a place for their "party". I came to a dead stop on the sidewalk as I finally made the connection that I should have made at the outset. If they were drinking, odds were that Xander wasn't the only one underage. None of the places I'd been to this morning would have condoned serving minors. The logical solution would have been to use The Silver Bullet, especially if Xander's father really was the owner. Except they wouldn't have needed to scout a location if they were going there. Which left one terrible possibility and explained Xander's intense worry when I said I'd snoop around—they'd planned to party in the woods.

"Damn it!" I cursed in frustration, drawing the evil eye of a passing mother with her toddler. I gave the pair an insincere apologetic smile, coupled with a wave.

Clearly I was starting to lose my edge after all, if I could miss such a glaring detail. As if to underscore the thought, the hairs on the back of my neck suddenly stood on end at the now all too familiar sensation of being watched. Resuming my stroll, I surreptitiously looked around for the cause of the unshakeable feeling. It wasn't my imagination. Someone was definitely watching me. But other than the odd town's person, no one stood out.

I picked up my pace, determined to lose the prying eyes before venturing to my new destination to search for clues. Unfortunately, the eerie sensation stayed with me, dogging my steps and threatening to crack my composure. Most troubling was that the only person aside from Detective Takashi that would have a vested interest in following me was the true killer.

I never thought I'd actually hope to run into the detective, but it was better than the alternative. The killer had already proved they didn't need the cloak of night to attack and arrows were a long-range weapon. My only consolation on that front was that they'd be hard pressed to retrieve the arrow without detection if they shot me now.

My heart rate continued to escalate, and I was seconds from breaking into an all-out sprint when I rounded a corner too fast and smashed into a pedestrian. "Oh shit! Sorry," I exclaimed as I simultaneously regained my footing and tried to prevent the other person from crashing into the ground.

"For fuck's sake! Look where you're going. You've ruined my cupcakes *and* my blouse. What's the rush, anyway?"

At the irritated question, I stopped searching over my shoulder for my stalker and faced the person I'd just stumbled into. "Kora?"

She stopped plucking at her blouse, which was now covered in a variety of frosting, and looked up. "Diana? What the hell are you doing here? And why are you in such a damn rush?"

"I um..." At a loss for a plausible excuse she'd actually buy, I searched nearby storefronts for inspiration. "I'm on my way to meet someone and running terribly late. Sorry again." I indicated her ruined treats and shirt and moved to step around her.

"It wouldn't perchance be Mr. Tall-Young-And-Dreamy, would it?" she asked, pulling me to a stop.

I slowly turned back to face her. "I don't know who you mean."

Kora rolled her eyes and flicked a clump of frosting from her ruined blouse. "Please, Hyacinth clocked that like a month ago. So... make any moves yet?" She sidled closer, a conspiratorial gleam in her blue eyes. "Don't tell me you haven't at least encouraged him. Guy's freaking *gorgeous*."

"And young," I snapped, in an attempt to nip this line of chit-chat in the bud. The feeling of being watched may have finally subsided, but that didn't mean I had time to indulge Kora's propensity for gossip.

"Pft. So you're a couple years older. You're both still consenting adults."

To my chagrin, my face heated at the comment, and her eyes lit up with triumph.

"Aha!" she shouted emphatically, nearly depositing her overturned cupcakes on the ground. "You *have* made a move. Alright, change of plans." She glanced around. "We're going to sit in front of that little café and you're going to spill all the deets while you help me eat all these smooshed cakes." She stared sullenly down at her blouse. "Maybe I can clean up a bit in the bathroom. Don't suppose you have a spare sweater?"

"I am *really* sorry for messing up your blouse, but I'm meeting someone, remember?"

She raised her golden eyebrows. "And who was that again?"

"Hyacinth," I said, grabbing the first name that came to mind.

She tsked. "Nope. We both know Hyacinth is presenting her group project today for ethics."

I could have smacked myself for forgetting. She'd done nothing but gripe about the damn project for weeks. And given the irony that it was for Ethics of all things, it was hard not to laugh every time she brought it up. "Fine. Xander," I mumbled.

"Sorry, didn't quite catch that." She smirked, an absolutely evil gleam in her eyes.

"His name is Xander," I said louder, my face flushing again. "And, okay, we've fooled around. A bit. Nothing serious," I added with a sour glare at my friend.

"Uh huh. Is that why you've been keeping him all to yourself? It's not like you to be shy about who you're sleeping with." I flashed to how fucking tasty Xander had looked this morning as he shook off the last tendrils of sleep. The thought had the unfortunate side effect of causing my ridiculous blush to deepen and Kora to cackle. "Oh, that's so cute! You *like* him."

"What are you, twelve?"

"Then tell me I'm wrong."

I opened my mouth to do just that, but nothing came out. Was that why I was so secretive of him? Was it more than the fact that we were investigating multiple murders together? I hadn't even realized until she'd pointed it out. And I wasn't sure how I felt about Hye "clocking it" at all. And Kora was right about me not being shy about who I saw, except... Except I *did* care for Xander. Somehow, his golden retriever energy had grown on me.

"Called it!" Kora flashed a self-satisfied grin. "And what's the real reason you're in such a hurry? I'm gonna go out on a limb and guess you're not actually meeting up with him, either."

I scowled at her. "That's a pretty long limb."

"That's what she said." She winked, and I groaned at having walked right into that.

"Seriously, you're twelve."

"Maybe, but I'm also right." My mouth fell open at her confident assertion and she flashed me another knowing smile. "When you're friends with the likes of you and Hyacinth, you learn to read between the lines. So, you can either double-down on your story of meeting up with the hottie that you're *totally* not banging. *Or* you can help me eat these melted cupcakes while you fill me in on all the juicy, dirty little details."

"Cupcakes don't melt."

She squinted at the compromised packaging. "Could have fooled me. Now about that sweater..." She hooked my arm and guided me to the cafe she'd indicated.

By the time I extricated myself from Kora, muted indigo tones mingled with bright swatches of orange and magenta in the sky. She might appear to be a perfectly normal sorority girl, but the woman could give lessons in interrogation techniques. I shook my head, still amazed at how much information she'd weaseled out of me about Xander. At least I'd managed to keep the knee-deep-in-murder aspect of our relationship to myself.

I huffed as I sagged against the damp wall and stared out at the nearby forest. Fog drifted in lazy tendrils near the ground, a harbinger of the bitter cold that would follow. So much for investigating the woods. I may have a high opinion of my survival skills, but I wasn't reckless enough to venture deep into the forest at night with a killer on the loose.

Dismayed at my resounding lack of progress, I pushed away from the wall and angled myself toward the nearest transit stop. Something shifted in my periphery and I turned back to the small field separating the fringe of town from the woods. It took some squinting, but eventually I spotted the likely source of the movement. A shape settled deep into the now very dead grass, looking like an indistinct blob of gray in the early dusk.

As if sensing I'd spotted it, the shape slowly stood to reveal a large canine, but with the sun setting, it was difficult to make out much more. My heart surged with hope and a touch of excitement. Had my companion finally returned?

Without thinking, I took a step toward it. Immediately, the animal stepped back, maintaining the distance between us. I took another step, unwilling to give up so easily. He glanced around as if my increasing proximity was making him anxious. That was weird. Surely he recognized me, even if we hadn't seen each other in a few weeks.

"Is something wrong?" I asked.

The canine went stock still and stared back at me, its ears twitching.

"Why haven't you come back?" I took another step, determined to find clarity for at least one mystery. The dry crackle of leaves reached my ears just as he spun around and bolted. "Wait!" I shouted as I tore after him.

Dense mist swirled around my feet as I raced past the tree line. He veered to the right, and I followed suit. My lungs burned with cold as I pushed harder to close the distance.

My canine companion wasn't just fast, he was abnormally fast. Still, I refused to be left behind. Then he vanished.

"Shit." I braced my hands on my knees and heaved for breath. When I straightened, I realized just how misguided my chase had been. Everywhere I looked were trees. Not so much as a hint of civilization. To add insult to injury, twilight had firmly set in while I'd run. Without even the dappled light to break up the darkness, the forest took on an ominous air.

I shook off my sudden unease at seeing just how far I'd ventured into the woods. Why had my companion fled in the first place? Was it a trap? I scanned the immediate area for any sign of which direction he could have gone. Search as I might, though, the encroaching winter had hardened the ground and any mud that might have betrayed his passing... or anyone else's.

A chill slithered down my spine that had absolutely nothing to do with the cold. One thing was for certain, companion or no, I couldn't stay here. I dove into the scraggly underbrush, clinging to the faint hope that I'd either stumble out into civilization or find some landmark to give me a hint of where I was.

When not even the muted light was enough to see by, I paused and fished a small flashlight out of my bag. It flicked on with a nearly silent click and a beam of yellow light shot out to hit the ground. Armed with the feeble light, I proceeded forward, careful not to step on any dried branches or fall into any hidden pitfalls. Not an easy task, given how blanketed the uneven ground was.

I swung the cone of yellow light in a sweeping arc. About ten feet ahead, where the illumination faded into obscure shadowy shapes, something caught the light in a flash of amber. I quickly brought back the focus and took another step forward. Right at the edge of clarity, two amber orbs glowed back at me.

"There you are. Please, don't run. You know I won't hurt you." Unlike before, when I took another step closer, he remained rooted. I lowered the flashlight a fraction, so it wasn't directed right at his eyes. Another fateful step and I was finally close enough to realize this was *not* my furry companion. The hair was significantly lighter, they were smaller, and most startling, he was a she.

"Well, this is awkward." I'd literally chased down some random other dog-wolf hybrid and gotten myself lost in the woods in the process. "Today really isn't my day," I sighed heavily.

Her ear twitched. Much like my canine visitor, the response felt like an understanding and subsequent response.

On a whim, I took another step closer. The canine simply titled her head to the side as I approached slower than cold molasses. Maybe they belonged to the same litter. If someone was illegally breeding hybrids, it was possible they'd gotten out together.

Suddenly, the animal's hackles rose and her gaze shifted from me to look out at the forest. An eerie quiet settled in the air. Then I faintly made out the whisper of a bow being drawn.

"Duck!" I shouted.

The canine immediately dropped to the ground just as an arrow thunked into the tree beside her, right where her head would have been.

"Run," I ordered, lurching forward. The canine didn't hesitate to vanish into the darkness on nearly silent paws. I ripped the arrow out of the tree and veered in a different direction, my flashlight held low. I stumbled through the darkness, wary of bringing the flashlight any higher than absolutely necessary. As it was, I was already a shining beacon.

The faint snap of a twig somewhere behind me cracked through the woods. Adrenaline coursed through my limbs, urging my already tired legs on faster. Another arrow thwacked into a tree trunk right as I zipped around it. Fear clogged my burning lungs as my run turned frantic.

The yellow arc of my flashlight swung wildly to bounce off trees and fallen branches alike. My foot caught on an exposed root and I stumbled forward, narrowly preventing myself from landing in a sprawl. The nearly inaudible whistle of an arrow passed overhead to embed itself deeply into the trunk in front of me. Liquid fear battled with the training I'd received years ago.

I pushed back the instinct to run, then lowered the beam of light to a barely distinguishable glow and quickly surveyed my immediate area. The arrow was buried deep enough that its owner couldn't be that far away, even with a high-powered bow. Which meant my time was limited and running out.

As quietly as I could and disturbing as few of the leaves as possible, I made my way to an ancient oak with heavy limbs, silently thanking every deity I could think of that I'd stumbled in front of what had to be one of maybe a dozen oaks in the whole forest. A branch hung low enough that if I stretched, I could just get a good grip. I took a deep breath and glanced in the direction the arrow had come. There was nothing to betray its origin or how much time I still had.

Now or never.

I would only get one shot at this, so I didn't hesitate. I abandoned my crouch to jump straight up. The trajectory could have been better and my torso scratched along the rough branch while my backpack weighed me down. The jump would have been easier without it, but I couldn't afford to leave anything behind to give away my position. I gritted my teeth and clawed my way onto the branch as quietly as I could. Every rustle of fabric and flaking piece of bark grated on my ears, but I persisted until I was fully up and able to shimmy my way toward the trunk. Once there, I reached for the next nearest branch overhead and did it again, then again and again until I was a good fifteen feet off the ground and nearly completely hidden by leaves.

My breath came out in a soft puff of fog and I finally dimmed the light all the way to nothing. Not a second later, there came the faint rustle of dead leaves from below. I held my breath and peered down at a cloaked figure thrown into sharp contrast by the faint pool of light at its feet. The figure walked up to the embedded arrow and pulled it out with a crunch of broken bark in one violent yank.

They eyed the tip and then slipped it into the quiver on their back, then resumed their search of the ground. My heart pounded loudly in my ears. I willed it to quiet as the hunter took a step away in the opposite direction. They ventured a few paces, then turned around and followed the same path I had to the large pine. I shrank against the trunk as they approached my perch. They scoured the ground a moment before looking up. From my hidden vantage, it was impossible to make out anything in the shadowed cowl. Their gaze searched the branches with an intensity that made my skin crawl.

My lungs were at the edge of their limit when I wrapped a hand around the arrow I'd retrieved. I was loath to part with the only tangible clue I'd obtained, but it was either that or wait for the hunter to shine a brighter light. As carefully as I could, I removed the arrow. I held it like a dart, aiming between a hole in the dense needles, then released with all the force I could muster without jeopardizing my perch.

I nearly let out a relieved breath when the arrow ripped through dry leaves a fair distance away. As I'd hoped, the noise captured the hunter's attention, and they slipped away to trace the sound. I continued to hold my breath for another minute before letting it out as quietly as my abused lungs would allow. I stayed in the tree, unwilling to give up my hiding spot on the off chance that my pursuer hadn't actually left. It wasn't until the cold had my fingers and nose completely numb that I dared venture lower.

By the time I dropped from the last branch, there was no telling how much time had passed. The sun had long since set and what little nightlife that was active in winter had long since resumed their nocturnal activities. I warily brightened my beam of light and surveyed the ground. Now I just had to get out of here before the hunter realized I'd sent them on a wild goose chase. As I carefully lowered myself to the ground, I couldn't help but hope that he didn't find the canine I'd been chasing along the way.

16

Deadly Mistakes

THE NEXT DAY, I went to class as normal, as well as the day after that, and the day after that. While I went through the motions of mundane life and avoided anything that might put me any more in Detective Takashi's view than I already was, I'd be lying if I said I wasn't worried. It wasn't just that I'd had a brush with the killer and had zero idea of how to tell Xander, he wasn't answering my texts. Any of them.

I understood that things were chaotic at his dorm and that the whole place was probably freaking out, but he'd promised to keep me in the loop. *As much as I can.* The phrase popped up ominous and unbidden, just like it had every other day. Was he hiding something from me? Not that I had any right to be upset given the enormity of the things *I* was hiding. But it was more than that. To my chagrin, I was... worried about him.

Maybe it was something I'd done? I immediately dismissed the thought, not because I believed I was too good to screw up, but because Xander wasn't the type of person not to speak out if something was wrong. He certainly hadn't had any qualms accusing me of murder to my face while holding a potential murder weapon. I'd call him reckless, except he

165

seemed confident in a way few people possessed. I tried not to look too closely at what *those* people—people like me, like Hyacinth, like my family—had in common. Whatever the reason, I just hoped that same confidence didn't lead him to do something he couldn't walk away from, assuming he hadn't already.

I stretched, cracking my back after I exited the transit at my apartment complex. It was probably all the stress making me so tight. But short of inviting myself to Xander's dorm—which I had every intention of doing this weekend, if he didn't provide some proof of life in the next two days—I just had to deal. A notification dinged on my phone and I fished it out as fast as my sweater would allow. My buzz of optimism that I'd somehow manifested a response simply from thinking about him shriveled as I realized it was a weather alert.

The phone was halfway to my pocket before the notification fully registered. I paused in the middle of the sidewalk just beyond the pool to stare at the screen. A weather notification. One that had been set up the moment I'd been given the device. Unable to stop myself, I looked up and searched the sky. Sure enough, hovering barely visible above the tree line, was the full moon, its ethereal glow unmistakable in the deepening twilight.

Dread sat on my chest. I hadn't been afraid of the full moon since I was five. Yet, here I stood, damn near trembling because of a ridiculous rock in space. No way was Xander going to let his dorm go forward with a damn party. He was way too smart for that, especially after Tor and Kai. Try to logic as I might, I couldn't help but tap out yet another message to Xander.

Don't do anything stupid. Stay home. Or come here. You can party another time.

Hopefully, he was at least reading them, even if he wasn't responding. I traded the phone for my keys and finished walking up the hill to my apartment. Once I was inside, though, the restless energy that had been plaguing me all day demanded release. So, I did what any other sane person would do—laundry.

I was putting away the last of the clothes when something slammed into the apartment door. A burst of adrenaline shot my heart rate up and briefly paralyzed my limbs. Then another crash came that sounded a lot like the plastic lawn chair outside had just met an untimely end. Normally, I'd leave whatever was making such a ruckus alone until it left, but that was before my canine companion, and before I'd been shot at in the woods. As quietly as I could, I slipped into the kitchen and grabbed the biggest knife I had before tiptoeing toward the door. I was inches from checking the peephole when an agonized whine had me moving double time.

I stabbed the knife into the top of the nearest end table and set to work undoing the locks as fast as my suddenly trembling hands could manage. I'd barely turned the handle when a hard thud on the opposite side sent the door flying open. A dark blur instantly barreled through the opening and I scurried out of the way. It thrashed about, the whining and snarling almost deafening in the enclosed space. Not wanting to alarm the neighbors, I shut the door, locking it for good measure. No sooner did the deadbolt strike home than the animal released a heart-shattering whine of pain and collapsed.

Now that he was no longer thrashing about, it was easy to see that the source of the chaos was, in fact, my furry friend. Similar to the first time I'd met him, his dark coat was dirty and matted. Then he shifted and revealed a smear of red staining the carpet. I let out a gasp and rushed closer, prompting a deep warning growl that stopped me in my tracks.

My companion attempted to heave himself back to his feet, but only made it about halfway before his legs gave out. This time, when he collapsed, I clearly saw the two broken arrows sticking out of him. Cold suffused my face as all the blood drained from it.

"Oh my gods," I whispered in horror.

I kept up a steady stream of soothing noises as I inched closer, careful to stay in his line of sight and keep my hands visible. When I was close enough, I could see that what I'd mistaken for mud was actually a shit ton of blood matting his fur. I could also tell exactly how labored his breathing was. The shots weren't technically fatal, but the blood loss would be if I couldn't stem the bleeding. Which meant the arrows had to go. I reached for one and he growled again.

"Sh, it's okay. I'm not trying to hurt you. I want to help, if you'll let me."

His head lolled to the side, and I saw the whites of his eyes as they rolled to keep me in sight.

Carefully, I touched the arrow sticking out of his shoulder, and he elicited a whine that tore at my heart. I choked back a sob and blinked away the tears pricking my eyes. "I know, I know, but it has to come out. They both do."

The series of whines and whimpers that followed tested my resolve in a way I never could have imagined. I placed a hand above the protrusion to hold him steady. I tried not to think about the sticky wetness that instantly coated my fingers as they sunk into the thick fur and gripped the shaft with my other hand.

"Deep breath." I wasn't sure if I was talking to him or me. Either way, I followed my own advice.

After a deep lungful, I tightened my hold and pulled. It was a huge gamble that it wouldn't cause more harm, but it wasn't like I had an arrow spoon on hand and pushing the shaft through wasn't an option. There was a moment of resistance, then the arrow popped free with a sickening squelch. The horrific sound was accompanied by a pained wail from my companion that most definitely would have been heard next door. He dug his claws into the low shag carpet, tearing it free as he attempted and failed to remain still against the agony.

I quickly wiped the gore off on my shirt and held the remains of the arrow up to the light. Horror settled like a stone in my stomach as I realized what kind of tip it had. Despite Xander's conviction that there was no way the arrows were poisoned, the modified target arrowhead was designed specifically for delivering exactly that. I glanced down at the heaving sides of my companion. One shot could fell an adult human. And he'd suffered two.

I pushed down the queasiness threatening to work its way up my throat and tossed the arrow aside. He was still breathing, still fighting. Maybe it wasn't too late. I recognized the shallow hope for what it was, but it was also all I had.

"Okay, one down, one to go," I said with all the confidence I could muster.

His sides heaved, and he gave a pitiful whimper, but otherwise didn't move.

I swallowed and rubbed my bloody hand on my pant leg. The one in his side would be so much worse, there was no telling if it had punctured something vital and he'd bleed out the second I removed it. But there simply wasn't time to find out, or even get someone way more qualified to be doing this. The longer the arrow stayed in, the more damage it would do.

"Ready?" I asked.

His only response was to close his eyes and dig his claws deeper into the mutilated carpet.

In one swift motion, I planted my hand firmly around the entry point and yanked the arrow out with all my strength.

He instantly convulsed and thrashed on the ground in pain. He kicked out with his back legs, ripping through my jeans to score the flesh beneath and sending me sprawling. I grit my teeth against the searing pain and pushed myself up, then limped to my room to retrieve anything and everything I had that could staunch the flood of crimson now pooling on the once beige carpet.

On the way to gather what meager supplies I had, I grabbed my phone. Xander had already proven he wouldn't answer my calls, so I tried someone I hoped would, someone who already knew about my unusual companion.

"Diana?" Jen's voice was like music to my ears. "Is Xander with you?"

"What? No. But I need you to come over as soon as possible."

"Why? What's wrong?"

"Remember my furry friend? He's back, and he's hurt. I didn't know who else to call. He... he's been shot."

"What?" Jennifer's alarm rang through the speaker.

"I pulled out the arrows. He's bleeding so much," I sobbed, my strained composure breaking.

"I'm on my way." She cut the call without waiting for further explanation. I just hoped she'd be here quickly.

I tossed the phone aside and stepped into the bathroom, where I turned the hot water on. While it warmed up, I grabbed every towel I could. I was fishing beneath the sink for the first aid kit when there was a distinct thump from the other room. I grimaced and tried to move faster. If he was awake enough to move, then he was definitely awake enough to hurt himself. I willed the trash can to fill faster with the steaming water and scrambled to shove all the supplies into a bag. Finally, the can was full, and I turned off the water.

"Son of a bitch!" A rough voice shouted from the other room, and I stopped dead.

I dropped the bag to the floor and glanced up at the vent that once again held my bow. *No time.* Without a second thought and still holding the steaming container of water, I raced back out into the living room where I immediately lurched to a halt.

My companion was gone. In his place stood the apparent source of the curse. My first instinct was to assume that the intruder had done something with my furry friend. Except, the man standing in my living room was filthy; grime, mud, and what looked startlingly like blood covered him like a second skin. No sooner did I have a chance to register his inexplicable presence than he turned, clutching his side, and I got a glimpse of his face.

The makeshift bucket slipped free of my grasp to crash to the ground and sent the still hot water splashing everywhere. The man instantly glanced up at the noise and I was met with all too familiar brown eyes. His dark hair was matted with dirt that dulled its natural shine and the muck coating his body had initially hidden the two gaping wounds: one in his shoulder and the one bubbling blood through his fingers at his side. Wounds that perfectly mirrored my companion.

No. It's not possible.

Suddenly, the door flung open, sending a spray of splinters out to join the already blood and water soaked floor, and Jennifer barged in. "What in the name of the moon were you thinking?!" she yelled, not at me, but at Xander. Xander who was standing naked in the middle of my living room, covered in mud and bleeding from two arrow wounds.

Xander is... My mind balked at the truth, unwilling to accept what my eyes were telling, what my *instincts* were screaming. But there was no getting around it—Xander was a werewolf.

My body jerked with the automatic reflex to retrieve my bow, to finish him while he was wounded, but my feet remained planted.

"Answer me, damn it!" Jennifer demanded, oblivious to my internal struggle. "What kind of moon forsaken game are you playing?!"

"I knew what I was doing," he said as he limped closer to the couch and snatched the blanket off, which he then wrapped around himself. He spared me a quick glance, but otherwise didn't address me.

Jen, however, would not be denied. "You could have gotten yourself killed!" she yelled emphatically, pointing at him.

Xander instantly spun on her, fury briefly overlaying his pain. "We don't have time for this. I don't need a lecture. I knew the risks. Now instead of berating me for *doing my job*, how about you help me?"

Jennifer paled and clenched her jaw, but otherwise didn't back down.

"The others are still out there," he continued.

"What?" she gasped, her anger now totally eclipsed by her concern.

"Someone needs to go get them. Make sure they are alright."

"Fine, but what about—"

"I'll be fine. Take care of them. Did you bring your phone?"

She nodded, already reaching for it as he continued.

"Good. I need to call my father." He took a step toward her to take the device and turned gray as a stone. Jen took her own step toward him and he held out a hand to stop her. "On second thought, you call Dad."

"But Xander," she protested.

He shook his head. "I just need time to heal. It wasn't that bad."

I begged to differ. He was still freely bleeding from the wound in his side and I finally knew exactly what was in those arrows. He shouldn't be standing at all.

He gave Jennifer a beseeching look. "Please, get the others. They can fill you in on what happened."

She only hesitated a moment before nodding in acquiescence. "I'll find them. Just..." She darted a glace over to me then returned to Xander. "Take care of yourself, okay?"

He dipped his head in silent agreement, and she walked back out the door. The second the door closed behind her, he collapsed.

"Xander!" The soggy carpet squished beneath my bare feet as I raced to his side.

17

The Truth Comes Out

I DROPPED TO MY knees beside Xander's prone form, checking for a pulse and making sure he was still breathing. His heart rate was abnormally high, but I wasn't entirely sure if that was due to his injuries or because of... what he was. On the flip side, his breathing was alarmingly shallow. Luckily, the shoulder wound had been a fairly clean shot. The wound in his side, however, was another matter. His movements had aggravated the wound so much that the edges were ripped and torn to the point that the only reason I knew an arrow had been involved was because I'd been the one to pull it out.

Now that I had a slightly better idea of what I was working with, I retrieved the meager medical supplies, more fresh hot water, and towels. His near-lifeless body barely even twitched as I wiped the muck away, then poured hydrogen peroxide into the hole in his shoulder. I glanced repeatedly at his face to see any sign of a response as the bubbles frothed out of the wound. Nothing.

Mercifully, the gaping hole in his side had finally diminished to a slow trickle. I shook my head as I stared at the ragged skin crusted with dark blood. It would have to wait

175

just a little longer. While I mustered the courage to attack the more grievous wound, I cleaned the rest of Xander. Suddenly, my mother's insistence that I learn emergency field care seemed like a blessing rather than the nuisance it had felt like at the time.

It took three fresh buckets of warm water to finish cleaning the last of the blood from him. A bathtub would have been infinitely easier, but I was loath to move him. His skin was pale, his breathing labored, and through it all, he'd yet to move once. I doubted that would keep. All that was left was the terrible hole in his side. I swallowed thickly and wrung out my last remaining clean towel. The damp terry cloth had barely touched the flesh two inches above the still bleeding hole when Xander's entire body spasmed.

He gasped loudly, and an iron grip encircled my wrist. Unfocused eyes, hazed with pain, stared blankly at me. Despite the bruising hold or the fact that if he squeezed any harder, he would likely break my wrist, I remained perfectly still and gazed back.

"It's okay, Xander. You're safe. I have to clean this wound, though." I had no idea if he understood any of what I was saying—his vacant expression certainly didn't look like it—but he released my hand, nonetheless. I spared him a brief glance before touching the marred flesh once more.

His side flinched, and he emitted a low, strangled sound deep in his throat, but he didn't fight me. It took twenty minutes to finish cleaning the muck off, then it was time to do the hydrogen peroxide again.

"You might want to brace yourself."

His jaw tightened, as did his fist. He gave a brief nod, and I started pouring liberally. Immediately he gasped again, then promptly dissolved into dry heaves. Blood seeped from between his clenched fingers, from where his nails had punctured his palm. Imminent tears stung the back of my eyes, but I didn't let his reaction stop me. I poured the rest of the bottle and waited until the last of the bubbles had popped before wiping away the now pink fluid. At last, he was completely clean, or as clean as he was going to get with a blanket wrapped around him.

"Xander," I whispered.

There was a muffled groan from where his head was buried in his arm.

I let out a sigh of relief. "Good, you're still awake." Though it didn't sound like he would be for long. "Do you think you could help me get you to the bed?"

His head rolled to spear me with one dazed eye. Without a word, he heaved himself off the ground, losing the tenuous blanket in the process. I slipped in beside him to try to take some of his weight and nearly collapsed beneath it. Xander may be on the leaner side, but he was dense. Part of me couldn't help but wonder if that was a Xander-thing or uniquely werewolf attribute. It wasn't like I'd ever tried to carry one before.

I shook off my surprise and started shuffling toward the bedroom, glad that the door was open and nothing was on the bed. The moment Xander's body touched the mattress, he was out. It took several minutes of pushing and shoving to actually get him under the covers, none of which seemed to faze him. Then all that was left to do was let him sleep and hope that he woke back up again.

I shut the door quietly behind me and surveyed the disaster in my living room. No way was I getting my deposit back. I sighed heavily and set to work cleaning the mess. The bloody towels went into the wash immediately and I'd never been so grateful to have the pathetic washer and dryer set that came with the apartment. I couldn't begin to imagine how I would explain the state of my laundry at a laundromat. Scrubbing the ever-loving shit out of the carpet took all of my focus, making it easier to push aside what I should really be worried about, and it wasn't the stubborn blood stains.

How could I have missed the signs? I'd been trained to recognize werewolves since birth. Maybe I'd been a little too accepting of his canine appearance, but he still didn't resemble any of the pictures I'd seen, or hell, the live one I'd encountered in Texas. But even thinking back, there weren't any red flags to indicate that Xander might be anything other than human. Except he wasn't, and I was at a complete loss for what to do. For fuck's sake, I'd had sex with him. If my family ever found out, I'd be disowned on the spot.

I stopped scrubbing as a fresh wave of horror washed over me. How was I going to tell Xander *my* truth? Before, it would have been easy to label my family as crazy fanatics that believed in myths and legends. Now? I'd be lucky if Xander didn't lunge for my throat on principle. Not that I could blame him. There was a reason I didn't want to follow my family's legacy of hunting.

A soft knock on the door brought me back to the here and now. Exhausted to my core, I pushed myself up and warily made my way to the front door. A quick peek revealed an anxious Jennifer wringing her hands and dancing from foot to foot. I unlocked the door and opened it to discover she was also lugging a bag stuffed to the brink of exploding.

"Diana," she said, squaring her shoulders.

"Jennifer." I stepped to the side so she could enter. "What do you have there?" I asked, closing and locking the door as well as I could.

She took a few steps inside, then let out a shaky breath as she lowered the overflowing bag to the floor. "Um, I wasn't sure what first aid stuff you might have, so I brought what I could find, as well as some food."

"Looks like more than a snack."

"Yeah..." She glanced at me, nervousness written in every line of her body, and I moved to block the knife stabbed into the table from view. "I imagine you have a lot of questions."

My fingers tingled as I reached behind me. "Not really, no." I wrapped my fingers around the handle, tugging it free. "Oh, you mean about how you are werewolves?"

Jennifer's eyes widened. "How did you..." she trailed off, stiffening as her senses finally registered the danger she was in. She darted a glance at the door, but even with preternatural speed, she wasn't fast enough.

I whipped the knife around, my gaze fierce as she swallowed so close to the blade that a thin rivulet of blood ran down her throat. "Back up," I ordered.

Terror flooded her brown eyes, but she took a step back and I went with her, keeping the blade steady. "We won't hurt you. I'm just here for Xander. We can be out of your hair and out of your life as soon as he can move." A different fear flitted across her face. "He is still alive, isn't he?" she whispered.

I considered my friend, who hadn't even tried to deny she was a monster. My mind rebelled at the term. I knew her. Knew Xander. Not once had either ever given me cause to believe they were monsters, except, of course, for the fact that they were apparently werewolves. "He's alive," I said at last. "Though by all rights he should be dead, and not just because he was dosed with enough wolfsbane to kill an elephant."

"I don't... I don't understand. What do you mean? What's wolfsbane?"

"I imagine Xander told you I was raised as a hunter. What he doesn't know is *what* I was raised to hunt." Jennifer began to visibly shake, not the best idea given how close the knife's edge still was to her throat.

"You're a werewolf hunter," Xander filled in.

Jennifer immediately glanced toward him while I kept my focus locked on her.

"Nice to see you awake, Xander. Your... cousin brought you food. Why don't you have a seat?" I tilted my head ever so slightly to indicate Jennifer should as well. I adjusted my stance to allow her to move, as well as to bring Xander into view. He was clutching a sheet around him and still looked like death, but he was upright and conscious. It took him a lot longer to get situated, but eventually, the pair sat side by side on the couch. I pulled the bag closer with my free hand to check its contents. Satisfied it held exactly what Jennifer said, I nudged it with my foot closer to the two.

Jennifer slowly leaned forward to grab the bag. When I didn't do or say anything, she began pulling out carton after carton of food. She set one in Xander's lap, but the most he responded was to grab it so it wouldn't fall to the floor.

He stared at me for a long moment. "Why did you help me once you realized what I am?"

"Why did you come here after you were shot?" I asked in return, meeting his blank stare with one of my own.

"Because I trust you."

I couldn't help but raise my eyebrows. "Trust? As in still do?"

"Yes," he said without hesitation. "I came here because you told me to and because I believed you could help."

A tightness eased in my chest. I flipped the knife around, catching it by the blade, then sent it sailing across the room to sink into the far wall with a resonant thud. Jennifer elicited a startled squeak as it flew past her ear.

"You were right. I can help and..." I paused. What I was about to say—to do—went against everything I'd ever been taught. But if there was one thing my training had nailed home, it was to always rely on my instincts first and what my eyes could see second. And my instincts didn't believe either of them would ever willingly harm me or anyone else, for that matter. "I'm glad you came here," I finished at last.

The worry tightening Xander's eyes softened and some of the tension in his shoulders eased. "Me too," he said softly.

I ran my hands over my face, then gave myself a good shake. "How are you doing? Not still bleeding, I hope."

"No, it seems to have stopped. Thanks to you."

I nodded and moved to the kitchen to retrieve utensils. "I hope you brought enough to share," I said, passing everyone a fork. No more knives until we got everything out in the open.

Jennifer still had an air of terror about her as she looked between me and Xander while we began tucking into the food she'd brought. "Was it you? Did you," she swallowed thickly, "did you kill the others? Did you shoot Xander?"

"No," Xander and I said at the same time. My heart soared at his certainty, and I gave him a small smile to show him my appreciation of his trust and support.

"But how do you know?" Jennifer huffed at him.

Xander finally looked away from me to meet her troubled gaze. "Because I know."

I was fairly sure there was a little more to it than that, which I had every intention of delving into *after* Jennifer left. "Let's start with the basics. You're both werewolves. I come from a long line of werewolf hunters. And I'm guessing that your entire dorm is also entirely werewolves."

"Yes," Xander said with all the calm that had clearly abandoned Jennifer.

"Are you two really cousins?" I hated to ask, but I still had a niggling doubt about why they were so close.

Xander chuckled, and Jennifer glared at me. "Yes," they said in unison.

I released a long breath and set my food aside. "Well, there's that at least." I glanced at Jennifer, noticing how much lighter her hair was compared to Xander's and made a connection that had been bugging me. "It was you that day, wasn't it? The canine that led me into the woods."

"You did what!" Xander turned a furious look on his cousin, who squirmed beneath his intense gaze despite being older. "What part of 'no one goes off on their own' did you not grasp?"

"She wasn't supposed to follow me!" she snapped, shooting me a nasty look. "When Anna let slip that a 'dog'," her face twisted into a derisive sneer as she made air quotes, "had been visiting her, I knew it was you. I just wanted to see what she would do."

I pulled up my knees and rested my arms on them. "You mean like save your life?"

She winced, but didn't back down. "I've seen horror movies. There is such a thing as two killers."

"You have a point. For the record, they shot at me too."

"What!" Xander shouted, gripping the sheet so tight he white knuckled and I was worried he'd give himself a stroke. "Why has no one told me about this?"

Jennifer hung her head. "I didn't want you to worry... Or get upset I was keeping tabs on your girlfriend. Thanks for telling me, by the way," she added with a glower directed at me.

"How about we address social pleasantries later? Xander needs to rest, and so do I."

"Fine," she huffed and started moving things around. "If you can spare a pillow or two, I can sleep on the floor while Xander takes the couch."

I barked a laugh, startling her out of her frenzied motions. "If you think I'm sleeping while two known werewolves are in my apartment, you're out of your damn mind."

"But..." She glanced at Xander, then scowled. "I'm not leaving him alone."

"He won't be," I countered.

"Be reasonable, Anna," she pleaded. "It's not like he's in any condition to be dangerous."

"Gee, thanks," Xander grumbled.

That was where she was wrong. "I'd say that makes the odds about even. Unless you'd like to try to convince me that an injured werewolf isn't still twice as deadly as a human." I raised an eyebrow in challenge.

Xander placed a hand on her leg and she tensed. "I'll be fine. Besides, the others need someone to look out for them while I'm recovering."

Judging by the sour expression on Jennifer's face, she didn't like that one bit, but it also didn't look like she was going to argue. "Fine. But I'm coming back first thing in the morning and I better be getting regular updates." She reached for the bag again. I hooked my foot in the strap and pulled it out of her reach. She bit back a snarl... barely. "I also packed his phone and some clothes."

I nodded, pulling the bag closer so I could fish out the device. Jennifer's gaze tracked my every movement, trepidation stamped on her face. I shot her a look of my own before tossing the device at Xander.

He caught it in the air and Jennifer let out an unmistakably relieved breath. "Thank you," Xander said softly.

"Don't thank me yet." Both of their gazes flicked to me—Xander's openly curious and Jennifer's once more fearful. Suddenly, I was struck by how truly outrageous the situation was. I was essentially holding two adult werewolves hostage on my couch, and I wasn't even holding a weapon. I stifled a bark of delirious laughter and turned my attention to Xander. "You message who you need to message, then that goes on silent. You need rest more than you need to comfort the ones who made it back safely." I shifted my focus to Jennifer. "That's your job, and I expect you to dissuade anyone from blowing up Xander's phone with well wishes, concern, or outright panic."

Xander's eyes shone with something I couldn't quite name, and he nodded. Then he turned to his cousin. "It'll be okay, Jenny. I trust Diana, and you should trust your initial instincts about her."

Jennifer deflated and nodded as well before giving me what was almost an apologetic expression. She pushed herself up and glanced at the bag beside me. "He'll need to eat. A lot. If he's going to heal. And... and you'll call me if you need anything?" To my surprise, she looked at me, not Xander.

"I will." I stood and escorted her to the door while she kept looking back at Xander. "He'll be fine," I assured her.

She took a deep breath and let it out slowly. "I believe you." She gave me a sheepish look. "Things are going to be kinda weird between us now, aren't they?"

"For a while, maybe, but we'll get through it."

A tentative smile curled her lips. Then she bid me good-night and was gone. I closed and locked the door behind her before turning back to my patient, not at all excited about the long night ahead. Undoubtedly, there would be tough questions and even tougher answers. There was no helping it though. This was a bridge we had to cross. Except Xander was already fast asleep.

I chuckled to myself and walked over to him, where I attempted to get him more comfortable. We could have our difficult conversation later. I brushed the hair back from his sweaty forehead, still at a loss for how the hell he was even alive.

18

COMPARING NOTES

TWO DAYS LATER, XANDER was recovered and awake enough to shower on his own. Which was for the best, because honestly, the sponge baths weren't really cutting it. I was also immensely relieved that he hadn't taken a turn for the worse, though I'd never heard of a werewolf that could survive a lethal dose of wolfsbane, let alone two. Sure, enough of the stuff could kill a human as well, but it was particularly toxic to werewolves, and as far as I knew, there was no antidote.

Xander came out of the bathroom still toweling his hair and wearing the fresh clothes Jennifer had dropped off. We made eye contact and he let out a resigned sigh. "I suppose we've put it off long enough."

I nodded and sat at the table with my fresh cup of coffee, gesturing for him to do the same. A weird mix of trepidation and excitement swirled in my chest as I watched him prepare his cup and make his way over. The task itself was perfectly mundane, but nothing about this situation belonged in the normal world. I'd never knowingly talked with a werewolf before. To my surprise, I was brimming with questions. How much of what I'd learned over the years was accurate? What was shifting really like? How long had his pack been here? Had they migrated to the states like the Texas pack had done from Germany? Did they even *know* the Texas pack? Just how big did territories get? To be fair, I didn't expect him to answer most of those. Best course of action would be to let him take the lead and wait for an appropriate opening to satisfy my burning curiosity.

"Before we get started," he said, rolling the steaming mug between his palms, "I just want to say that however this conversation goes, I appreciate everything you've done for me and I'm glad to have met you."

The odd fizzy feeling filled my chest once more. I refused to examine it more closely until I'd cleared one thing up first, though. I cleared my throat and took a sip of the hot liquid for courage, then met his beautiful brown eyes. "Now that you know the truth about me, do you think I killed your friends?" No, not just friends. "Your packmates?" I clarified a little awkwardly.

He studied me for a long moment and I fought the urge to fidget. Finally he blinked. "No. I don't. I might have had my doubts in the beginning, given how much you seemed to know about the murder weapon, but I don't think I ever really believed you did. That's, um, part of why I came by that first night. To judge your character." His cheeks darkened and he dropped his gaze to the table. "Sorry about that, by the way."

I chuckled and his head shot up. "Honestly, given everything else, that might actually be the least weird thing, and I can't exactly fault you. I *did* con my way into your dorm. Though now I get why everyone was giving me odd looks at the time."

"Yeah..." A smile warmed his face and I relaxed. "You kinda stick out when you're the only human in the building." He took a sip. "In all seriousness, I am sorry. Though now I can't help but wonder how you didn't know what I was from the outset."

"I think part of me did. It was actually my first knee-jerk conclusion. But it didn't make any sense. As far as I knew, there were no werewolf or even wolf packs in the area. Plus, you didn't look anything like the werewolves I grew up learning about or even the one I'd seen previously. I guess when they say everything is bigger in Texas, they mean *everything*." We both chuckled at that.

"They are something else down there. But I see what you mean. We're not really built the same." He hesitated then went on. "Not to put too fine a point on it, but we don't exactly resemble the average dog either."

I let out a huff of air. "True. I rationalized your larger stature as being the result of a wolf-dog hybrid. But honestly I think I was just being willfully ignorant."

A frown creased his brow. "How so?"

"I think I mentioned before that part of the reason I came to Blackwell was to get away from my family. That's actually most of the reason. Growing up, I never really liked what my family did, though I was made to believe it was necessary. As I got older though, I realized that I didn't want *any* part of it. It was actually on a hunting trip in Texas that I hit my breaking point." I stared into my mug, suddenly not the least bit thirsty.

"What happened?" Xander asked softly.

I closed my eyes and for once, didn't shy away from the memory. "I'd just turned seventeen and my father, Jeremiah Harker, decided it was past time that I had my first kill. My uncle had a line on a possible werewolf causing trouble east of El Paso. We tracked them down to a stretch of woods between the miles and miles of nothing out there. My uncle and father worked together to herd it toward me, harrying it with unpoisoned arrows." I paused and swallowed thickly. I hated this next part.

"When it burst through the shrubbery where I was stationed, nettles, brambles, and blood coated its body. There were at least three broken arrows sticking out of it. I already had my arrow nocked and ready to fly when it turned to look at me. In all my training, no one had ever covered their eyes beyond the yellow glint. Where I'd expected it to look at me with savage animosity, it looked at me with... fear." I exhaled a long breath. "So much fear. I couldn't do it. This thing wasn't a killer. What was the worst that it had done? Harry some cattle? Sure, it was huge and could probably tear me apart without a second thought. But, at that moment, it was just a creature trying to survive like the rest of us."

"What did you do?"

I shrugged and sipped at my rapidly cooling coffee. "Lowered my bow and gestured for it to run. When it didn't immediately take off, I fired a shot over its shoulder. Not long after it left, my uncle and father arrived. Both were disappointed and pretty angry, but they chalked it up to nerves. The whole flight back to Washington I had to put up with my father lecturing me about the risk and shame of hesitation. A week later I told my parents I didn't want anything to do with the family business and started applying for schools on the opposite coast."

Xander hissed between his teeth. "Can't imagine that went well."

"No, it did not. That's why I started so late. It took quite a bit of convincing. My father still believes I'll come around, but I think my mother is finally getting it, though she hates what it's done to our family."

"Damn, Diana, that really sucks." Xander's warm hand covered mine. The fluttering in my chest returned and I gave him a weak smile.

"Well, that's my stupid sob story. Your turn. What happened that first night?"

To my disappointment, he removed his hand to run it through his hair, upsetting the drying waves. "I really wish I knew. I still feel so stupid for letting us get herded onto the campus."

"How about we play the blame game later? Just start at the beginning," I encouraged gently.

"You're right." He took a deep breath, before continuing. "Running during the full moon or at least shifting isn't really optional. We'd never had any issues before and weren't expecting any this time. Per our usual routine, we made our way to the woods where Katie was killed in small groups and clusters."

"Sorry to interrupt, but I'm not following. You say routine like you've done it dozens of times, but I never heard any howling before that night."

His lips quirked into a crooked grin. "We were pretty good about staying quiet. Not getting to howl during a run does take a lot of the fun out of it, but not enough to risk exposure." His face fell and he dropped his gaze to study the table. "Something spooked the party. Before I knew it, we were headed full tilt toward the campus and into the most unnatural fog I'd ever smelled. It didn't take long for us all to get separated."

I sucked in a breath as understanding dawned. "That's why you were howling, to try and find each other."

He nodded.

"I must have been smack dab in the middle of everyone. That's why it sounded like the howls were chasing me."

Xander snorted. "Given that moon forsaken fog clogging up all our noses, none of us would have ever known you were there short of tripping over you." I winced at his unfortunate choice of words, but held off interrupting again. "Anyway, once we heard Joey's yelp, we all made our way back to the dorm. Then Jennifer and I set out to see if we could figure out what happened."

"And you found me," I filled in.

"We found you," he echoed with a slight smile that surprisingly touched his eyes.

"Fuck," I exhaled, slumping in my seat. We sat in silence for a few minutes while we each absorbed the other's tale. Finally, I gave him a shrewd look. "One more question, for now, anyway."

"Go for it."

"You said you came by that first night to get a grasp of my character. I get that. What I don't get is why you kept coming back."

His face turned red faster than I knew a face could. He coughed and struggled to clear his throat.

"Was it because you still doubted me? I know the whole 'finding a hidden bow and arrow thing' didn't help, but that was way after."

He laughed and even to my ears it sounded forced. "That would be the logical reason. But no. I kept coming back because I couldn't stay away. I really liked you and you didn't seem to have a problem with me in that form."

I scowled at him.

"Look! I know it was wrong. Okay?" He looked so damn miserable, I couldn't help but chuckle.

"Not anymore wrong than a werewolf hunter not recognizing the werewolf obnoxiously taking up two-thirds of their bed."

This time he chuckled. We stared at each other for a long minute, each wearing a slight smile. Part of me actually found his behavior sweet and a little endearing. Definitely still fucked up, but then so was most of my life.

Xander was the first to break our moment. He stood and reached for my now stone cold cup. "Refill?"

"Thanks, that'd be great. There should be plenty." He grabbed my cup and took it with him back to the kitchen. While he walked, I watched for any hint that his injuries hadn't finished healing or were causing problems.

"You could just ask," Xander said without turning away from pouring the scalding liquid. I stiffened, and when I didn't immediately respond he cocked his head to the side to look at me. "I can feel you watching me."

"How are you feeling? I know werewolf healing is impressive, just not *how* impressive. And I've never heard of any *were* surviving aconitum napellus."

"About that," he said as he set down the refreshed coffees along with some milk and sugar, "what exactly is it and why is it so fatal to werewolves?"

"It actually has a lot of names. The more common ones are monkshood and... wolfsbane. It's a species of highly toxic flowering plant. It's technically also poisonous to humans in the right doses, but it's rare." I could see the questions building behind Xander's eyes, but he let me continue uninterrupted. "As for why it's so lethal to werewolves or how you survived, I have no idea. Nearest I can guess is some kind of natural resistance or immunity. Though it's the first I've ever heard of one."

Xander alternated between sipping his coffee and tapping his full lips as he pondered the conundrum. Only once he'd polished off the last dregs of his cup did he break the silence. "I think you might be onto something with the immunity bit. A lot of the older werewolf families that can trace their lineage back to immigrating in the 1600s or before have names that describe special attributes they have. Over time though, they've gotten diluted and forgotten."

"What about your lineage? How far can you trace that?" I asked, suddenly intrigued that both of our family lines were equally ancient.

He smirked. "All the way back to the Cherokee. My ancestors actually witnessed the first settlements in the area." His upbeat demeanor turned more dour. "Though at one point the werewolf part of the tribe was almost completely wiped out. Only a few survived."

I smacked my forehead. "Holy shit. That's it!"

Xander startled at my exclamation. "What's it?"

"In the early 1700s, the Harkers came to the colonies from Europe. I might have my dates mixed up, but if I'm remembering correctly, there's a record around that time of them wiping out an entire pack." I held out my hands, my excitement about history briefly eclipsing my good sense to be ashamed of my ancestors committing genocide.

Xander stared at me skeptically. "And?"

"And they used wolfbane they brought from Europe! That was before they knew there was a similar species here they could use. What are the odds that the reason your ancestors survived was because they had this unknown immunity? My ancestors would have been none the wiser, which is why we have zero records of any werewolf packs in this area for the last couple hundred years. And yours likely would have heard them use that name and adopted it for the survivors."

Xander shook his head and I was about to launch into further explanation of my admittedly out-there hypothesis when I realized he was laughing to himself. "You really do love your history, don't you?"

My face burned as my good sense finally caught up with me.

"Hey, don't be embarrassed," Xander said, leaning across the table to tilt my chin up. "It's awesome you're so passionate." His expression turned dreamy and his voice softened even further. "I bet you would love the archives at the House." He cleared his throat and sat back, taking the tingling warmth of his nearness with him. "So, now what?"

"I'd like to keep seeing each other, if that's still on the table," I offered nervously.

The way his face lit up was all the reassurance I needed. "Oh it's definitely on the table. And me too. I meant more, what do we do now that we know each other's big secret? Did you still want to help me save my pack?"

"Right. *That.* I do want to help, but..." I trailed off, not sure the best way to explain what would likely need to happen next.

"But?"

"I need more information. Which means... going home. My mother has already demanded I visit sooner rather than later and apparently my crazy-ass uncle has hatched another scheme. It could be related. Probably not, but either way, the Harker histories could still shed some light or my mother might have some news about another family operating in the area."

Xander's brow furrowed so deep his eyebrows connected. "Aren't you forgetting that your Detective Takashi's number one and possibly only suspect? And how safe is it for you to go back there? You said so yourself, they weren't exactly pleased when you left the first time. What if they don't let you come back?"

The worry in Xander's questions had my heart melting. "I'm less worried about how I'll get back to Blackwell than I am with how I'm going to get out of it without Takashi finding out."

His bright smile returned and he leaned on his elbows. I mirrored his stance, bringing our grinning faces closer together. "Did you know," he said in a conspiratorial tone, "that werewolves are really good at keeping secrets?"

I barked a laugh. "You don't say."

"Oh, yes." He nodded with a serious expression. "Jenny and I will cover for you with Takashi. I'll even loop in the rest of the dorm if I have to."

"You know, you're kind of amazing." My smile broadened and I leaned even closer, causing me to hover over my seat.

"Aw, you're too kind. You're pretty impressive yourself."

I caught the sparkle in his eye the second before he pressed his lips against mine. With that one simple move, all the doubts wriggling in the darkness settled. We could do this. We could defy the odds. We could save his pack. And werewolves weren't the only ones who excelled at elaborate cover stories. Hunters were every bit as skilled. Which meant I'd be calling in another favor.

19

RETURNING HOME

I STEPPED OUT OF the hired car and stared up at the massive red brick facade of the Harker ancestral home. The clouds merging overhead gave the imposing structure an ominous cast that sent a shiver down my spine. It wasn't that I was afraid to come home so much as I had no desire to step foot inside a place steeped with blood. But I wasn't here for me.

Squaring my shoulders, I approached the heavy oak doors gilded with iron and layered with so much magic that the hairs on my arms stood on end. Before I could reach for the handle, the door swung inward. To my surprise, it wasn't our butler, Leon, or one of the other household staff, but my father. All the courage I'd cultivated on the flight and subsequent drive withered beneath his scrutiny.

Luther Harker was not a tall man, but that didn't make him any less imposing. His strong jaw was clenched with a disapproval reflected in his eyes. Even the gray of his hair was steely. While his main responsibility was maintaining the Harker finances, he was no less skilled or deadly than any other of our line.

"Hello, daughter. I see your mother had the car called for you. Have you finally returned to fulfill your familial obligations?" He raised an eyebrow that underscored his derisive tone.

"Nice to see you too, father. Why, yes, school is going splendidly. Thanks so much for asking," I said with forced cheer as I shouldered past him.

He sniffed and shut the door with a hollow thud that echoed through the foyer, then wordlessly gestured for Minnie, one of the maids to take my things.

I smiled at her in thanks and relinquished my carryon, then turned back to my father. "Where is mother?"

Before he could respond, a woman that personified elegance swept into the room. Today, her dark chestnut hair was pinned in a tasteful bun and her burgundy pantsuit was tailored to perfection with a cream chemise. "Diana, darling, I'm so glad to see you. How was your flight? And classes? We speak so sparingly these days, you must fill me in on everything." She kissed both my cheeks then captured me in a fierce hug.

I shot my father a look over her shoulder as I returned her embrace. "Thank you for asking and thank you for the car, though I could have taken a taxi."

"But why would you when I can send the car?" She pushed me back and smiled warmly. "Come, let's catch up in the parlor." She hooked her arm in mine and I smothered a disappointed groan. I'd hoped to find her in the library, which was ultimately where I needed to be, though some of the information would be kept in the vault.

Once we were settled and established with refreshments, I filled her in on my course work and how classes were progressing. Yes, I was still on track to graduate in the next school year. No, I didn't have any professors I didn't get on with. I was still glad I hadn't opted for the dorm experience.

"And any romantic interests?" she asked, sipping her Lady Grey tea.

I'd had every intention of saying no, but keeping those kinds of secrets from my mother had never been something I was good at. I hadn't even been able to come out to her as bisexual before she'd already deduced my sexuality and started setting me up with any and all offspring of reputable families.

Her eyes widened over her cup when I hesitated a fraction too long. "You do! How marvelous. Tell me all about them. How did you meet? Have you been seeing each other for long? What do you like most about them?"

"Who are their family?" My father's dry question cut through my mother's happy euphoria, earning him a scathing look. I twisted in my seat to find him lurking in the doorway.

"Luther, dear, perhaps you'd be more comfortable sitting... outside." Her smile and tone were genuine enough despite that she'd just dismissed her husband with the politest of "fuck offs".

I quickly ducked my head before he could catch me smirking. Where I'd expected an equally passive aggressive retort—per their usual—there was only the sharp click of his heels followed by the diminishing sound of his steps. "I see he's in a *mood* today," I said cautiously.

My mother released an aggrieved sigh. "Your uncle has been up to his usual ill-conceived plotting again. Monopolized the archives for days and kept going on and on about how he'd finally found the answer and the perfect place to test it."

I set my cup aside. "Please tell me it's not Texas again."

"Mercifully, no. He seems to have finally grasped that one man cannot take on such a large pack."

"I take it he still hasn't made any headway with the other hunter families?"

My mother snorted and I couldn't help but smile that she didn't feel the need to be so impeccably proper with me. "Besides, you know how the other families are. The Van Helsings won't touch anything that's not a vampire. The Youngs up to their noses in magical chaos. No one wants to work with the Gagnons after what happened at Mount Logan. And the day any of the Mayumi leave Japan will be the day we've all lost."

"So basically, the larger families are too good to work with him and the smaller ones think he's insane."

"Oh, darling, they *all* think he's insane, and rightfully so. But..."

I instantly straightened. "But?"

She shook her head as if she couldn't believe what she was saying. "He might actually be onto something this time."

"What do you mean? Uncle Nemo may be a fine hunter in his own right, but none of his schemes actually pan out. Just look at what happened on the Texas hunt."

She raised an eyebrow. "You mean the Texas hunt that you returned from and immediately disavowed your heritage. That Texas hunt?"

"You know it wasn't like that, mother," I said with a heavy sigh, slumping in my seat.

"Actually, Diana, I do not. Your father was disappointed you didn't get your first kill, your uncle was adamant it was jitters, and *you* refused to talk to anyone about the matter."

"No, I refused to be bullied into becoming a hunter like everyone else in this family," I countered. I could see the same old argument about all of my wasted potential brewing on my mother's face. To my surprise, she schooled her features and waved a dismissive hand.

"Whatever the reasons, I know my daughter well enough to know that when you've made up your mind about something, there's no changing it. Best to let you steer your own course and hope that you'll at least ask for help if you need it."

My chest warmed at hearing her profound change of heart since our last "discussion" even while I inwardly cringed. I did need help, but I didn't trust that asking for it wouldn't lead to me being sucked back into the life. After clearing my unexpectedly tight throat, I reached for my mother's hand. "Thank you. That means a lot to me."

She gave my hand a gentle squeeze, then set her cup aside. "Anyway, as I was saying, your uncle's latest bout of madness might actually be brilliance. Though it might be easier to show you than to try to explain." She stood and made her way toward the same entry my father had lingered in before.

"Where are you going?"

"To the archives. We can catch up properly at dinner. I imagine now that I've dangled that carrot, you won't be satisfied until you know everything. Especially since it involves some obscure history." Her eyes twinkled knowingly as she said those magic words. History? Obscure? Count me in. I practically launched out of my chair, nearly toppling the delicate china off the end table, and fell in step beside her.

We wound our way past the grand staircase, through a locked and warded door, and down a significantly more humble flight of stairs to reach yet another locked door. My mother went through the motions of disarming the magical and mundane securities, until the last obstacle was clear and we could safely step into the Harker family archives. There were books in here older than several countries and even civilizations, though the ones from before the Ottoman Empire weren't really in a state to be handled. Many of the books didn't even mention werewolves, like the ones covering the Demonic Wars.

I stepped into the large circular room lined entirely with shelves, paintings, and memorabilia. This place had once felt like a magical haven with untold knowledge. But the more I consumed, the less the space felt like a sanctuary and more like a tomb. A feeling reinforced by its proximity to the Harker armory and training areas. Still, books were books, and I couldn't resist gliding the tip of my finger along the aged spines of the books not secured behind glass. It was actually to one of those reinforced cases that my mother went up to. She punched in the code and pulled on some protective gloves, then carefully removed a tome that would have been right at home in a medieval monastery.

My mother set the monstrosity of a book on the podium in the center of the room with a heavy thud. I let out a low whistle as I moved closer to where she was carefully flipping the aged pages by their corners.

"Damn. I can't say I've had the pleasure of perusing this beastie before." I tentatively traced an elegant section of calligraphy. The writing didn't look like any modern language, nor did it appear to be Latin. "Always assumed that since it wasn't part of the regular studies, it wasn't pertinent to werewolves."

"You weren't alone in that assumption. Not that it doesn't cover werewolves, but that it isn't really pertinent anymore. It's not like we need to know their migration patterns during the Renaissance or the pack sizes during the Persian Conquest. Here we are." She gently pressed the pages apart and pulled out a magnifying glass from within the podium.

Even with the magnification and spelled glass translating the page, I still had to squint and read quite a bit before I realized what I was supposed to be looking at. "Mom, that's a footnote."

"Yes, it is," she replied with pursed lips in a tone that suggested she was every bit as exasperated with my uncle as everyone else.

"He must have camped in here for ages to find that. And, honestly, how life-altering can a few lines in a footnote really be?"

"I know, I know. I had exactly the same thought. Just take a look." She passed me the magnifying glass and stepped aside so I could get closer.

With a significant amount of skepticism, I did as she asked. Seriously, only Uncle Nemo would find the key to ending all werewolves in a fucking footnote. I shook my head and studied the section more studiously. It was only after I read the referenced area in conjunction with the footnote that the reality of what I was seeing sunk in. I stiffened as dread ran clammy fingers down my spine and prayed my mother would interpret the reaction as surprise rather than fear. For the first time in likely ever, Uncle Nemo really had found something and it was nothing but bad news.

I flicked my gaze up. "Do we know if this is true? People believed all kinds of ridiculous things about celestial bodies back then."

My mother shrugged. "Who can say? Your uncle at least seems convinced and your father's not far behind. Whether it's true or not, he already has a pack picked out to test it."

"Where?" I asked a hair too quickly, prompting her to raise an eyebrow.

"If I didn't know any better, darling, I'd mistake your curiosity as interest." My mouth opened and shut several times, but I couldn't find any words to push out. Finally, she laid a calming hand on my arm. "Don't worry, I'm not going to demand you rejoin the fold. You're every bit the strong, independent woman I raised you to be and fully capable of making your own decisions. But I also recognize that a lifetime of habits don't vanish overnight or even a few years."

I couldn't help but relax in the light of her understanding and subtle support. Perhaps our relationship wasn't so far gone after all.

"As for what pack your uncle has his sights set on, he hasn't deigned to share that information yet. Though he did mention that it was relatively small and that he'd been trimming it down to ensure that should his scheme fail, the odds wouldn't be totally against us."

I nearly choked and struggled to swallow. "Us?"

She rolled her eyes and gently shut the book, which she then replaced in its secured case.

"Mother..." I began in a warning tone to get her attention when she still hadn't answered. "What do you mean by 'us'?"

She let out a huff as she removed the gloves and put them away. "I may not agree with most of what your uncle does, but he's still family. While I don't expect you to join, it's not like he's garnered support from anyone else. We can't very well let him do this on his own."

"Why not?" I asked, my voice climbing along with my pitch. "We always have before."

"Don't be juvenile, Diana," she said, swanning past me toward the armory.

"It's a perfectly reasonable question," I insisted as I stalked after her. The scents of well oiled leather, fresh wood shavings, and tangy metal assaulted my senses. I'd had a love/hate relationship with this room my whole life. But not even the comforting smells could mask the undercurrent of death.

She tossed me a challenging look over her shoulder before reaching for a compound bow mounted on the wall. "Then use reason to answer it. Let's say the footnote is accurate. We can't very well miss an opportunity like this."

"And if the notes are a fabricated exaggeration? An unrelated anomaly?" I countered.

"Then your uncle will need all the help he can get if he expects to walk away still breathing. Either way, it's an all hands on deck type of situation." She bounced the bow in her palm as if testing the weight, though we both knew it was perfectly balanced. "I just hope he doesn't insist on his seven year old son being there. I will have to put my foot down about that," she mused to herself.

I blanched at the prospect. No child, hunter-born or not, needed to be present for that kind of massacre. "Surely not."

She simply hiked a shoulder in response. Then without warning, she plucked another bow from its place on the wall and tossed it to me. I reflexively caught it, my fingers wrapping around the familiar leather grip. "Now let's see if my champion archer can still best her mother."

I was still staring at the bow in a daze when she walked back the way we'd come. This was so much worse than I could have imagined. How was I going to explain to Xander, to Jennifer, that the deaths had only just begun? That no one was safe? Because the Harkers were coming... All of them.

20

────◄○►────

NEED A RIDE?

ONCE I WAS BACK in Blackwell, there was only one thing I wanted after my ludicrously long flights–Xander. But seeing as how he wasn't my ride from the Asheville Regional Airport, I'd have to wait a little longer to get my arms around him. I'd just stepped into the pickup area when a familiar voice called out.

"Do my eyes deceive me, or is that what I think it is?" Hyacinth teased from where she was leaning against her black cherry BMW.

I rolled my eyes and walked to the trunk of the sedan, which she popped open with a quick press of her key fob. The paint glimmered a deep red as it hit the light then transitioned back to black. I placed my carryon inside, followed by the distinctive case. Logically, I knew it was beyond reckless to bring my compound bow back with me, but I couldn't shake the feeling that I'd need it. Especially after everything I'd learned.

Hye snorted. "I see. It's fine when *you* do it, but a terrible idea when I do it."

"Oh, it's still a terrible idea," I replied, still questioning my sanity. I was a murder suspect, for fuck's sake. With *this* type of bow as the murder weapon.

She gave me a calculating look that made me anxious. How long had it been since her last transfusion? Because the way she was looking at me now was throwing major predator hunting prey vibes. "Then why?" she finally asked.

"I honestly don't know." I shut the trunk with a tad too much force, but thankfully, Hye didn't call me out. From there, I bundled myself into the passenger seat of the car which was every bit as frigidly cold as outside. "Damn, Hyacinth, how are you not a popsicle?"

She shrugged and finished buckling while I cranked up the heat, but I didn't miss the way she pulled her thin leather jacket tighter. Worry spiked through me. When *was* the last time she'd had her magical hit? And while we were at it, was it my imagination, or had the interim between gotten shorter? Just how much longer did she have before she became the thing she despised? How much longer until my friend was gone forever?

I cleared my throat and endeavored to push the troubling thoughts away. "Thanks again for covering for me. Did Detective Takashi give you any trouble while I was gone?"

"Surprisingly, no." She shifted gears and angled the car into traffic exiting the airport. "Though it would have been nice if you'd bothered to tell me that your boy toy was going to be practically camped at your apartment."

"Shit," I hissed. It hadn't occurred to me that *both* of them would think the best way to hide my absence would be to go to my apartment. While the Van Helsings strictly hunted vampires, I didn't want her anywhere near Xander. I wouldn't put it past her to make an "exception".

She tossed me a smirk. "Didn't think I'd find out about you fucking a freshman? Whatever happened to that chick from the bar? Thought y'all hit off well enough."

"Gods, Hye, you can't call women 'chicks'. It's demeaning. And while we're at it, don't call Xander a boy toy. He's an adult and *not* a freshman."

"So he *does* have a name." She snickered in triumph as she merged seamlessly onto the highway at a speed well above the limit.

I groaned and dropped my head back.

"Oh, lighten up." She smacked my leg. "He's cute enough, I suppose. Though not really my type."

Panic swirled in my chest at her casual mention of "type". She'd taken one look at him and known he was a werewolf. She had too. But then, how could she? *I* was the one trained to recognize them and even I'd missed it. Forcing myself to calm down and stop jumping to paranoid conclusions, I continued the conversation like I would have had Xander been anyone else.

"Pretty sure you don't have a type. When's the last time you dated again?" I teased. Hopefully, she couldn't hear how forced it sounded.

She made a noncommittal noise that was contradicted by the way she tightened her grip on the steering wheel. Oh yeah, my friend was lonely as hell. "Dating is a waste of time," she said after an awkward lull.

"Maybe, maybe not. You could always give it a try. Might surprise yourself."

"Not likely. Besides, my longest relationships are with family like you or they end up with a stake through their heart sooner rather than later." Interesting that she categorized her victims as relationships, but I wasn't going anywhere near that with a ten-foot pole. Luckily, she was too focused on getting around a car *not* trying to break the speed barrier to notice my look of astonished skepticism.

I shifted in my seat and searched for a safer topic than murder investigations and Xander. Unfortunately, what I settled on wasn't much better. "So, I really don't owe you another favor for having my back with Takashi?"

She shot me a scandalized look before quickly returning her attention to the road. "Covering with the cops for another hunter is *not* a favor, it's the job." I neglected to point out that I wasn't a hunter, at least not anymore, but it was probably a moot point, given the bow currently sitting in her trunk.

Officially out of things to talk about, I slumped in my seat and stared out at the trees whizzing past. We'd been so close once, but now we had almost nothing in common beyond shared history. If we'd been normal friends–normal *people*–we likely would have let our friendship naturally die out. We just didn't want the same things from life. While I cared for Hyacinth and worried about her chosen path, it was exhausting being someone's moral compass. Especially when they didn't bother to listen to you most of the time.

She glanced at me, her expression curious. "Did you find what you were looking for?"

Wasn't that a loaded question? And one whose answers would have to be shared carefully lest she decide to join the fray. "Yes... and no."

"Well that's clear as blood."

"That's not really how that saying goes."

She made a snarky face. "You could just be less vague and answer the damn question."

"Mnegh." I stuck my tongue out, then we both giggled. And for a shining moment, we were the silly girls we'd once been. "Well, if you must know, I learned that my Uncle Nemo is just as crazy as ever. Though it was really nice to see my mom."

"Yeah?" she asked with a note of optimism. "You two patching things up?"

I paused to think about it, then nodded. "Yeah, I think we are. She didn't try to talk me into coming back to the life. She even said she respected me for making a decision and standing my ground."

"Whoa, that's huge." Hyacinth would never admit it, but her voice said it all. She'd always been envious of my relationship with my mother. Fortunately for us both, my mother had treated her like a second daughter as often as possible. Though I doubted even Hye realized it was to compensate for how awful my mother believed her parents were. "Dare I ask about his highness, Lord Harker?"

I snickered at the ridiculous title Hye had bestowed upon my father when we were seven. "As cold as ever. Still not happy about my decision to leave. I actually didn't see him much beyond passing in the hallways."

"At least there's that. What about your Nancy Drew mystery? Make any headway on that?"

Now the real test. Could I outright lie to Hyacinth without her catching on? "Same as you, really. No packs in the area for the last couple of centuries, supernatural or otherwise. And according to the hunter gossip my mother had, no other hunter families have been operating in the area either."

"Damn, there goes my theory that the dead kids might have been some other kind of supe."

I swiveled to face her so fast I nearly gave myself whiplash. "Did you think it might have been vampires?"

Hye let out a full body laugh so hard I feared for her ability to see the road. "Oh, that's rich. Like I didn't scope out the whole fucking town when you said you were going to school there."

"You did?"

She gave me an incredulous look. "Of course. And I regularly do sweeps. Can't have my best friend going to a college crawling with vamps." She reached over again and jostled me in a rare show of affection.

While my heart warmed at learning how much she cared about my wellbeing, guilt writhed in my stomach. For all her lovely sentiments of friendship, I couldn't trust Hye with the truth. She'd kill Xander on principle.

We pulled up at my apartment complex and Hye looked at with a twinkle of mischief in her eyes. "Sure you don't want me to come in? We could for a bit. Go over a plan of attack to get Takashi off your back for good."

I shook my head. It wasn't anything she hadn't suggested a few times during the drive. "No, I'm good. Just want to get settled back in."

"Oh, right. Your boy–fuck buddy," she quickly corrected herself, "is probably waiting to help you 'settle in.'" She smirked and I rolled my eyes.

"Fuck buddy is not all that much better than boy toy." I angled a look at her, not that it remotely fazed her.

"That's not a denial," she quipped, popping the trunk.

"Gods, you're the worst," I mumbled as I retrieved my bag and walked toward the short covered passage that led to my apartment.

"I'd say I try, but it comes naturally!" she shouted after me.

Rather than reply and give away that she'd made me laugh, I waved over my shoulder. I was a little disappointed to discover Xander wasn't already there. Probably just as well, since I still wasn't sure how to explain my decision to bring my compound bow. Then again, I had a shit ton of bad news to share with him. I set my things down on the table and pulled out my phone to text him.

A subtle knock at the door made me pause mid-message. I set the phone aside and walked over, dubious about what excuse Hye would give for coming in anyway. When I opened the door, though, it was Xander on the other side, looking every inch his bubbly, ridiculously hot self. I didn't even bother to restrain my smile.

"Have you been staking out my apartment for when I return?" I asked in a mock serious tone.

He hunched his shoulders, his cheeks darkening. "On a scale of one to ten, how creepy would it be if I said yes?"

"I'd say about a two on the creepy scale, but a ten for stupidity."

He chuckled and stepped inside.

"I'm serious, Xander," I admonished as I closed the door. "What if you weren't the only one watching? The hunter has proven multiple times now that he doesn't care if the sun is out. And your people need you."

He closed the distance between us, cupping my face with his obscenely warm hands and I couldn't help but melt into the touch a little. "Right now, my people need you too." That was it, my perfect segue to share all the horrible things I'd learned. Before I could utter so much as a syllable, his lips brushed against mine and my thoughts fled.

I wrapped my arms around his neck and leaned into him, inviting him to deepen the kiss. True to form, he didn't disappoint. The gentle brush of his plush lips turned harder, needier. His tongue slipped past my lips to curl around mine in a sensuous glide that instantly had me moaning and burying my fingers in his soft hair. We could have kissed like that for a minute or an hour. I wouldn't be able to tell the difference.

"Diana," he whispered, his voice raw and sounding every bit as wrecked as I felt, and we still had all our clothes. An oversight easily remedied.

I stole another kiss that had my insides fluttering in antici-pation. "I want you."

He searched my face with those intense brown eyes that had captured my attention from the moment we'd met. "Are you sure?" The soft question made my heart flip, and honestly, I wasn't even fighting it anymore. Every time we came togeth-er, it felt inevitable and right. But I could also hear the real question: did I really want this? I'd been raised a hunter. He was a werewolf. We were giving star-crossed, forbidden lovers a run for their money. But that didn't change my answer.

"Yes."

Rather than belabor the point and keep asking if I was certain, he took my answer at face value. He captured my mouth in a fierce kiss that made my toes and fingers tingle. Then he slid his hands around to cup my ass and lifted me. I wrapped my legs around his waist without further prompting and continued to devour his mouth as he walked us toward the bedroom.

I was relieved to see that we were both past the slow-ly-strip-each-other point as we each shed our clothing like it was on fire. Hurried or not, I still took the time to appreciate how fucking gorgeous Xander was. While I wasn't a shallow person by any means, there was no denying how attractive I found him. Part of it was likely due to the natural sex appeal werewolves exuded, but most of it was simply because he was him. The way his raven's wing hair swept over his sienna forehead, partially obscuring his warm brown eyes. It was how he moved with purpose and confidence, so at home in his body, it put everyone else to shame. More than anything, it was the way he looked at me, touched me, as if I was the only person he *wanted* to see and he could convey that with his fingers.

Despite how quickly we'd ditched our clothes, neither of us seemed in a hurry to accelerate past making out. His hand glided up my torso, while he nipped and kissed along the seam where my neck met my shoulder. Every time he moved, it caused the hair on his legs to rub against my smooth ones, and I shuddered at the sensory overload. Then he abandoned my neck to close his mouth over my nipple, while he caressed the other with his other hands. I'd never believed women who said they could orgasm from nipple stimulation, but between the obscene heat of his mouth, the expert swirls of his tongue, and talented fingers, I was well on my way to being a convert.

He nipped at the increasingly sensitive bud before flipping his ministrations. I let out a sharp cry and arched into him, desperate for more, but not wanting him to stop either. I raked my nails down his back until I could dig them into the perfect globes of his ass. He half grunted, half growled and lifted his head enough for me to see his eyes blown wide. While I was captive to his gaze, he slid a hand between my thighs and delicately stroked my folds before slipping a finger into my wet, aching core.

I moaned as he twisted the digit, as if he knew all my sweetest spots and ground against his hand while I conquered his mouth with needy abandon. Then he added a second finger, and I gasped at the perfect fullness. Without warning, my climax ripped through me and I clenched around him. He kissed along my collar as he milked my orgasm for all it was worth. When he finally pulled back, he was panting and his erection was pressing promisingly into the junction of my thigh.

He slowly slipped his fingers free and sat back on his heels. Then, in what was quite possibly the hottest move I'd ever seen, he raised his fingers to his mouth and sucked them clean. It was probably my lust-addled imagination, but I could swear he moaned.

"Please tell me you have condoms," he said breathlessly, his gaze even hotter than his touch.

I snickered. "Thought werewolves couldn't get STDs. Not that I have any."

He grabbed my leg and playfully nipped at my calf. "We can't."

"If you're worried about an unplanned pregnancy, I have one of those fancy IUDs. Don't even need to remember to take a pill."

"Yeah, I'm not sure I really want to test the efficacy of an implant against werewolf genetics. But there are other reasons to use protection." His searching gaze was at odds with the smile on his lips. "Is this your roundabout way of saying you don't have any?"

"I do. But now I'm curious about these other reasons."

His cheeks darkened again, and he glanced away. "In any of your training, did you learn about bonding?"

I pushed up to rest on my arms. "Sure. Some accounts say it's real. Some say it's not." I shrugged.

"Oh, it's real. And for whatever reason, penetrative sex–un-protected–seals the bond. And..."

"And you think you could bond with me?" I finished for him with a mix of awe and incredulity.

He gave a self-deprecating chuckle. "At the risk of sending you running for the hills, I know it. When I told you before that I couldn't stay away, I meant that I *really* couldn't. The need to be near you is unbearable sometimes. Hence staking out your apartment until you returned."

"Wow. That's–"

"A total mood-killer?"

I shook my head. "I don't really know what it is, besides a lot. And you're sure? With me?"

He nodded. "I, uh, asked a few other mated pairs in the pack about the symptoms and it lines up."

"Damn." I wasn't sure what to do with that bomb. Normally, he was right. I'd be out of here in the blink of an eye, but... I kind of felt it too. Didn't I? I had no idea if humans could even reciprocate the attachment, but there was still that sense of inevitability. "I guess the only thing left to say is thanks for the honesty and consideration."

He blinked. "So, not a mood-killer, then?"

I couldn't help but smile at his sudden optimism. "Definitely not. Besides, I'm not finished with you yet. I've been dreaming about this for too long for you to stop now."

"Been dreaming about me, huh?" he teased as he leaned down to kiss me with the same level of intensity and single-minded focus as he had since the beginning. Abruptly, he pulled back. "Condoms."

"Night stand."

He promptly reached across to pull open the drawer, snickering when he pulled out the glass dildo.

"Shut up," I said, my face heating at the memory of the first time he'd seen it.

He replaced the toy and grabbed a condom from the box. My impatience reached new heights as I waited for him to roll it on. He'd scarcely straightened when I tackled him back onto the mattress. I straddled him and sank down into pure bliss.

Road Trips & Revelations

We lay on the rumpled sheets, leisurely mapping each other with our hands while we exchanged intermittent kisses. To say I was sated would fall short of the reality that I was completely and utterly–albeit happily–exhausted. It was one thing to "know" werewolves had impressive stamina. It was entirely another to get to experience that stamina first hand. Like *wow*.

Xander's fingers trailed down my side, and I shivered. "Well, that went better than expected."

"What did?" I asked, lifting my gaze from his chest.

His face turned a dark red, immediately piquing my curiosity. "Nothing," he mumbled.

"Oh, no you don't." He tried to fend me off, but I still managed to pin him beneath me. "Spill."

His warm hands coasted lightly over my hips, gently holding me in place. Meanwhile, he obstinately refused to meet my gaze. "I haven't, you know, had sex-sex before." His blush deepened, and he shyly met my gaze. "You're, uh, my first."

"Xander!" I smacked his chest lightly. "Why didn't you tell me?"

"I didn't want you to think I was too inexperienced," he grumbled, ducking his head again.

I shifted to lie on his chest and look at him over my crossed arms. "That wouldn't have mattered. I might have been a little less pushy, though. Maybe taken things a little slower."

He snorted. "I don't think 'slow' was in either of our vocabularies." He combed his fingers through my hair and I hummed contentedly. "I missed you."

The fizzy-feeling once again returned with a vengeance, and I positively beamed at him. "I missed you too."

His phone rang, completely shattering the tender moment, shortly followed by my phone pinging several times in rapid succession. "Sounds like responsibility is calling," he groaned.

We rolled apart to check our respective devices. Sure enough, I had several messages from Jennifer, Hyacinth, and, surprisingly, Kora. Ironically, all of them were asking about Xander. I huffed and flopped back down, determined to wallow in sated comfort a little longer. But reality had an insufferable way of intruding on my joy. I really should have told him everything I'd discovered first thing instead of letting myself get distracted.

"Full moon at midnight. You've got to be kidding me."

I lurched into a seated position. "What is it? What's wrong? Have they found Kai?"

Xander shook his head. Then whoever was on the other end stole his attention again. "No. Don't you dare. I'm warning you. Under absolutely no condition should you–" A pounding on the apartment door cut him off. "For fuck's sake," he growled, tossing his phone aside.

"What is it?" I asked, my concern mounting as he yanked on his jeans and stalked toward the bedroom door without bothering to button them. Not wanting to be left behind, I wrapped the sheet around me and scrambled after him. "Xander, what's going on?"

Instead of answering, Xander glowered and opened the front door. "Jennifer," he deadpanned.

I didn't even have a chance to be embarrassed before my irate friend waltzed inside. "Seriously, Xander?" she asked, giving us each an incredulous look. "Our packmates are *dying*, your biggest rival is stirring the pot, and you think now is a good time to be having nookie?"

"Hey! Dial back the attitude," I snapped. "First of all, call it sex like an adult. And second, Xander is entitled to a momentary reprieve, *especially* given everything that's going on. And last, you do not get to march into *my* apartment like you own the damn place and start condemning everyone in it."

Jennifer and I glared at each other, her mouth working to find words that never came. I'd have settled for her at least looking chastised in lieu of an apology, but that didn't happen either.

"Enough." Xander's stern command cut through the standoff and we swiveled to face him. "Jenny, I know a lot is going on, but try to remember that we're all on the same side. Diana is helping us and she's your friend."

Jennifer grumbled something that might have been an apology (finally), but I'd have needed supernatural hearing to make it out. At last, she let out a huff and seemed to force herself to drop her shoulders. She glanced at me. "I really hope you found something useful, because shit just got a lot more complicated."

"Because it wasn't before," I muttered.

"Okay, fine, I was wrong to storm in here and berate you both, but just because you know about werewolves, doesn't mean you know anything about pack politics." She turned back to face Xander. "As I was saying on the phone, while you've been here, Victor has already come and gone from the dorm. He's undoubtedly halfway back to the House by now and I don't need to tell you the shitstorm he's going to kick up in your absence. He'll kill your support. We need to leave now to have any chance of mitigating the fallout."

Xander shot me an anxious look. "Diana, we're going to need you to come. You're the most qualified to explain the danger facing us."

"But...I just got back." I gestured wildly at the pair of them, nearly losing my sheet. "And What about Takashi?"

"She has a point," Jennifer chimed in. "Just because the detective didn't come sniffing around while she was away the first time, doesn't mean we'll get as lucky a second time. Also, there's a little detail you're forgetting."

"What would that be?" Xander asked.

I already had a pretty good idea of where this was going. "That I come from an ancient line of werewolf hunters and you'd be taking me to the very heart of your pack's territory."

Jennifer cocked her head and twisted her mouth. "Not to mention she threw a damn knife at my head."

"It was *past* your head, not at it," I corrected her. "If I'd been aiming for your head, I wouldn't have missed."

She scoffed. "And yet, I don't find that reassuring."

"You're right. I'm sorry. That was extreme, even for me. Just try to remember that you weren't the only one processing life-altering information." She gave a shrug that could have been acquiescence. Given we didn't really have time for anything else, I'd take it. "She's not wrong, though. You have no reason to trust me and I haven't even told *you* what I found yet."

"I know. I *know*. But assuming you're willing to go, we'll figure it out. Hell, it might be safest for everyone if some of the dorm came as well, and the rest camped out here. Would be easy enough then to distract and divert the detective should he come around."

"I suppose," I replied noncommittally as I chewed on my bottom lip.

Xander stepped past his cousin and rested his hands on my exposed arms, making me realize how cold I was. "Hey," he said softly. "I know it's a lot and we don't have the luxury of time to think of alternatives. *I* trust you and I really think it would make a world of difference if my father heard what we're up against directly from you.The question is, do you trust me?"

I searched his face and only found sincerity. Was I worried this would blow up in all our faces? Yes. Was I anxious about meeting Xander's father and probably mother? Hell yes. Could I think of anything better? Nope. "Okay, I'll go." I released a nervous chuckle. "Guess it's a good thing I'm already packed. Though I should probably leave the bow behind."

Xander darted a glance at the table where my things from yesterday still sat, his gaze zeroing on the oblong case. I mentally kicked myself. Hadn't actually told him about that bit yet. "Actually," he said, snatching me out of my self-recrimination, "bring it. What better way to make sure they truly understand what we're up against than showing them what an expert archer can do." He returned his gaze to me, looking a little sheepish. "That is, if you're okay with that."

I glanced between him and Jennifer, who looked surprised but not like she disagreed. "If you think it's a good idea, I'll bring it. And as loath as I am to have people I don't know in my space, especially without me, I trust you and I trust your pack. I just want them to be safe."

Surprise flitted across Jennifer's face. Xander, on the other hand, looked like his heart was now in a puddle on the floor.

He stole a quick kiss and stepped back only to be replaced by Jennifer swooping in to give me a fierce hug. I squeaked at the incredible force now crushing my ribs.

"Jenny! Human!" Xander scolded.

"Oops," she conceded, lightening her grip and letting air back into my lungs. "Sorry about that. I just... I didn't realize how out of sorts I was when I learned you were a werewolf hunter. So, since you two are clearly... you know, and he's a werewolf, does that mean we can still be friends?"

This time, I captured her in a tight hug. "Absolutely. And I promise not to throw any more knives in your direction."

"Gee thanks," she scoffed. We laughed nervously as we parted while Xander stood there with a goofy smile.

"I'll pop back to the dorm to tell the others the plan and give you a chance to get ready. I'll also see if anyone else wants to make the trip with us. We'll see how many that is once they know you're going back to meet with Alpha." She turned to go and Xander pulled her up short.

"Let's try to keep the panic to a minimum. Encourage anyone who wants to go to the House to carpool... in a separate car." He glanced back at me. "We're going to be having a pretty intense conversation on the way there. The last thing I want is for someone to hear something out of context and cause another mutiny. We've had enough of those for a lifetime."

Jennifer nodded sharply and let herself out. Once she'd gone, Xander's shoulders sagged, and he ran both his hands through his hair in an obvious sign of frustration and anxiety. Before I could comfort him, though, a question was buzzing in my mind.

"Xander."

He glanced up from his sightless study of the stained carpet. "Yeah?"

"I thought I was going to talk to your father."

"You are."

I licked my lips and tightened the sheet. "Okay, but Jennifer said that I would talk to the Alpha. Am I doing both?" One was bad enough. But an actual werewolf *Alpha?* That sounded like an epically bad idea and made me infinitely less inclined to bring the bow, though I'd be more likely to need it.

Xander's expression was confused for a moment, then he huffed out a laugh. "My father *is* the Alpha," he said as casually as if pronouncing his father was a mechanic or a doctor, then walked toward the bedroom.

22

THE HOUSE

During the drive, I filled in Jennifer and Xander on everything I'd learned during my visit home. There was the expected disbelief, followed by outrage, and ultimately fear. They also let me know what to expect when we arrived, both in terms of the "House", which was apparently a proper noun, and my meeting with the Alpha. Despite their reassurances, though, I still couldn't wrap my head around Xander's father being the Alpha. The connotations of it were immense, and I was struggling to parse fact from fiction.

"What about the whole Alpha-control thing? Is that real?" I asked in my list of endless questions.

Xander and Jennifer shared a look in the front seat while I waited eagerly in the back. At last, Xander was the one to answer. "It's real. Going against a bonafide Alpha is damn near impossible. What an Alpha says, goes. No questions asked. Packs can't afford the doubts that come with conventionally democracy."

I puzzled over that. "Sounds a little dictatory to me."

"Don't think of it like that. It's more a measure of complete trust that the Alpha has the best interests of the pack in mind when an outright order is issued. The..." She fidgeted in the driver's seat as she struggled to come up with a word. "The *need* to follow those orders is a kind of self-preservation. Survival instinct, if you will."

I glanced over to Xander. "Yeah, I'm still not sure if I'm following."

He let out a long suffering sigh. "It's a way to minimize chaos. Think what would happen if werewolves didn't have any kind of desire to follow leadership. Besides, it's not infallible. If a pack's faith in their Alpha is shaken enough, the control can be circumvented." He shared another glance with Jennifer. "We, uh, had something like that happen over the summer."

I immediately straightened up. "What? Why?"

"The crux of it is that my father is planning to step down as Alpha."

"Huh," I mused aloud, "I wasn't aware that Alphas retired."

Xander met my gaze in the rearview mirror. "They don't. At least, not by choice."

I let that sink in before jumping to my next question. "And you want to pick up the mantle. But I was under the impression the title wasn't hereditary. Or do I have that wrong too?"

"It's not." Jennifer's hands tightened on the steering, causing it to creak. "Xander will have to fight for the right to call himself Alpha just like anyone else. The political part is making sure he has enough support to back him in the ring. Which could mean fewer contenders or other *weres* stepping in to eliminate his competition."

Fear wrapped around my heart so hard and fast, I let out a grunt. I'd read how brutal werewolf fights were. And even if the accounts of Alpha battles were grossly exaggerated, that still put them as extremely violent and potentially lethal. Before I could give voice to my worry and start pumping them for details on his competition, Jennifer turned off the road onto what appeared to be a long gravel driveway.

"We're here," she said as the trees obscuring the view gave way to reveal a massive plantation style house, with pillars and all.

I swallowed hard. "Are you sure my being here is okay?" I asked for the hundredth time, though it was definitely too late to think about turning back now. Not when each second brought us closer to the front door.

Xander swiveled around to face me as we pulled to a stop. "If anyone says or does anything untoward, you tell me immediately. You are here as a guest and a consultant, and I will not have you disrespected." His fierce tone had Jennifer and I both a little taken aback. He paused in the act of opening his door. "Bring your bow. I have a feeling we'll be needing a demonstration to drive the point home." Then, without a backward glance, he exited the vehicle and approached a woman with a similar skin tone and dark hair pulled over her shoulder in a braid.

"That's Maria Wolfsbane, Xander's mom and the Alpha female of the pack," Jennifer said softly as the woman smiled broadly to reveal laugh lines around her mouth and eyes. She then embraced her son tightly before turning a penetrative gaze on the vehicle.

As we stepped out of the car and walked around to the trunk the other two cars in our little caravan pulled up. Xander had explained that while they didn't live at the House, it was customary to stop by in a show of respect prior to going to their respective homes in the town of Stonelake that we'd passed.

"I'll grab your bag, but I'd leave the box for the bow. Better to show strength walking in for anyone that might be watching, than have to dig it out in your private audience," Jennifer said so quietly I almost didn't hear. She glanced at me briefly, then dropped her head again. "I know this isn't your world and you're not used to seeing things from this side, but please don't do anything to fuck this up for Xander. He's worked so hard to prove himself and recent events have already shaken people's faith enough as it is."

I gave a quick nod to convey my understanding and hoped to hell and back that she wasn't steering me wrong as I slung the small quiver over me, followed by the bow. I hesitated a moment before grabbing the arrow I'd pulled from Xander what already felt like a lifetime ago. Even carefully wrapped, I worried about any lingering remains of the deadly toxin. Either I'd be walking out of here in one piece or I'd never walk anywhere ever again. With that dire thought in mind, I turned to greet the handful of people that had congregated on the front porch.

"Mom, this is Diana Harker." Xander held out his hand for me. I accepted the warm display of unification as I stepped closer. "Diana, this is my mom, Maria."

I extended a free hand. "It's a pleasure to meet you, Mrs. Wolfsbane."

She took my hand with both of hers and smiled. "Please, call me Maria. Not even the stuffiest in the pack call me Mrs. Wolfsbane. I know you've had a long drive, and while normally I would encourage you to get settled first, unfortunately, time is not on our side." She gave my captive hand a gentle squeeze and released it. "If you'll follow me, I'll take you to Alexander. Hopefully, though, we'll have some time to catch up later. It's not every day my only son brings home a girlfriend."

"Mom," Xander hissed under his breath, but it did nothing to diminish the knowing twinkle in the older woman's eyes.

She turned and led the way inside. It was then that I'd realized Jennifer wasn't with us, but the other two from the porch were still there—a tall woman with fair skin and astounding red hair and a burly man with golden hair and stunning blue eyes. "Um..." I began, glancing around for my missing friend and completely ignoring the history decorating the walls.

The woman placed a gentle, yet startlingly warm hand on my arm and leaned closer. "Don't worry, Jenny will be around afterward. I'm Charline and that's David." She gestured to the blond man who was currently having a very animated conversation with Xander that was causing his adorable blush to appear.

Xander glanced up, catching my eye, and maneuvered closer. "Sorry about that. Normally, I'm better about doing *all* of the introductions. David is currently acting as my dad's Beta and will hopefully end up being mine when the time comes." Pride radiated off of Charline and David. It was true that I didn't fully grasp pack politics, but it didn't take a werewolf to know that was a big deal.

"It's nice to meet you. I look forward to getting to know you." The pair shared a knowing look, then split apart with promises to catch up with me later. David increased his pace to join Maria as she led us around a grand staircase while Charline ducked her head and slipped off into what appeared to be a kitchen. "What was that about?" I asked softly.

Xander shook his head. "Nothing. David's just giving me a taste of my own medicine."

"Uh-huh." I glanced toward him as we continued down a hallway. "Did you tell your mom we're seeing each other?" I asked, not that it really mattered, but I couldn't figure out when he';d have had the opportunity, as I thought we were fairly new.

His cheeks bloomed red. "Not exactly."

Before I could press for clarity, Maria was opening one of the many doors dotting the hallway. "Here we are." She gestured for the rest of us to enter, then followed, closing the door behind us.

To my surprise, there was another young man already waiting inside. He turned to face us, a scowl darkening his face when his gaze landed on me. He couldn't have been more than a few years older than me, was of average height, with muddy hazel eyes, tanned skin, and messy brown hair. One look was all it took for my instincts to clock a threat. This had to be Xander's rival for the position of Alpha. I was so distracted by the man that I missed the person I'd actually come here to meet.

"It's so good to see you safe," an older man with a striking resemblance to Xander said as he embraced him. "I wasn't sure what to think from Jenny's report and your account wasn't any better."

"I know. I'm sorry, dad. So much has been going on." Xander returned the tight hug and I braced myself for the imminent introduction. At last they parted, and the older man turned to face me.

"Won't you introduce me to your friend?"

A brilliant smile illuminated Xander's face. David coughed something I didn't quite catch, which resulted in Xander shooting him a frown and his father smiling. "Dad, this is Diana Harker, former werewolf hunter and the woman who saved my life. A couple times," he added with a cheeky grin. "Diana, this is my dad, Alexander Wolfsbane."

I shifted the bow hanging on me and squared my shoulders. I could have lived without being called a werewolf hunter, former or otherwise, but it *was* why I was here. "Good day, sir. It's an honor to meet you." I fought the urge to curtsy like some pretentious debutant. Meanwhile, the other young man seemed to be actively stopping himself from saying something.

Xander's dad–what did I even call him?–stepped to the center of the sitting room. "I'm glad you could join us, Miss Harker. Before we begin, I'd like to thank you for helping my son and sharing whatever you're able." I blinked. It hadn't occurred to me not to tell them any and everything they wanted to know. They'd need it in the battle ahead.

"I don't know how much Xander has shared with you, but I want to make one thing clear. While my family raised me to hunt werewolves, never in my life have I actually shot or killed one. I left that life behind because I want nothing to do with it."

Mr. Wolfsbane nodded, his expression thoughtful. "That is encouraging to know. I'm still coming to terms with the fact that werewolf hunters, specifically the Harkers, are not only real, but are still around and practicing." He walked toward a wall lined with books and seemed to study their worn bindings. "I've heard the stories, of course, but I think, like most of us, I believed they were exaggerations meant to frighten pups into behaving."

"If only that were the case," I interjected sadly.

"Tell me, is it true the Harkers have twin daggers with wolf's head pommels and rubies for eyes?" He glanced over his shoulder at me and it took everything I had not to fidget beneath that intense gaze. Xander clearly came by *that* honestly.

"Yes, though I've never personally handled them. They're both a family heirloom and a symbol of our vocation. Last time I knew of anyone using them was shortly after the Harker's moved to the American colonies. Though they're still kept in pristine fighting condition."

He expelled a long sigh. "That matches with what I've been able to scrounge up in our histories." He turned back and gestured for me to take one of the wing-backed chairs. We both sat, along with Xander and his unnamed rival, though David opted to remain leaning against the wall by the door. "I believe it's past time that we heard what you came to share."

Right. This was it. I shared an anxious look with Xander. I touched the tip of my bow that I'd leaned against the chair as if to reassure myself, then began. "We were able to deduce that it was a hunter picking people off. To get a better idea of who that hunter might be, I went home to see what I could find. While I was there, my mother all but confirmed that it's my Uncle Nemo who's been stirring up trouble."

A sharp hiss to my side made the hairs on the back of my neck stand up, but I didn't stop.

"But it's worse than that. Normally, my uncle would be easy enough to stop, as the rest of the hunting community thinks he's insane. He's always been after the perfect kill and has come up with some pretty wild schemes in the past."

"What's different about this time?" Mr. Wolfsbane asked.

I took a shaky breath. "This time he has history on his side. How familiar are you with the impact a solar eclipse has on werewolves?"

The group shared a collective look until he finally shrugged. "We've lived through a couple. Nothing seemed out of the ordinary, though."

"It's possible you didn't have cause to know what would be out of the ordinary. According to an obscure reference my uncle found dated centuries ago, during a full solar eclipse, werewolves..." I hesitated, not sure how well what I was about to say would be received. Secretly, I hoped Xander's dad would outright refute it, but I wasn't holding my breath.

"Go on," Xander encouraged me.

I gave him a weak smile in thanks, then returned my attention to his dad. "Werewolves lose all of their supernatural abilities during the eclipse. No super strength, no enhanced senses." I steeled my resolve. "And no healing."

"What?!" The other man launched out of his seat, prompting Xander to do the same. "That's impossible!"

Mr. Wolfsbane shot the man a scathing look. "Sit down, Victor. If you cannot hold your peace during these types of proceedings, you'll be excluded from future ones."

Victor appeared to shake beneath the weight of Mr. Wolfsbane's words, then begrudgingly resumed his seat.

"I can see how we would miss that. How long will this last?" Mr. Wolfsbane asked.

"Only for as long as the moon obscures the sun," Xander chimed in. "We believe that our abilities will gradually wane as the eclipse begins, vanish altogether during the height, then slowly return as it ends."

His dad ran a hand over his wary face, highlighting stress lines I hadn't noticed before. "That's something at least. A few minutes isn't long in the grand scheme of things."

"It's long enough," I countered.

Victor scoffed. "It's one man. Even without super strength, one hunter is no match for a pack of wolves." His cocky attitude snapped the last of my reserve.

"It won't be *one* man." I turned a meaningful look on Mr. Wolfsbane. "All the Harkers will be there. My uncle, possibly his wife, definitely my father and mother. With all of their support, it's possible he'll even convince other hunting families to join his crusade. Every one of them has trained their entire life to hunt and kill werewolves. They know what they're doing and they'll be using these."

Without preamble, I kicked the arrow I'd bundled so that it rolled across the area rug, unraveling until it came to a stop at Mr. Wolfsbane's feet. Most of the room recoiled in shock while he studied the blood stained arrow without touching it.

"I pulled two of those out of Xander less than two weeks ago. It's a miracle he's alive at all. It only took one to kill the others." I stood and walked over, carefully picking up the arrow to reference as I explained how it worked. "If you look at the tip, you'll notice a slim reservoir. The shot itself isn't intended to be deadly, just pierce its target. From there, a poison made from monkshood is injected into the victim. Depending on where they were shot and how much of the poison made it into their system, it can take anywhere from minutes to hours. But it's always fatal."

Mr. Wolfsbane gingerly took the arrow from me and studied it intently. "I'm not familiar with monkshood."

"You might know it by its other name. Wolfsbane."

23

UNIQUE INSIGHT

To say I was kicked out of the room after that might be an exaggeration, but it's what it felt like. Part of me understood that they needed time to absorb the information and come to terms with it. I just hoped they didn't take too long. The next full solar eclipse was less than a month away and time was precious.

Xander encouraged me to check out the yard or the orchard while they spoke about next steps and he would come find me, so that's what I did. Mostly, I was hoping I'd run into Jennifer and wouldn't be left wondering on my own in the heart of werewolf territory. They'd both assured me on the drive here that none of the others, including the pack members that had opted to return from Blackwell, knew what I was, but that didn't exactly put me at ease. At least I'd been allowed to take my bow and quiver with me when I'd been shown the door.

As I walked along the edge of the barren orchard, I spotted a few people. Some of them gave me curious looks, but most paid me no mind. I wasn't sure if it was normal or not for so few people to be at the central hub of a werewolf pack. Was it a symptom of the recent troubles Xander had alluded to? Was it quiet by design because I was coming here? Or was it simply the season and no one was home? Could they smell from that far away that I wasn't one of them? It was virtually impossible to stay downwind the whole time.

Whatever the reason, no one bothered me as I meandered past the last row of apple trees into dense forest. I still got flashes of the large house between the trees, but admittedly had fallen into my own whirling thoughts as I walked. Had a hunter, let alone a Harker, ever been *invited* to pack lands? To the house where the Alpha lived? Granted, I wasn't exactly here on the best circumstances, but it didn't change the fact that he'd trusted me enough to wander on my own. The same would never be said for my family if the roles had been reversed. Even though I hadn't met that many werewolves since learning the truth, one thing was becoming abundantly clear: they were *not* the monsters I'd been raised to believe they were. What's more, I was falling in love with one of them.

That was a heady thought. While it wasn't the first time it had crossed my mind that I was falling *hard* for Xander, it still had the power to pull me up short. No one from my world could ever know. Not about Xander, not about the dorm, and definitely not about this place. It was a fact that was equally thrilling, as it was disheartening.

"And just when it seemed like my mother and I were patching things up," I mumbled to myself.

"What about your mom?" Jennifer asked, rounding a tree off to my side and pulling me out of the sudden funk.

"There you are. I was wondering if I'd be able to find you."

Jennifer ducked her head. "Sorry. I didn't mean to bounce like that. Closed meetings are, well, closed. I was just touching base with some of the early arrivals to see how things have been going here. Thought for sure you'd be at the house, not wandering around out here. But Charline said you weren't there and Foxy knows everything."

I raised an eyebrow. "Foxy?"

"It's a long story. Maybe she'll tell it to you. When I popped in, she was practicing her scone recipe. What do you say? Wanna sign up to be official taste testers? It's a position that fills up quick around here." She gave me a serious look and I couldn't help but laugh. Considering the kind of appetite werewolves were reputed to have, I didn't doubt it.

"Sounds like a plan to me." We hooked arms, careful not to get twisted around my bow and set off back toward the house. "How much longer do you think Xander will be?"

She shrugged. "Who can say. I doubt he'll want to leave you on your own for long, though."

"Why's that?" I asked.

"Because you have no business being here," Victor snarled as he stepped in our path, blocking the way.

"Get lost, Victor," Jennifer growled, her hold on me tightening to the point of pain.

His withering glare shifted to her. "Being a human lover is one thing, but to bring a moon-bitten hunter to the *House*? Xander's got some nerve. He'd have lost support when the others found out he was pursuing one of them, but when they learn the truth about what she is, where she comes from?" He let out a sinister laugh. "We won't even have to have to an Alpha battle, the pack will beg me to take over."

Jennifer released me and advanced on him, fury written in every line of her body. "You shut your fucking mouth. Or did you not see what happened to the last wolf that thought he could divide the pack like that?"

Victor's face darkened with a menacing smile. "Oh, I definitely saw. And I learned from Johnathan's mistakes." He shifted his gaze back to me. "As for you, thanks for the information, but you've out-stayed your welcome."

On cue three others–two guys and a girl–stepped from behind trees to join him. My heart sank as I realized that not only were they some of the few people that had noticed my passing, but they'd been stalking me and I'd been completely oblivious.

Jennifer widened her stance and looked around at the others. "Get behind me," she ordered as the sense of danger ratcheted up to a thousand.

I warred with the logic of doing what she said and embracing my training. Even outnumbered, I could do significant damage with the target arrows I'd brought. Nothing poisoned like the one I'd left in the sitting room, but no less lethal with the right shot. And as the detective had pointed out, I was one hell of a shot. Before I could decide on the right course of action, another body barrelled between the trees and sent me sprawling.

I twisted to avoid landing on my bow and injuring myself. From my spot on the ground, I could just make out Jennifer spinning around to try to keep all of them in sight and still stay between them and me. Fear strangled my lungs and tangled my limbs as I tried to get off the ground and join the fray. What kind of asshole ambushed one of his own? I was still working on getting my footing under me when another growl snatched my attention.

Xander burst into the scene, flanked by two others, and made a beeline for Victor. "Are you out of your mind!" he shouted as they went head to head. Reading about *were*-on-*were* violence was one thing, but nothing could have prepared me for the ferocity that erupted. The worst part was that I had no way of determining who was on what side.

I got jostled into a tree right as I stood upright and nearly lost my bow. The guy that had bumped into me barely spared me a second look before he lunged for Jennifer. She spun around just in time to knock him in the side of the head with her arm. Not that it really slowed him down. More concerning was the fight raging between Xander and Victor.

I wasn't sure what I'd missed, but those were undeniably claw marks in Xander's arm currently dripping blood on the forest floor. Victor advanced on him and it appeared everyone else was too busy fighting their own skirmishes to help. Xander drove his elbow upward into Victor's jaw, but not before earning himself another set of bloody scratches.

Whatever indecision was holding me back evaporated. I nocked an arrow in the same fluid motion I'd done a thousand times over. Xander snarled, but before he could do more, I set it free. The arrow flew over the others scrapping it out on the ground and passed close enough to Victor to clip his ear.

"Enough!" I shouted.

Fury clouded Victor's face while everyone else froze. Xander smirked and a little ember of pride burned in my chest.

"You seem to be under the mistaken impression that I'm incapable of defending myself. Allow me to correct you." I knocked three arrows, carefully holding them in place between my fingers. It had been a long time since I'd successfully pulled this stunt and I wasn't at all confident that I could do it now, but they didn't know that. "Back up and back off."

When none of them complied. I adjusted my trajectory and prayed my skills wouldn't fail me now. I released the arrows, and they split off to hit three different trees, all conveniently close to the assholes he'd brought with him. Warily, they eyed the embedded shafts. "I said, back up."

Xander turned his smirk on Victor. "You heard the lady. Go chase your tail somewhere else."

Victor bared his teeth. "You can run and tell daddy, but it won't stop me from challenging you for Alpha."

"I didn't think it would. And I have no intention of telling my father about this... misunderstanding. Way I see it, getting your tail handed to you by one of the humans you detest so much is embarrassment enough."

Victor spared me a hate-filled glare, then waved for the others. One by one, they peeled away to disappear deeper into the forest. Only when the last of them had gone did Xander relax.

"Fuck. This is all we need," Xander groaned. He scrubbed his face with both hands and finally seemed to realize he was bleeding. He pulled off his shirt and immediately wiped his arm clean. Luckily, it looked like a shallow wound and not as bad as I'd first thought.

Jennifer glanced after where the attackers had disappeared. "Maybe it was a mistake to pardon everyone who sided with Johnathan."

"I'm going to pretend I didn't hear that." Xander didn't look up, but the undercurrent of anger in his voice was unmistakable.

The color drained from Jennifer's face, and the others that arrived with Xander looked equally chastised. At some point, someone was going to need to fill me in on exactly what drama had occurred over the summer and who the hell this Johnathan character was. But that could wait. Right now, Xander needed to get bandaged up.

"Why don't we head back to the house?" I suggested into the tense quiet.

Jennifer gave me an appreciative look, and nods of agreement made their way through the small group.

"You can go on ahead. I'll join in a bit. I'm going to get cleaned up, and then I need to talk a few things over with

David." My face must have betrayed my disappointment, because Xander walked over and cupped the side of my face. "I promise I won't be long." He pressed his lips softly against mine and I wondered if everyone present could tell I had a kaleidoscope of butterflies fluttering wildly in my chest or if it was just me.

Someone cleared their throat, prompting Xander to release me. "What would you like us to do?" a guy with dirty blond hair asked.

Xander glanced around at the inquisitive faces. "First, let's make sure we collect these arrows. Don't want to start a panic." He gave me a wink and a cheeky grin. "Then I'd like you to keep an eye on our troublemakers. I'd rather history not repeat itself. I would appreciate one of you making sure Diana gets into the House safely."

Each bowed their head and wandered off to follow through with their assigned tasks, with the exception of one who lingered nearby. Jennifer was actually the one to pull the arrows free.

"And to think I thought you were scary with a knife," she said with a grin as she handed them over.

"That's nothing," I blustered. "You should see my ring work."

She and Xander chuckled, then stepped in the same direction... away from the house.

"Where are you going?" I finished holstering the arrows back in the quiver. "I thought you were going back to the house to clean up first."

He glanced beyond me toward the house, then at Jennifer. "I'll clean up at David's. I don't want to put this off in case more trouble tries to sprout up while I'm away. Nate will see you back to the house."

Despite my best efforts to stifle my disappointment, my shoulders still slumped. "Okay. I guess I'll wait for you there."

"Promise I won't be too long," he reassured me before they both resumed walking.

I trudged back to the house, this time keeping a sharp eye out for anyone taking too much of an interest in my presence in spite of my silent sentry. I still couldn't believe I'd dropped my guard so much as to not at least be on alert for being followed. With each step closer, my disposition soured further. I reminded myself that this wasn't a happy "meet the family" type situation. People were dying. More would likely die before all was said and done. And all of that was on top of whatever had happened previously that left this place feeling like a powder keg.

"Oh, I know that face," a charmingly Southern voice said.

I glanced up from where I'd just pushed through the back-door to find Charline, the woman with red hair, giving me a knowing look. I glanced the way I'd come and could see Nate hightailing it back to the woods, then returned my focus back to Charline and her odd comment. "Huh?"

"Come with me and we can talk about it." She waved for me to follow her deeper into the house, but didn't wait around to see if I would. We took the same path as I had earlier when I'd left until we arrived at an absurdly small kitchen, given the size of the house. "Have a seat, and I'll fix you a plate of scones. Coffee or tea?" she asked over her shoulder.

"Uh, tea. What did you mean you 'know that face'?" I asked as I made myself comfortable at the equally tiny breakfast table.

"You could say I have a unique perspective on things." She slid a plate filled with different scones between us, as well as a cup of steaming water and a silver tin filled with different types of tea. She waited for me to pluck out a packet of

Irish Breakfast before continuing. "As for the face, I know it, because I've made it. The 'this is not going at all how I imagined' face. Or, as my friend Sara prefers to call it: 'oh shit, I'm human.'" She laughed and I relaxed slightly.

"That obvious?"

She gave me a wistful look. "Unfortunately."

"But why would you have made that face? Aren't you..." I trailed off, not sure if it was rude to assume she was a werewolf like everyone else here, but I'd seen the way her eyes caught the light.

She laughed again. "Yes, I'm a werewolf, but I wasn't always. It's actually a recent development." I did a double take and this time her laughter filled the room and her very round belly threatened to tip the table. "Sorry," she said, wiping her eyes, "you just looked like a long-tailed cat that realized they were in a room full of rocking chairs."

"Uh..." I began, not entirely sure what that meant.

"Don't mind me. The point is, I know what it's like to be one of the only humans in a place like this." She plucked up a scone, took a bite, and immediately made a face. "Still too dry. Cursed confection, I *will* conquer you," she grumbled to herself while I tried to wrap my head around the fact that I was sitting at a table with an honest to goodness *bitten*-werewolf.

I subconsciously sipped my tea. "If it's not too rude, can I ask when it happened? When were you–"

"Bitten?" she finished for me. "Not long before the summer equinox. I won't get into the nitty-gritty of it, but things were a little touch-and-go there for a while. Luckily, it all worked out." She rubbed her belly absently and I could practically see the pride emanating off of her.

I lowered my voice and leaned closer. "Did David?"

"Oh, heavens no! That man would have died before putting me in harm's way. As it was, he nearly *did* die, because of the bite. Side effect of the bond." She shrugged like it wasn't a big deal, but the haunted look in her eyes betrayed her.

"Wait, so you're a bitten werewolf *and* part of a bonded pair?"

"Yep," she said, biting into a different scone and wrinkling her nose. "Try one of these. I can't tell if it's the hormones messing with my tastebuds or if they really are that dry."

I did as she asked, testing a cranberry one with some kind of drizzle. One bite was all it took to have me practically melting in my seat. "It's the hormones," I said around a mouthful of the best scone I'd ever had in my life.

Charline huffed and dropped her latest bite with a pout. Then she glared at her belly. "You better be glad I'm so excited to have you for all that you're making me suffer."

I chuckled and washed down the last of my scone with the tea. "So, how does it all work?"

"I'm going to assume you don't mean where babies come from," she said with a wink. "The bitten part wasn't great. To be honest, bitten werewolves are rare as hen's teeth."

"Why is that?" I asked. Given the horror stories I'd been raised with, I'd been inclined to believe nearly all werewolves were bitten.

"It's two-fold, really. Modern packs view it as barbaric, mostly because of the other reason we're so rare. Not every-one survives the bite or the change."

I was about to say that sounded terrifying, but then some-thing she said registered. "Wait, you said we."

She nodded and sipped her own tea. "I did. My friend Sara was bitten back in February. It's how we both became part of this world." She must have seen something on my face, because she added, "While there are a few things I wish I could do over, all-in-all, I don't have any regrets."

I teased the tag of my tea bag. "Are things easier now that you're a werewolf?"

She let out a long sigh, and I lifted my gaze to meet hers. "I wish the answer was that it didn't matter. There are a handful of mixed couples in the pack, but with David vying to be the pack's next Beta, my being human wasn't helping matters. Just goes to show that every culture has their prejudices, even progressive ones."

I mulled that over while I sampled another outrageously delicious scone. Xander's goals were even higher than David's, and judging by the interaction in the woods, his attachment to me was definitely hurting him. I understood that being bitten wasn't a guarantee, but it didn't seem to be all bad. Werewolves weren't anything like I'd been taught to expect. And I wasn't exactly risk averse. But it did lead me to another question.

"What about the bond?" I asked.

Charline smiled knowingly. "I was wondering when you'd ask about that."

"Why's that?"

"Oh, honey, I've seen the way Xander looks at you. If he hasn't completed the bond yet, he's well on his way. Has he talked to you about it?"

I shifted in my seat. "He's mentioned it in passing. What's that like?"

She got a dreamy look in her eye. "It's the most amazing thing I've ever experienced. I often marvel at how lucky I am to experience it at all when so many others haven't. I only wish I could have appreciated the connection blooming *with* David instead of months after the fact. It would have saved us both a lot of trouble," she added under her breath.

"So, it's true that humans can't reciprocate the bond."

"Sadly no. It's purely a werewolf thing. Oof," she said all of a sudden, her face twisting. "You'll have to excuse me. The little bun is kicking my bladder again. I swear, all I do is eat and pee these days," she grumbled to herself. "I'll be back shortly."

I watched the pregnant woman waddle out of the kitchen, griping in what I assumed were yet more Southernisms with each step. In the silence left in her wake, all I had to keep me company were my thoughts. Most of which my family would lock me up and throw away the key if they knew about it. But then, this wasn't their life, it was mine. And I'd be damned if I wasn't going to live it.

24

—◆◇◆—

KORA TO THE RESCUE

HOW THE HELL WAS I expected to focus on anything as trivial as standard deviations and statistical anomalies with an imminent massacre on the horizon? But final exams didn't care that the next full moon was only a couple weeks away. Nor did they give two shits that it was also going to be a solar eclipse. Okay, that was a lie. A full solar eclipse was a big deal for anyone and I'd already heard about countless watch parties.

Finally, the lecture ended. I bagged my notes and made a beeline for the door. With my last class of the day finished, I was at liberty to go back to my apartment. If I was lucky, Xander would be waiting for me and I could get lost in his warmth like I'd wanted to do since we got back. I was still miffed at his insistence that we keep up appearances by continuing to go to class, even if it was logical.

I stepped out of the college of business and took a deep breath of the crisp air. Given how the temperature kept yo-yoing, it was a wonder it hadn't snowed on top of everything else.

"Hey, you! Where are you off to in such a hurry?" Kora's chipper voice froze the relieved breath in my lungs.

249

I turned a smile on my friend as she finished bounding up to me. Her blond hair was styled into a messy bun that I knew for a fact took her hours to perfect. "Nowhere," I lied through my teeth.

"Perfect. Then you have plenty of time to hang out with the crew," she said, falling in step beside me and subtly herding me toward the heart of campus and away from the transit buses. "I've already confirmed with Millie and Sabrina—you remember her—that they're good to join us at the Student Union's Winter Fair. I'd have included Hyacinth, but it seems she's out of town again."

Worry briefly eclipsed my irritation. Hye had gone home again? It wasn't that I expected her to tell me every time she did, but the fact that she hadn't told me she knew I'd disapprove. Fuck, I'd been so wrapped up with Xander, werewolves, and eclipses that I'd forgotten to keep tabs on her. When had her last "transfusion" been again?

"Uh, Earth to Anna. Are you even listening to me?" Irritation sparked in Kora's eyes and vanished just as quickly. Truth be told, it was usually an endeavor to pay attention when she babbled on like that. But that had always been a challenge when most of my conversations before I'd come to Blackwell had revolved around much more serious topics—like how to kill a family of monsters and not end up on the evening news.

"Sorry, a lot on my mind," I said, guilt gnawing at me as I realized that with everything going on lately, I'd all but abandoned the friendships I'd worked so hard to build.

We parted to go around a cluster of students moving too slowly. "Wouldn't have anything to do with that young stud you've been spending so much time with, would it?" she crooned as we came back together.

I had all of half a second to wonder how she knew I'd been spending any amount of time with Xander when the absolutely last person I wanted to see walked up. Detective Takashi was bundled up against the biting cold in a long coat and a thick scarf. Even with his head down against the wind, there was no denying his trajectory.

"Miss Harker, fancy running into you here," he said, stopping in front of us. To my infinite embarrassment, Kora didn't even try to hide her open perusal of the detective.

I gave him a thin lipped smile and throttled the urge to snarkily ask where the fuck else I would be. "You must have excellent timing. I just got out of my last class. Exams are going to be brutal. So I really should be on my way. Lots of studying to do."

His steady gaze said luck had nothing to do with it. "Funny you should express such concern for your classes. I feel like I haven't seen you around lately. It's almost like you haven't been here at all."

"Oh, that's because she wasn't," Kora chimed in. The detective's gaze sharpened and we stood in a tense stalemate while Kora kept talking. "I can't believe I forgot to ask how your trip home was! And I expect all the deets about what you were up to over the long weekend." She shimmied her shoulders suggestively, no doubt assuming *that* absence had something to do with Xander, then she seemed to realize something was off.

"Traveling, Miss Harker? Surely your friend is mistaken. Especially since I distinctly remember telling you not to leave town."

"What?" she asked, alarm causing her voice to rise. She stared at me with wide eyes brimming with hurt. "Why didn't you say anything?" I broke my staring contest and gave her a pleading look to understand.

"It would appear our Miss Harker is in the habit of keeping secrets," Takashi commented dryly.

Anger flashed in Kora's bright blue eyes and she rounded on the detective. "I'm sorry. Who are you again?"

"Kora, this is Detective Takashi, I've been helping with a case he's working on," I interjected before she could give him a full-blown scathing rebuke. She might come across as flighty at times, but she believed in sisterhood and would be damned before she let a man talk like that to another woman like that, and certainly not a friend.

She raised a dubious eyebrow, clearly not fully buying it. Probably would have helped if I'd included that it was about a string of murders, but that was more likely to get me into trouble than to clear things up. The last thing I wanted was to drag her into a murder investigation, least of all one that involved supernaturals. "Is this about when you hit your head?" she asked.

"Um, yeah," I responded falteringly as I wracked my brain to recall how much I'd told her about that night.

She stepped closer and dropped her voice while eying the detective suspiciously. "Anna, are you in some kind of trouble? You could have come to me. I would have helped."

The sentiment was sweet and I could tell how hurt she was that I'd left her out of something so big. I wished I had the time and brainpower to make her understand that I hadn't kept it from her out of any ill will. But time was in increasingly short supply. Especially with the detective eying me like I'd just gone from suspect numero uno to having committed murder right in front of him. Before I could say anything, the detective turned a placating smile on Kora.

"I'm sure your friend will be happy to explain her absence to you at a later time. If you wouldn't mind excusing us, there are a few things I'd like to discuss with Miss Harker."

Kora looked between the two of us expectantly. "Go ahead."

"In private," he added.

It was a toss up if Kora would comply without argument or insist on staying to protect me. Judging by the hard line of her clenched jaw, things didn't look like they'd be going in the detective's favor.

"It's okay. I'll catch up with you later," I said, gently squeezing her upper arm.

She darted another suspicious glance between me and the detective. "If you're sure..."

"I am. Go on and enjoy your evening. And give my best to the others. This could take a while, and I don't want to hold you up." I mentally crossed my fingers that she could hear my sincerity. I'd have to come up with a reasonable explanation for all of this, including leaving her out of the loop, but I'd need more time for that.

"I will. We'll catch up another time," she added, giving me a pointed look before continuing on toward the Student Union.

I fought the urge to rub my temple in exasperation. Of all the times for the detective show up. I did not have the fucking bandwidth for this bullshit. The Eclipse was less than two weeks away, my family was going to be popping up any time now, my friend was pissed, and all I wanted to do was go home to my boyfriend, get fucked into oblivion, and forget about all of it for a few hours.

"Miss Harker, if you would be so kind as to accompany me back to the station. I believe there's quite a bit we need to get caught up on."

The emotional overload from the last few months hit its peak and I snapped. "Actually, I will *not* be so kind. I have been nothing but cooperative during your investigation—without legal representation, I might add—and I'm done. If you want to talk to me about anything from here on out, you can do it through my lawyer. No more stalking me or ambushing me on campus."

"I would strongly advise against this," he said in an ominous tone.

"Yeah? Well tough. If you don't like it, then you can arrest me now and charge me properly." I held out my wrists for him to cuff. After a few moments where he didn't so much as twitch, I raised an eyebrow. "No? Then, if you'll excuse me, I have better people to spend my evening with." I dropped my arms and spun on my heel to head back toward the transit station.

"We're not finished, Miss Harker," he called after me.

It twas tempting to flip him the bird as I stalked off, but I figured I'd pressed my luck enough as it was. Seriously, daring him to cuff me? What was wrong with me? Instead, I spun enough to shout back, "We are today."

Unfortunately, the transit ride gave me plenty of time to second guess my decision to blow off the detective. There was a reason I hadn't invoked wanting my lawyer before now and it had nothing to do with being innocent. If I called the family lawyer, then my whole *family* would know—lawyer-client confidentiality be damned. I glanced up from glaring murderously at the sidewalk to find Xander standing outside my door.

"Thank fuck," I said once I got closer. I caught a flash of his brilliant smile before I slammed my mouth against his, pressing him into the still closed door. His natural heat permeated my thick jacket as he pulled me tighter against him and deepened the kiss. I didn't even care that we were making out on the front porch for all to see. I just wanted more.

"Bad day?" he asked with a lilt of humor when we finally pulled apart for air.

"The fucking worst." I reached past him to unlock the door and we shuffled inside where I dropped my bag. "Look, I know we had plans to, well, make a plan, but I'm going to need something else first."

His brown eyes darkened with lust and if the tent in his pants was anything to go by, we were definitely on the same page. "I'm at your service."

I smiled wickedly then yanked all my layers off in a move that I was honestly shocked worked. Then I launched myself at him, letting his searing touch banish the chill already pebbling my skin. I was pretty sure I would never tire of how easily Xander carried me to the bedroom with my legs wrapped around his waist.

He set me down once we were by the bed and I shimmied out of my jeans while he stripped. I stole a moment to appreciate the sheer fucking sexiness of his athletic body, then scrambled across the bed to rip open the nightstand. For a hot second, I was tempted to say fuck it and nix the condom, but decided against it. I set out the foil wrapped packets and turned back in time to watch Xander crawl up the bed like he was stalking prey. And it was *hot*.

My need reached critical levels and I didn't give him the chance to finish making his way up the bed before tackling him to the mattress. His hands on my bare back were absolute heaven and I craved the way his mouth owned mine. Abruptly, he dialed back the intensity and brushed my lips with more tender kisses. Then he flipped us so I was laid out beneath him and continued his methodical exploration.

Despite how good it felt to have his mouth anywhere on me, it wasn't what I wanted. What I *needed*. In an effort to reignite the fiery maelstrom, I flipped us back. To my dismay, he chuckled and gently tucked my hair behind my ear. I made a frustrated sound at the back of my throat.

"What's the matter?" he asked, his face scrunching with gentle concern.

"I'm not made of glass," I grumbled, straightening up and sitting on my heels.

"And I'm not human." he sat up, mirroring me. "Hey, talk to me. Tell me what you need."

I ran my hands through my hair, at a loss. Telling him I wanted it hard, fast, and dirty wasn't going to fly. I could see it in his eyes. He was too worried about hurting me. Hell, I'd be lucky if I could convince him to pull my hair. I hated that he was right. Compared to his werewolf nature, I *was* fragile. I let out a hard breath.

"What?" he pressed when I remained quiet.

I snagged my bottom lip between my teeth and shot him an anxious look.

"Please look at me." I reluctantly did so. I don't know what I'd expected to see, but it certainly wasn't a calm, open expression. "Tell me what you need."

"I... I don't know. I just know that I don't want gentle and you're afraid of hurting me."

"Diana." It wasn't until he said my name so firmly that I realized I'd dropped my head again. I dutifully lifted my gaze once more. His small smile threw me. "All you had to do was say so."

"Really? You're not worried about hurting me?"

"Of course I am. But that doesn't mean I can't or won't give you what you need."

My eyes began to sting and fuck this whole day. I would die before I cried during sex. Or almost sex.

He shifted closer and leaned in to kiss me. I was fully prepared for a gentle brush of lips that might evolve into more. What I got was scorching, toe-curling, fuck-me-sideways, how-did-I end-up-on-my-back kiss. Xander looked down at me with a cocky smirk while I blinked up at him completely stupefied.

Fuck fizzies or butterflies or what have you. I was a total goner for this man. And the way I saw it, the fact that he was a werewolf was a bonus. I had zero doubt that I was sporting a shit-eating grin as I pulled him back down for another ravening kiss. I buried my hands in his hair to keep him there and shifted beneath him. Then he angled his hips just right and I gasped. I didn't know what was better, that I now had friction where I wanted it most or that he'd yanked my head back to expose my throat.

I moaned into him as I ground against his thigh, desperate to have him pushing through my swollen folds. His hands were everywhere, teasing, pulling, pinching until it felt like my body was vibrating. Then his mouth followed. He laid open-mouthed kisses along my collar onto my breasts and down my abdomen, but just when I thought he'd go further, he lifted his head and gave the wickedest grin I'd ever seen on his face.

He plunged two fingers deep into me at the same time he leaned down and sucked a bruise out on my neck. I practically levitated off the bed. It was only his weight on top of me that kept me grounded. His fingers continued to twist and thrust while he lavished attention on my neck and torso. He angled his thumb to work my clit in time with pushing in and out of me and stars danced across my vision.

My release didn't hover closer, it barrelled toward me like a freight train. Then he sank his teeth into the sensitive skin between my neck and my shoulder and all thought fled. All but one—the sudden overwhelming desire for him to not just mark me, but *truly* bite me, ramifications and all. Before I could dissect that much further, he pulled his fingers free and I groaned at their loss. Thankfully, he didn't make me suffer long.

Xander reached for the condoms and either he really was that fast or I was already beyond blissed out. In no time flat, he'd rolled on the rubber and speared into me in one smooth motion. I caught a glimpse of the unadulterated pleasure on his face before he placed my legs over his shoulders and set a punishing pace.

Every muscle tightened, blurring the line between pleasure and pain. He buried his length again and again, stroking my already sensitive nerves into an aftershock orgasm that bled into another and another. I was on the verge of tapping out or passing out when he pulled free and I realized that was the last thing I wanted. As if he knew exactly where my head was at, he didn't leave me wanting.

Leveraging his considerable strength, he turned me over and angled my hips back so I was on my knees. I cried out when he plunged back in. He placed the flat of his hand on my back to push me down into the bedding while he used his other to hold my hip in a bruising grip that I absolutely reveled in. He coaxed out two more mind-altering orgasms before his rhythm finally faltered. He yanked my head back by my hair and caught me in a savage kiss as he found his release.

As I pulsed around his softening cock, I ached to know if we really were fated mates. To experience that indescribable certainty that Charline had spoken of with stars in her eyes. One thing was for certain, fated or not, I never wanted this to end. And if I had my way, it never would.

25

A Dangerous Ask

I COULD LIE NAKED in bed with Xander forever, but we still had a massacre to prevent and those plans weren't going to make themselves. We'd already wasted a whole night; we couldn't afford to waste the morning as well. Begrudgingly, I left the cocoon of warmth and braved the cool air.

"Ugh, why can't reality stand still?" Xander grumbled as he rolled over and tracked my movements.

I chuckled. "I was literally just thinking the same thing."

His gaze slid down my body and all it took was seeing the slight crease in his brow to know what he was looking at—the bruises his fingers had left on my hips. "I won't insult you by asking if you're okay. If I can trust you enough to take you home to meet my father, then I trust you enough to tell me if something is too much."

I swayed closer to him, loving the way his gaze turned hungry. "Good. And for the record, I feel amazing." I leaned down to steal a quick kiss, then danced out of reach before he could pull me back onto the bed. If he succeeded, we'd never make any progress and his pack was counting on us.

I wandered back toward the dresser and debated my next move. "Shower?" I asked over my shoulder.

There was a pause, then we both said, "Coffee."

"Plus, I think the shower would be more of a distraction than a benefit," I added with a smirk.

He slipped out of the sheets and stepped up behind me, wrapping his hands around my waist. "Have I told you how beautiful you are?" He mumbled as he nuzzled his face into the side of my neck.

"Xander," I chastised lightly as I felt his erection nudge my ass.

"Hmm?" He hummed, adding gentle kisses and nibbles.

My errant thought from the evening before returned with a vengeance. Except it wasn't errant at all, nor was it the first time it had crossed my mind. If I was being honest with myself, the idea had been low key percolating in my subconscious since I'd learned the truth about him.

"I have a weird question for you," I began tentatively.

He spun me around and planted a wet kiss on my cheek. "Anything." His sunny smile gave me the confidence to continue.

"What would you say if I asked you to bite-bite me?"

He stiffened, and I was pretty sure marble statues were softer. Even his warm brown eyes hardened into something closer to petrified wood. "Absolutely not." He dropped his hands from waist and turned away. "How could you even ask me that?"

"It was just a question," I replied defensively.

"No, it wasn't. I know you well enough by now to know that you don't deal in flighty hypotheticals. If you asked, it's because you were seriously thinking about it. Do you know what you're asking?"

Being defensive wouldn't help matters, and it wasn't like he was wrong. "Of course I know."

He snorted and turned away again, so I maneuvered to be in front of him, forcing him to see me.

"I know it's not a guarantee. It's possible I wouldn't turn."

"You're leaving out the part where it's incredibly painful and you. Could. Die." His glower and the shadow of hurt in his eyes made me doubt the desire more than any danger ever could.

"I could also be immune. You never know."

He scoffed. "Literally never heard of anyone being immune."

"Doesn't make it impossible," I countered. "Besides, you're forgetting the part where I could turn. It's not exactly like we have statistics we can reference for this. And if you say you do, I know you'll be lying. Way I see it, there's a fifty-fifty chance either way."

Disbelief exploded across his face. "And you call *those* good odds?"

"I mean, they're not the worst."

"Un-fucking believable. How long have you been thinking about this? No. Scratch that. I don't want to know. What I *do* want to know is why. Is it the enhanced abilities? Is it the ulti-mate fuck-you to your family? Come on, Diana, what's your logic for carelessly risking your life?" Coming from anyone else, I'd have called his concerns fair, but from him, they just felt cruel.

"So I could be with you," I said, softer than I'd intended.

The anger left his face to be replaced with his usual gentle-ness. "You don't need to be a werewolf for us to be together," he said just as softly.

"Don't I?" I wrapped my arms around myself, hating the surge of insecurity. He opened his mouth to give me an empty platitude, though I doubted he'd see it that way, so I rushed to speak ahead of him. "Your pack will never accept an alpha with a human partner."

He finally closed his mouth, his jaw clenching. I appreciated that he didn't try to refute it.

"I know it's dangerous. How could I not? Hell, I know most of the nuances and idiosyncrasies that come with the change as well. But I saw firsthand how your influence is suffering because of what's going on in Blackwell. My being human would all but kill whatever backing you have left."

His hands fisted by his sides, and a frustrated growl rolled out of him. "Who I'm with doesn't have any bearing on my ability to lead." He reached for his pants and tugged them on aggressively.

I mirrored him and pulled on a shirt. "Don't be naïve. Just because it shouldn't, doesn't mean it won't."

His low, agonized cry tore at my heart. "Then I'll make them get on board. It's a battle for the position. And when I win, they won't have a choice but to fall in line."

I walked closer until I was once again in his space and brushed my fingers through his hair. "No. That's not the kind of man you are, my love."

He wrapped his arms tightly around me, just shy of crushing, and dropped his head to my shoulder. "I won't let you take this risk for me. If it comes to it, I won't compete for the title."

"Don't you dare say that. You are a born leader. I've seen it in the way you care for the *weres* at the dorm and I have no doubt your pack will be all the better for having you in the position. Besides, no way you can let that asshole Victor undo all the progress your father has made as Alpha."

"Mangy jerk totally would," he grumbled against my neck.

"And my turning wouldn't just be for you." He raised his head to meet my gaze, his expression curious. "It'd be for me too. Not as an anything to my family. My choices are my own."

His eyebrows came together as he considered me. "What aren't you saying?"

My face heated, and I tried to look away, but he filled my vision. "I, uh, talked to Charline while we were at the House. So I have an inkling of what I'd be in for."

"Oh? Did she mention she almost died? And David too, thanks to the mate bond."

"She might have left that part out, but it does bring me to my other reason." I took a moment to build my courage to say what I wanted to next, stealing strength from Xander's warm touch as he rubbed my back. "Do you really believe we're mates?"

He took a breath large enough to expand his chest, causing it to press against me, then let it out. "Honestly? Yes. Selfishly, that's a big reason why I *don't* want to put you in that kind of danger. The uncertainty is too great. Not to mention there's also the horrific possibility that you *do* turn and go mad from it."

Well, that certainly wasn't an outcome I'd considered. Not that it changed anything. I still believed it was worth the risk. "She didn't mention that either. She did mention the bond and how beautiful it is. If we really are destined to be a mated pair, I don't want to experience that second hand. I want to feel the connection take root *with* you," I said earnestly.

His mouth opened and closed a few times until he finally said, "I don't really have an argument for that." Rather than embrace what felt like a small victory, I waited for the other shoe to drop. "Can we table this for a bit?" He immediately put a finger over my lips to stop me from replying. "Just until things settle down. I promise to think about it in the meantime."

"I suppose that's fair. It's a lot to consider, given everything else that's going on, and I promise to keep thinking about it as well. I won't make any rash decisions like going behind your back and getting Jennifer to do it," I conceded with a playful smirk.

"Are you *trying* to get me to kill my cousin?" he teased back before sealing his mouth over mine. His lips moved as if we had all the time in the world. I opened for him, loving the way his tongue leisurely stroked my increasingly sensitive lips before slipping past them. All too soon, the intimate glide stopped, and he pulled back. Right on cue, his stomach growled.

I laughed. "Right. Coffee, food, then plans."

"One more thing real quick," he said with a smirk I couldn't decipher.

I tipped his nose with mine, hoping that this one more thing was another kiss, or even better, mutual orgasms. "Hmm?"

"Doubling *way* back, did you say you love me?"

I lurched back to look at him, my face heating once again. "What?"

"You totally did!"

"I don't know what you're talking about," I sidestepped as I extricated myself from his embrace and attempted to escape into the living room.

"I mean not in so many words, but the sentiment was definitely there," he teased.

"Weren't we having breakfast? And I'm pretty sure Jennifer said something about wanting to be included in the planning. I should probably call her while the coffee is brewing." My destination was so close, I could practically smell the ground beans and frying bacon.

"Hey," Xander said, capturing my arm and guiding me back to him. "For the record, the feeling's mutual." He cradled my face with both hands and gave me possibly the sweetest kiss I'd ever had in my life.

"Yeah?"

"Oh yeah. I've been nose over tail in love with you for weeks, months even. Or was repeatedly showing up at your apartment posing as a dog, crashing your date, and taking you home to meet the family too subtle for you?" he added with another teasing grin.

I pushed against his chest. "You're the worst."

He shrugged. "Eh, I grow on you."

I returned his smile, feeling so light I could float away. "That you do." I closed my eyes and pressed our foreheads together, appreciating the soft intimacy of it. "Xander, there's a good chance I might be in love with you."

He kissed the tip of my nose and gave me a brilliant smile. "Does that mean I can have all the bacon?" He dashed for the door faster than I could grab him.

"It absolutely does not! That bacon is for sharing, you greedy werewolf!" I shouted as I scrambled to catch up before he could follow through with the threat.

26

MISSION RECKLESS

"I STILL DON'T UNDERSTAND why you think this is a good idea," Xander said for what was probably the fiftieth time over the last two days.

I glanced at Jennifer for support, but she just held up her hands in the universal leave me out of it gesture. Since I was clearly on my own in this, I turned back to Xander. "Because if there's a chance we can stop all of this before the eclipse, even if it's a small one, we should take it. He's already shot at me once."

Xander threw his hands up and resumed pacing the small living room of my apartment. "Yes, please, let's tempt fate again."

"It will be different this time," I insisted.

He halted his pacing to scowl at me. "How? So he can actually hit you this time? You said it yourself. Wolfsbane can be lethal to humans too in the right quantities and we don't know how much he's using. Even if it wasn't a fatal shot, it could still be lethal."

I sighed, exhausted with arguing in circles. If our conversation about our possible mating bond wasn't at the forefront of his mind, then I'd eat my bow. I got it, I really did. Over the last couple days, he'd explained that even without cementing the bond, losing me could still result in a slow, painful death by heartache for him. But what he refused to grasp was that this was *not* a reckless suicide mission.

I moved to intercept his pacing and took his hands. The mix of emotions in his deep brown eyes squeezed my heart. The last thing I wanted to do was hurt him, but I also couldn't stand idly by when there was a way to keep him and his whole pack out of danger.

"Please try to hear what I'm saying," I began, squeezing his hands. "I know that you're worried, but this is what I was trained to do. Things will be different this time because I know what I'm up against. I won't be going in blind."

"How do you know your uncle will even be out there?" Jennifer asked from the sidelines.

I glanced at her. "Because his mission this whole time has been to thin the herd. He isn't completely convinced that the eclipse *will* weaken you. On the off chance he's horribly mistaken, he'd rather face smaller odds. Trust me, he'll be there."

Xander's defeated sigh snatched my attention back to him. "There's nothing I can say to stop you from doing this, is there?" he asked.

"I promise I'll be careful. And if I'm being totally honest, I think he's more likely to capture me than to kill me. I'm still a Harker, after all."

The sudden sharpness in his eyes told me exactly how he felt about that. "At least let me go with you. We already know I'm immune."

I shook my head. "Resistance to the poison doesn't make you immune to a head shot. I won't put you in danger like that."

"Oh, but it's perfectly alright for *you* to be in that kind of danger," he countered, his voice rising.

"Uncle Nemo won't kill me." I scrubbed my face. I hated arguing with Xander. How did I explain to him more than I already had that I needed to do this? My family was the reason his friends and packmates were being haunted, had already been killed. If there was *any* possibility of mitigating further bloodshed, I had to try.

Jennifer's phone chirped, but Xander's angry gaze didn't shift away from me. "That's Sandy at the dorm. They're getting restless and wanting to know where you are." Xander probably had a hundred messages on his phone that said the same, but he'd silenced it hours ago.

"You should go," I said gently. "They need you. I'll be careful, I promise."

He squared his shoulders. "Fine. We've already established that you're going to do whatever you want." I opened my mouth to argue that it wasn't like that, but he held up a hand. "I want regular updates. And if as much as an hour goes between them, I'm coming for you myself."

Clearly, this was as close to a compromise as we were getting, so I nodded. He ran his hands through his thick hair and I struggled to make peace with the fact that we were parting on bad terms. Then he closed the distance between us, mashing his mouth down on mine. I melted against him, sinking into his natural heat, and kissed him back fiercely.

"I'm begging you, don't take any risks that aren't absolutely necessary. Yes, you're a trained hunter, but so is he. I love you, Diana, and I'm not ready to lose you."

I wrapped him in the tightest hug I could. "I love you too and I won't."

He stepped away and Jennifer took his place, wrapping me in a fierce hug that threatened to crack a rib. "We're just a call or text away. You're not alone."

My heart swelled. Even when I'd been training with my family, the expectation had always been that I would hunt on my own unless backup was absolutely needed. To have this kind of unwavering support would take some getting used to. I gave her a final squeeze, then broke the hug. "Be careful getting back to the dorm. Shoot me a text when you get there?" I said to Jennifer, but I was looking at Xander. He nodded, and I had to hope that was enough. We'd be okay. Once they'd gone, I went to my room to get changed.

I pulled my cowl up against the chill and wondered yet again if the ironic Red-Riding-Hood was a little too on the nose. Then again, it wasn't like I had another cloak I could have worn for this and the eye-catching color would actually help in my mission. I let out a breath that fogged in front of me and checked my bow again. The compound bow would have been my preferred choice with its more significant firepower, but I really did not want to know how sideways things could go if I got caught out here with the same kind of bow responsible for killing the others. So, recurve it was. At least this time the sun was still out and wasn't in any danger of setting while I was out here.

I took another bracing breath, shot off a text to Xander and Jennifer, and ventured deeper into the forest. The plan was to start where I'd been shot at before and work my way out in a spiral. It was a gamble, for sure, but it had the highest chance of triggering an encounter.

Two hours and several update-texts later, it was looking more and more like my genius plan was a bust. My stomach was growling, my arms were tired from walking at the ready, and even my well-worn boots were failing me if the ache in my feet was anything to go by. I swung the bow over me and massaged my biceps. Being so tense really wasn't conducive to accuracy, but I wasn't ready to throw in the towel yet. I'd give it another hour, then start working my way back to civilization and, more importantly, food.

My disappointment was starting to get the better of me when I stepped over a raised root. My foot came down on an icy patch and shot out from under me, sending me crashing down. At the same time, a thunk came overhead. I glanced up from my sprawled position to see an arrow embedded in the trunk precisely where my head would have been.

I scanned the surrounding woods as I scrambled to my feet. Another arrow passed inches from face. I recoiled so fast I nearly landed on my ass. Panic tangled with adrenaline as I darted behind a tree trunk. I chanced a glimpse and spotted a green-hooded figure way too close for comfort. What was worse, it wasn't my Uncle Nemo. Whoever they were, they were too short.

I spun back around, swinging my bow free, and plastered my back to the tree. *Fuck. Fuck. Fuck.* So much for reassuring Xander that my uncle wouldn't kill me. Not only was it *not* my uncle, they clearly had no qualms about eliminating me permanently. I strained to hear any signs of movement—leaves shifting, a twig snapping, something—but it was damn near impossible to hear anything over how loud my heart was beating. One thing was for certain: this little mission was over.

Finally, I heard the scuff of a shoe on bark. Without hesitation, I nocked an arrow and set it loose in that direction, then sprinted for all I was worth. I didn't bother trying to mask my run. They already knew I was out here. Instead, I ran in a haphazard zigzag pattern, letting the terrain dictate my turns, and taking care to dodge behind trunks whenever possible. The faint whistle of a loosed arrow tickled my awareness. I veered to my right just as it thwacked into a tree so hard it was still vibrating. I fought the irrational urge to glance behind me to see where they were. The fact that I'd been able to hear the arrow in time meant they were much closer than I'd anticipated and turning around would only slow me down.

I surged forward, slipping on leaves wet with melting ice, and endeavored to put more distance between us. I spotted an aged oak and nearly sighed with relief at the familiar tree. Ironic that I'd ended up here again, given the circumstances. Unfortunately, going up wasn't an option this time. Instead, I darted behind the large trunk and stole a few precious moments to lose my identifiable cloak. Rather than leave it in a heap on the ground, I hooked the hood on a knot high enough to be convincing from a distance.

Assured that it would stay and looked at least moderately body-like, I took off once again. While it was tempting to set up an ambush, I didn't know how much ground I'd lost, and it was more important to get out of here in one piece. This time, I didn't sacrifice stealth for speed. Setting up the decoy wouldn't do me any good if I was making enough noise to alert anything within a half mile.

The eerie quiet grated on my nerves. Every step was made with caution and purpose. Whenever I could, I raced along exposed roots to gain more distance before venturing back onto the more treacherous terrain of fallen leaves and traitorous twigs. A distant thump made me freeze for a solid second. The other hunter had most likely found my cloak. That bode well. They'd likely think they'd hit me and wouldn't be in as much of a hurry to retrieve the arrow. It also meant that I had more of a head start.

I continued to cautiously make my way through the forest until I was fairly certain there was enough ground between us that it didn't matter how much noise I made. Then I swung my bow across me and ran with everything I had left. Mercifully, the sun was only just starting its decline and my footing wasn't guesswork.

A familiar line of trees came into view, but I didn't dare slow down or breathe a sigh of relief. I pushed harder, determined to make it onto open ground before they could realize they'd been duped. I hopped over a fallen log and landed in a crouch on the ground lower than I'd expected. An arrow slammed into a tree ahead of me. I swerved, the shot of adrenaline renewing my flagging energy. Just a few more yards.

Another arrow. This time so close, I felt the fletching graze my cheek.

Ten more feet.

Dirt sprayed as an arrow punctured the ground where I was about to step.

Five feet.

It was probably my panic-fueled imagination, but I swear I could hear their ragged breath as they closed in.

Inches. I burst through the treeline at full speed, a stitch in my side threatening to slow me down, and nearly collided with Xander.

"Diana?"

"Run!" I shouted, grabbing his arm and pulling him after me. He stumbled a few steps, then we were both racing toward my apartment. Neither of us slowed until we were inside and the door was firmly closed and locked.

"What the hell is going on?" he asked while I peered through the blinds to see if my attacker was brave enough to come into the open.

"What are you doing here?" I asked in turn.

"You missed your last check in. I told you what would happen," he growled ominously.

I stepped away from the window, mostly confident that the hunter wouldn't sacrifice their cover to continue after me. More than anything, I wanted to drink a gallon of water and catch my breath, but there was no time. I turned to Xander.

"We have a problem," we both said at the same time.

27

THEN THERE WERE TWO

XANDER AND I STARED at each other. The fact that we both had a problem did not bode well and I seriously doubted it was the same problem. It also didn't help that I was still trying to catch my breath after my brush with death.

"You go first," he said, walking to the kitchen and grabbing me a glass of water, which I chugged.

I took a few moments to regulate my breathing while I debated how to start. In the end, I settled for the direct approach. "There's more than one killer."

"We know that. Your family is going to be here for the eclipse." He crossed his arms, frowning. We'd barely touched on the topic of what *I* would do when it came to stopping my family, but it wasn't like I could get them to see reason.

I shook my head. "No. There's *always* been two killers."

"What do you mean? Who else could it be besides your uncle? I thought you said none of the other hunting families were willing to work with him."

I set the empty glass down. "And they won't. He's too unpredictable, too zealous even for them. But he's got someone working for him. Short, slender. It was hard to get a good judge

275

because I was running. Maybe he enlisted my second-cousin George. Or it's possible it's my aunt, but I can't see her leaving her seven year old with someone so she could follow her husband's latest scheme."

"Sounds like there's no love lost there."

"You don't know the half of it. Shame the Harkers don't believe in divorce. They should have split years ago. And they're not the only ones," I grumbled under my breath. Judging by the sympathetic expression on Xander's face, he'd still heard. I straightened and went to refill the glass. "The long and short of it is, this throws all of our plans out the window. I know my family, how they think, how they hunt. This extra hunter is an unknown variable. What's worse? He's a damn good shot."

"Diana..." Xander's warning tone rumbled from deep in his chest. Was kind of a shame he was mad, because it was sexy as hell.

"I wasn't reckless. So you can drop the tone. The second I realized it wasn't my uncle, I devoted all my energy to getting out of there." I neglected to mention that revelation had come *after* the attempted head shot. Xander was on edge enough. He didn't need to know how close I'd come to dying or how many times.

"Full moon at midnight," he cursed, running his hands through his hair and causing the dark, silky waves to stand up in odd directions. "This is bad."

"Understatement of the century." I drained a third glass and set it down on the counter.

He gave me a miserable look as I walked around the peninsula. "It gets worse." He glanced around until he spotted the dining table and walked over. "Mind if I use this?" he asked, gesturing at the laptop charging.

"Go for it." He opened it and I leaned over to key in the password. "It's all yours. What do you need it for?"

He slid down the bench and patted the vacant seat beside him. "Jenny forwarded this to me. Someone at the House sent it to her."

I schooled my features and braced myself for whatever "it" could be while he signed into his email and queued up a video. The quality wasn't great and he had to turn the volume all the way up, but finally I realized what we were watching. Or more specifically, who.

The image jumped as the recorder moved to a better position, revealing a fuzzy Victor standing in the middle of a small crowd. Unfortunately, whoever was taking the video had missed the first part and we were coming into the middle.

"--the audacity to bring someone like that *here*, to our home, our refuge. We can't trust someone who would do that. Xander put all of our lives in danger by bringing not just a human, but a known hunter to our door."

Oh, fuck. He was talking about me. I glanced at Xander who looked like he was going to be sick.

"It gets worse," he said in a whisper.

I returned my focus to the screen.

"And let's not pretend like we think this behavior will change. We all know that he intends to continue Alexander's work." Xander's sudden growl almost made me miss what Victor said next. "What have the exchange program, enrollment at the university, and mingling with the town gotten us? Nothing. No, not nothing, worse than nothing. They've cost people their lives. Valuable members of our community, gone forever.

For too long the focus has been on expansion and integration. Why? When will the pack come first? Now is the time to regroup, not double down on something that's clearly not working. If nothing else, think about the children that have already lost their lives. Kids who will never see the moon again, never hold their loved ones, never grow up. If you still think Xander should be running this pack, then I challenge you to consider this. If he was so well equipped to lead, why did any of them have to die?"

I reached out and slammed the laptop down.

"There's more," Xander said miserably. Defeat blanketed him like a funeral pall.

"I don't need to hear it and neither do you." I lurched out of my seat. "Does that asshole really believe *he* could have saved any of them? I doubt he even knows their fucking names!"

Xander sighed and dropped his head into his hands. "He knows their names," he mumbled.

"Okay, fine, so he knows their names." I squatted beside Xander so I could see his face. "But he doesn't know what you've gone through here, doesn't know everything you've done to keep them safe. You're one man—*were*. It can't be helped if people didn't do as they were told. You've done everything you could."

Anger flashed in his eyes. "And it still wasn't enough. As it is, I can't even get the remaining people at the dorm to return to the House for the eclipse. They're insisting on staying and fighting."

I placed a hand on his forearm. "Because they believe in you. We'll protect them, Xander. Together." I drew circles on his arm with my index finger, hoping to relax him a little more, because he was totally going to blow his top at what I said next. "Which brings me to my next point."

His eyes narrowed to slits. "Don't you dare say it."

"Come on, Xander. How can you still say it's not worth the risk after that bullshit?" I gestured at the laptop.

He stood, meeting me glare for glare. "We said we would table this until after."

"Well, I'm untabling it. If you're going to have even the smallest chance to succeed your father we either can't be together or I can't be human. So which will it be?" I softened my tone and reached for him. "You've explained the risks and I probably understand the process a lot better than most people who end up becoming werewolves. I'm strong. I'm healthy. My odds of surviving the change are pretty high."

He looked at me disbelievingly, shaking his head. "Odds? There are no odds for this. For moon's sake, there are barely even records. Just because two people recently survived the change doesn't make it a precedent."

"I think we have different definitions of precedent."

"Just because you're young and healthy doesn't ensure any-thing. So were they. Sara ended up going feral and she almost didn't come back from it. That's one of the worst things that can happen to a werewolf. She lost all sense of self. As for Charline." He stopped and pain flickered across his face. "She was on the brink of death. By all rights, she shouldn't have turned at all. It was a damn miracle she survived her first change."

"But that won't happen to me," I argued.

"You don't know that!"

"Yes, I do. Their changes were dictated by trauma. Mine won't be. I'm going into it with eyes wide open. With someone I trust. Someone I love." I wrapped him in my arms and held him until I could feel the tension starting to leave him.

"But what if you don't turn? What if..."

"We could 'what if' until the eclipse, but in the end it doesn't matter."

He pulled back enough to look at me. "What makes you say that?"

"Because whether I turn or not, if things go sideways during the eclipse, we're all dead anyway."

He kissed my cheek and held me close. "I hate that you're right. I hate even more that it's about something so nihilistic."

Excitement surged through me. "Does that mean you'll do it?"

He sighed heavily, before stepping all the way back and letting my arms fall away. "Yes, but only after you answer me one more thing."

I took a deep breath and worked to school my face. "Okay."

"Are you really sure you want this?"

I laughed. It probably wasn't the most appropriate response, but it couldn't be helped. "Xander, we've been over this ad nauseum–"

"We've covered a lot, yes," he cut me off. "But have you really considered the ramifications if we go forward with this? And I'm not just talking about being stuck with me. You'll be giving up your life, everything you've worked for, trading it in for a new one. I get that you don't agree with what your family does, but you can't tell me that translates to you hating them."

"I don't hate them," I admitted quietly.

"It's one thing not to want to follow their path for you, but if you do this, whether you turn or not, there's no going back. You'll be cutting ties with them. Permanently."

I swallowed hard. I'd had similar thoughts about keeping Hyacinth at a distance to protect Xander and the others. Why hadn't it occurred to me in more depth that a more extreme version would apply to my own family. He was right, even if I didn't turn, this was a betrayal they'd never forgive. Though that was assuming we'd live long enough for me to regret the decision.

Xander cupped my face and I blinked free a sudden tear. "I'm not saying these things to upset you. And I won't pretend that the thought of you not coming out of this doesn't scare the fur off me. I just want to make sure you really know what you'll be giving up. Once we do this, any chance you have at a normal life will be gone."

"You're right, and maybe I didn't consider the *full* ramifications. But I've never had a normal life. And if I'm being honest, I don't think I want one. I've spent the last four years trying desperately to carve one out, to force myself to assimilate. Then you came into my life and..." I shrugged and gave him a shaky smile. "I'm more myself than I've ever been. You give me that. I don't have to be ashamed of my past or downplay the things I know and can do. With you, I just get to be me. Life is full of sacrifices. Giving up my family will be hard, but not hard enough to risk losing you."

He leaned in and pressed our lips together in a kiss. Not one of fiery passionate ones that made my heart pound and my toes curl. One of the sweet intimate ones so full of connection that I'd be willing to sell my soul if it meant it never had to end.

"Okay," he whispered, his breath ghosting across my face. "That's what I needed to know."

I wrapped my arms around his neck and hugged him tight. "Thank you for trusting in us. I'll get what's left of the first aid kit and wait for you in the bedroom."

"I'll be a few minutes. The change isn't exactly a fast process."

"I know. I'll give you your space and privacy." With one final kiss, I left him to it.

I made sure not to completely shut the door so he could nose his way in when he was ready. In the meantime, our conversation played over and over again in my head. It didn't change my decision, but it did force me to consider how to go about severing ties with my family and any other people that could pose a threat to the pack. Human, non-hunter friends were probably safe enough to keep. People like Kora,

Milliscent, and any number of the other friends I'd made since coming to Blackwell. It wouldn't be easy, but it'd be worth it.

The door swung open, startling me. I got my errant nerves under control and stood to greet my furry companion. A smile tugged on my lips as he padded inside and he tilted his head, conveying his curiosity.

"Sorry, I kind of miss hanging out with you like this. It's also a nice change that you're not covered in mud or dripping blood from a mortal wound."

He huffed, closed the distance separating us, and sat.

I couldn't help but admire his luxuriously dark fur and wonder what mine would look like. Nearest guess was that it echoed natural hair color, so my coat would likely be dark as well, though it wouldn't have that raven wing sheen. Looking at him now and knowing everything I did, it was mind boggling that I hadn't put the pieces together sooner.

He let out a low whine and nosed my hand, alerting me to the fact that I'd just been standing there staring.

I took a deep breath. "I haven't changed my mind."

He opened his jaws and I had a small moment of panic at seeing how sharp his teeth were. No amount of bracing myself would eliminate how much those sinking into my flesh was gonna hurt. He angled his head forward and I moved my hand out of reach.

"Not there. I want to make sure I don't lose any mobility or range of motion in case I have to use my bow before the eclipse." It went unsaid that I might have to use it during as well. "I've thought about it and I think either the side or back of my thigh stands to cause the least amount of issues, though the bite will still need to be shallow to avoid hitting an artery."

He nodded and stepped back to give me room to remove my pants, leaving me in my black boyshorts. Once again he closed the distance and I turned around to lean on the bed. He licked the back of my thigh and I had to stifle a giggle, because it tickled.

"There's good," I said over my shoulder, then the giggle I'd tried to suppress escaped. "I suppose it's too soon to make a joke about this decision biting me in the ass."

He violently blew air out of his nose, causing the sensitive skin on the back of my leg to pebble.

"Yeah. Too soon. I mean, you have to admit, it is pretty funny. Talk about an origin story. Not that I'm thinking about origin stories, or heroes, or villains. Not that you're not a– Ow!" I yelped as his teeth sank into the meaty part of my leg which turned out to be *way more* sensitive than I would have expected.

I'd have given anything for the tears not to pool in my eyes, but there was no stopping them and they fell freely to dot the duvet with dark smudges. I sniffled then immediately set to cleaning and bandaging the wound. It wasn't until I was nearly finished that I realized Xander had left.

Panic eclipsed any lingering pain as I stumbled out of the room, favoring my right leg. When I spotted him still on all fours and covered with sweat, I let out a relieved breath. "Thank the gods, I was worried you'd gone."

He stood on legs that were honestly as shaky as mine and walked over. "I would never." He brushed the hair away from my face and gazed intently at me. "How do you feel?"

"A little butt-hurt," I teased to which he scowled. "I'm fine. You did a great job making the bite shallow. Though I suspect it'll be at least a few days before we know if it's taken hold."

"Probably. Just in case, I'm staying here tonight." He kissed my forehead and I couldn't think of a time I'd ever felt so cared for and cherished.

"I wouldn't have it any other way. Why don't you find us something to watch and I'll heat up some leftovers? Then we can curl up on the couch."

He smiled for the first time in what felt like hours. "That sounds perfect." And for at least a little while, it would be.

28

FAMILY DRAMA

IT HAD BEEN FIVE days since Xander had bitten me. So far, there'd been no sign of infection and my quad had stopped smarting every time I sat down two days ago. What really sucked was that Xander hadn't been here for any of those days. He'd been at the dorm doing his level best to prepare everyone who insisted on staying for what was to come. While I understood that adding me to the mix right now wasn't the smartest thing with Victor's smear campaign in full swing, it didn't mean I was happy about it. On the upside, I would see him later today, assuming he could get away.

I stood in the living room of my apartment and looked around for something to do. I'd already oiled my bow, done the dishes, tried yet again to get the bloodstains out of the carpet, and folded all my laundry. Hell, I'd even dusted, and I *hated* dusting. Finally, my gaze landed on my laptop and I wracked my brain to see if there were any class assignments I hadn't finished or turned in. I was on the verge of signing into my student portal to triple check when my phone rang.

I launched across the sofa to snag it off the end table and answered without checking the caller ID. "Hey," I said, only a little out of breath.

"Don't 'hey' me, young lady."

All my excitement that Xander was calling to say he'd be coming over early withered at my mother's crisp tone. "Mom, hi. Uh, what prompted this?" Part of me hoped she was calling to say they'd decided not to support my uncle and wouldn't be joining him on the hunt after all.

"Don't play coy with me. How could you not tell me you were a suspect in a murder investigation!"

Oh, fuck. "It's not–"

"I understand wanting to be independent, but this is not something you should have to face on your own. This is what family is for. Do you really hate us that much?"

"No, of course not," I interjected before she could keep talking over me.

"It certainly doesn't look that way from where I'm sitting. I've just gotten off the phone with Alvarez and he's filled me in on everything so far. Honestly, I don't know what's worse, the attitude of that incompetent detective or the fact that you actually sat down and spoke with him without a lawyer present. More than once! We raised you to be smarter than that. *I* raised you to be smarter than that."

"I'm not an idiot, Mother. Cooperating seemed like the best course of action, especially since I had *nothing* to do with the murders. Things escalated when more kids turned up dead."

She made an undignified sound. "Be that as it may, you still should have contacted us the second it went from giving a general statement to a more thorough inquiry."

"Yeah, well, things got a lot more complicated when it turned out the murdered kids weren't human. Which made a lot more since once I found out Uncle Nemo was involved."

"Do not get me started on your uncle. Literally, the only halfway commendable thing he's done is keep the news out of the papers. What kind of moron leaves bodies lying around in the open like that? No wonder the rest of the hunting community wants nothing to do with him."

That was my opening. "Mom, are you sure no one outside the family is working with Uncle Nemo?"

"Of course not, darling." Exasperation filled her voice.

"Well, it might not be someone from one of the other families, but *someone* is working with him."

"Of all the asinine... Your uncle should be committed for the stunts he's pulled recently. Honestly, I'm liable to kill him myself when we arrive in a few days on principle for allowing you to be framed for his tactless hunts."

I nearly fell off the couch as I straightened. "A few days?"

"Naturally. Your uncle finally came clean about where this hunt is supposed to occur and the Eclipse is practically around the corner." She paused, then said evenly, "I suppose it's too much to hope that you've changed your mind and have decided to participate."

Oh, I'd be participating alright. Just not on the same side as my mother. The air left my lungs in a whoosh as that revelation truly sank in. I wasn't just forsaking my family, my legacy, I would be actively opposed to them. They'd get hurt, possibly die, and I could be the one responsible.

"Diana, are you still there?"

"Yeah, mom," I croaked, my throat unexpectedly tight. "And I haven't changed my mind. But..."

"Yes?"

"Are you sure you need to come? I get talking Dad out of it might be impossible since Nemo is his brother, but do *you* really need to be here for the hunt? We both know it's probably all going to go sideways. There's no reason you should have to pay for Uncle Nemo's sins." It was a long shot, but I'd hate myself forever if I didn't at least try.

"Diana, darling, what's really going on? You've already shown more interest in this hunt than you have in any of the others over the last five years. I recognize it's in your backyard and you're far closer to it than I would like, but you've never had an issue with whether or not I've joined a hunt."

"I... I can't explain it." I clutched the phone tighter and scrambled to come up with something, *anything,* that might convince her. "You're the one who always taught me to follow my instincts, and I don't have a good feeling about this."

She sighed, and I knew my desperate plea hadn't worked. "We can talk about this more when I get there. Your father and I will arrive late Thursday and will be staying at a cabin about twenty minutes outside of Blackwell. It would be nice to have dinner together before we leave again on Sunday. As a family."

"Yeah, mom. I'll see what I can do."

"I love you, Di."

"Love you too, Mom." Defeat weighed heavy on my heart as I hung up and tossed the phone back onto the end table. Why hadn't I considered that she'd be in the middle of everything? That my dad would? That in order to save Xander and his pack–and possibly me–they'd have to be stopped?

The phone beeped, but I couldn't bring myself to check it. I was too lost in my whirling thoughts. It wasn't until there was a knock on the door that I realized I'd been staring at the wall for over an hour. I stood and walked over to unlock it.

"Coming," I called. When I opened the door to find Xander on the other side, an errant sob escaped.

"Hey, baby, what's wrong?" he asked, reaching for me and kicking the door shut behind him. His thumbs brushed along my cheeks, making me realize I'd started crying.

"I talked to my mom. They're still coming. Xander, I don't want anyone in the pack to die, but I don't want them to either."

He pulled me into an embrace, and I rested my head on his shoulder while he softly stroked my hair. "You knew they were coming, that they'd be part of the hunt."

I sniffed. "Yeah, but I guess part of me believed that they'd leave Uncle Nemo to fail on his own. But they're still coming." I sobbed heavily and buried my face against his neck as emotion washed over me. Through it all, Xander remained steady, letting me get it out and offering soothing sounds while he rubbed my back.

Finally, I pulled away and wiped my face. "Sorry about that."

"You have absolutely nothing to be sorry for. None of us could have foreseen things happening like this." He rubbed his thumb along my trembling lips, then dusted them with a chaste kiss. I appreciated he had the decency not to say "I told you so." Not that my family coming changed things. I'd still fight for the werewolves and I still would have asked him to bite me. It just made it so much harder.

"We should probably change the bandage," I said with another sniffle.

"Okay, we can do that." He took my hand and led me to the vanity area where I had the first aid supplies out. "When's the last time you changed it?"

"Two days ago. It looked good. No discoloration or abnormal swelling. Actually, it hasn't bothered me at all today."

He glanced at me in the mirror and I latched onto the hope in his eyes with everything I had. "Come here," he whispered. I gave him a funny look at the unexpected request and stepped back into his waiting arms. I don't know what I was expecting, but it wasn't for him to bury his nose in the crook of my neck and inhale deeply. When I glimpsed his eyes in his reflection, they were wholly wolf.

My breath caught, and I whispered, "What is it?"

He tilted his head up so I could see his smile, which did all kinds of funny things to my heart. "Your scent is changing. It was hard to tell with it basically being everywhere in your apartment, but it's definitely different."

"Yeah?" Hope I scarcely dared to entertain swelled in my chest.

"Yep," he replied, his smile growing. "What do you say we take a look at that bite?"

"Yes. Oh my gods, yes," I said emphatically, all but pushing him away as I twisted to grab the bandage secured with medical tape.

He chuckled. "Easy. Let me." He squatted down and looked up at me with a smile glimmering in his perfectly brown eyes. His warm hand coasted up the inside of my thigh, teasing the edge of my pajama shorts. The moment was simultaneously one of the sexiest I'd ever had the pleasure to experience, and the most intimate. He placed a kiss just above the bandage, lingering so that his breath made the skin prickle with anticipation. "Whatever happens, Diana, know that I love you with all that I am."

"I love you too, Xander," I whispered. We continued to stare into each other until my impatience got the better of me. "You going to rip that bandage off, or are you waiting for a written invitation?"

He ducked his head and chuckled. Then he slipped a nail beneath the edge of the tape and pulled in one quick motion.

"Ow!" I yelped. When he didn't respond, I searched out his face. To my horror, his eyes were wide and his mouth was hanging open like he couldn't believe what he was seeing. "What? What is it? Is it bad? Did it get worse?"

He shook his head, still slack jawed. "No, nothing like that."

"Then what?" I asked irritably.

He glanced up at me, his earlier grin teasing the corners of his mouth. "It's gone."

"What do you mean 'it's gone'? That's impossible. Even a bite that small would take at least two weeks to heal."

"I'm telling you, it's not there. There's barely even a scar."

"You're lying." He gave me a sour look as I twisted to examine the back of my leg. I could clearly see the outline of the medical tape where it'd puckered the skin beneath, as well as how pale the covered area was. What I didn't see was any sign of the bite. I squinted and could just barely make out the silvery outline of teeth. "Holy fuck, it's gone!"

"Told you."

I spun back around to give him a piece of my mind concerning his flippant attitude to find him smirking. "Xander, it's completely healed. What does that mean?" Hope and excitement spluttered in my chest like a flame determined to burn despite the wind.

"I think it means the *were*-virus has taken hold. You're one of us now."

29

Ties That Bind

WE GAVE IT ANOTHER couple of days, but there was no denying that the wound was entirely healed and my senses were heightening. Already my sense of smell was picking up nuances I'd never noticed. My strength hadn't increased much, but it was only a matter of time. Even my eyes were more sensitive to bright lights. Now it was a waiting game to see how I handled the change on the full moon.

Xander had spent the last hour or so walking me through what to expect and I had to admit that even with everything I knew, it paled in comparison to reality. No wonder people who hadn't grown up with other werewolves went mad or broke with reality. The experience was too new. Too different. Too traumatic. And that was my life now.

I forcefully dragged my thoughts out of their spiral. Worrying about how I would handle the change would only increase the likelihood that something would go wrong. "Honey?" I asked over my shoulder as I poured the steaming water into the cup.

"That'd be great, thanks," Xander said.

I placed the tea bags in the cups and brought them over to where he was already settled on the couch. His grateful smile filled me with a warmth that defied the chill outside. Though oddly, it hadn't been bothering me as much as it usually did.

He hummed in contentment as he sipped the scalding liquid. "And you said you're meeting with your family tomorrow for dinner?"

"Yeah. There's a restaurant on the edge of town my mom found that is apparently up to her standards."

"Are you sure that's wise? I'm not saying that you shouldn't, but the timing could be better. The eclipse is the following day." His concern was touching, but ill-placed.

I set my cup aside to let it cool some more. "You have to understand, it will be more suspicious if I don't go or try to cancel at the last minute. At least if I'm meeting them in a public place, there's less chance of them discovering something they shouldn't or attempting to sway me to join them for the hunt."

"I wish I could be there for you."

I cupped his downcast face. "You're sweet to say so and I love you for it, but the others need you more. Are you sure you or Jennifer can't convince more of them to leave town?"

He shook his head, drained his cup, and set it aside. "They won't go, though I was referring more to the opportunity to meet your parents."

I sat back and stared at him in surprise. "What? Why would you want to do that?"

"Oh, I don't know.." He tugged me closer until I was straddling his lap. "Maybe because I'm in love with their daughter and it might be nice to meet two of the people who helped make her who she is."

I snorted. "The bad parts, maybe."

"You don't have any bad parts," he replied with a smirk, followed by a kiss.

"I most definitely do," I argued back, wrapping my arms around his neck and bringing him in for another kiss.

"Subjective," he mumbled, then deepened the kiss, his hands digging into my sides and grinding me against him. We continued to make out like a pair of horny teenagers, our hands dipping beneath hems without removing any clothing. He nipped at my lip and looked at me with lust-hooded eyes. "You forgot about your tea."

I pressed into him, loving how his body reacted. "I can think of better ways to relax." The light caught his eyes, making their amber depths burn. I slid off of him and dashed for the bedroom. He was right behind me, catching me inches from the bed. I squealed in delight, then spun around in his hold to claim his mouth.

Our lips came together in a needy rush that set my skin on fire, then gradually simmered down into long indulgent kisses that in no way diminished how much I wanted this man. He trailed his thumb over my bottom lip and I slowly opened my eyes. Our gazes met, then in a silent understanding we removed first my shirt, then his. I ran my hands up his chest, luxuriating in the warm strength that had always emanated off of him. Not just physically, but strength of character. Werewolf or not, Xander was a *good* man.

He kissed along my neck and shoulder while I continued to explore his torso, then his defined shoulders and sculpted back. His fingers trailed lightly up my back, leaving a wake of goosebumps. He deftly undid my bra clasp, and I shrugged out of the insubstantial garment, eager for the skin to skin contact I craved. His hum was more of a low growl as I pressed my breasts against his chest.

He guided me backward onto the bed, his intense warmth blanketing me from head to toe. Then, with exaggerated slowness, he removed my leggings, tugging one leg free at a time. His hungry gaze sparked a flush of heat everywhere it landed, causing my breath to catch. Unable to restrain myself, I sat up to reclaim his luscious mouth. He indulged me in a tantalizing kiss before gently pushing me back onto the mattress and hooking his fingers in the band of my panties.

I angled my hips up to help and reveled in his appreciative gaze. He coasted his hands up my bare legs, leaving a trail of featherlight kisses up onto my quivering abdomen, then he stepped back. I propped up on my elbows and watched him just as hungrily unzip his pants and work them down his defined legs. When he pulled down his briefs and his beautiful cock popped free, I sucked in a breath, my nostrils flaring as if I could soak him up from here.

He stepped closer to the bed, but before he could do more, I swiveled around so I was facing him and swallowed his swollen head. His moan was all the encouragement I needed to take him deeper. I stopped just shy of my gag reflex and pulled back to swirl my tongue around the mushroom cap then along the thick vein on the underside of his shaft. Xander threaded his fingers through my hair and thrust shallowly into my mouth. I hummed my approval, then hollowed my cheeks, prompting a deeper groan out of him.

I continued to lazily lick and suck until a slight tug on my hair had me pull off. When I looked up at him through wet lashes his face was such a mixture of unbridled lust and adoration that it nearly undid me. I wiped my mouth and his heated gaze flicked to my undoubtedly puffy lips.

"You're so incredibly beautiful," he whispered with so much awe, it felt like I was actually glowing.

I scooted farther onto the bed to give him room. "Come here," I beckoned him, though he was already crawling across to meet me. Once again our tongues tangled together and I got lost in the sensations of just being near him. He held me close, his arms wrapping as firmly around me as mine did him. I knew in my soul that we'd never let go if we could help it. He was my person and I was his.

He shifted against me causing his erection to tease along the seam of my lower lips. I reflexively angled my hips to take him in. He broke our kiss and looked down at me. "Shouldn't we..." His glanced toward the nightstand and the condoms within.

"Not tonight," I whispered just as softly. We looked into each for a moment, another silent understanding passing between us. If things went sideways during the eclipse, this might be our only chance to know if the bond would really take hold.

He gave an almost imperceptible nod, then recaptured my mouth in an unhurried kiss that spoke volumes about how much time we wished we had. While he delved into my mouth and sucked on my lips, his hands caressed my sides, eventually encouraging me to wrap my legs around. I hooked my ankles over his back, aching to be as close as physically possible.

My eyes threatened to flutter shut as he rubbed his length along my aching folds and teasing my clit with just enough pressure to make me writhe. "Xander..." I half gasped-half begged.

"I love you," he said as he looked at me with those gorgeous brown eyes and slid home where he belonged.

I fought to keep my eyes open, not wanting to miss a second of the intense pleasure dancing across his features. I adjusted my legs and lifted my hips to meet his slow thrusts as we settled into a rhythm without urgency. This moment was infinite, completely outside of time. There was only us, our breaths mingling and our bodies moving as one.

The intensity increased until I was clinging to him like he was the only thing keeping me together. He corkscrewed his hips and I gasped as my orgasm came out of nowhere, crashing over me in wave after wave. Xander kept moving, holding me tighter, as he simultaneously sought his release and kept me flying. His pace faltered, then with a final deep thrust, burying his entire length, he came so hard that I climaxed again.

He rested his forehead against my sweat slick shoulder. Once he regained his breath, he peppered kisses on my fevered skin. I traced the contours of his back while I placed my own kisses on any part of him I could reach. When he finally pulled out, the absence about undid me.

He must have seen the disappointment on my face, because he leaned down to give me a gentle kiss. "Don't worry, I'll be right back." He helped me lower my legs, which were more jelly than useful at this point. As promised, he was only gone for a moment before he was curling up with me under the covers.

I traced his stubbled jaw with my index finger, my heart equal parts heavy and lighter than it had ever been. We continued to stare at each other, neither of us willing to break the silence. There was no telling how much time had passed when surprise flashed across his face. I was about to ask when a strange warmth pulsed in my chest. It wasn't so unlike how I usually felt when I was with Xander, but it was also so much... *more*.

I gasped and covered my mouth at the same time as he chuckled. "It's... beautiful," I whispered, for fear it'd shatter it. How could something feel so delicate and yet so strong?

"Words really don't do it justice," he said with just as much awe.

"So, it's true. We really are mates."

He tucked a rogue hair behind my ear and smiled softly. "It would seem so. And the bond will only get stronger once you've had your first change." A hint of sadness swirled in his eyes and I snuggled closer.

It had worked. I was officially a werewolf, and we were bonded. And in thirty-six hours, none of it might matter. We held each other tightly for the rest of the night, though I don't think either of us slept.

Anxiety plagued my steps as I exited the transit and made my way to the restaurant. Thankfully, the semester was officially over and many of the students had left for Winter Break, making the college town feel borderline desolate. Part of me was relieved that so many people had left to celebrate the holidays at home, because it meant fewer possible witnesses or casualties during the eclipse tomorrow. The other part was dismayed for almost exactly the same reasons. Fewer witnesses meant a greater likelihood that tomorrow would turn into a gruesome bloodbath.

I rounded the corner onto the street that would take me to the place my mother had picked out and wished yet again that I could have convinced her to meet earlier. Being out so close to dark made me nervous. Xander had assured me that my feelings were more than likely the anticipation of turning. He'd also emphasized that it was fairly normal and nothing unusual to be concerned about. However, that was small comfort considering I was meeting with my family.

A short distance away, I caught sight of my mother standing in front of what had to be the poshest restaurant in all of Blackwell. She wore dark crimson, flowy pants that gave the illusion of a floor-length skirt when she stood still and a fitted cream cashmere sweater with pearl accents, layered with a stunning long wool coat. I couldn't help but smile. While I'd never been one for fancy clothes that were more expensive than practical, I'd always admired my mother's impeccable sense of fashion.

"Hey, Mom," I said once I was close enough that I didn't have to shout.

She spun around from her perusal of a building across the street. "Diana, darling. There you are." She wrapped me in a hug that I returned fiercely, but cautiously. While I hadn't really experienced any increased werewolf strength yet, now was not the time to chance it. "You're late," she whispered in my ear before pushing me back to arm's length. "And where is your coat? Aren't you freezing?"

"Pft, I've been here long enough to acclimate," I replied flippantly, while mentally kicking myself. Why *hadn't* I put on a coat?

She eyed me dubiously. "I suppose. At least you look decent and that sweater appears cozy enough." I released a silent sigh of relief that she wasn't going to dig further into my inadequate attire.

"Where's Dad?" I glanced around, but didn't see anyone even resembling him. "Is he inside already?"

Irritation flared in my mother's eyes and pursed her lips. "Your *father* would not be persuaded to join us for dinner."

"Couldn't tear him away from scheming with Uncle Nemo, huh?" I chuckled and she made an indignant sound.

"We should get our table before someone else claims it," she said imperiously.

I stifled the urge to chuckle again and to inform her that I seriously doubted there was any danger of that given Blackwell's current ghost town status. She led the way inside and I was right behind her when a flash of sunlight pierced past a retracted awning to blind me. My pupils dilated so fast, I lost my bearings and my sight.

"Gah!" I shouted, throwing my hands up. Distantly, I could hear my mother's concerned voice.

"Diana. What happened?" she asked, worry evident in her voice.

I tried to blink away the spots in my vision, but the tears welling in my eyes made it difficult. "Just momentarily blinded." I waved absently at the offending shop. I didn't have to see my mother's face to know she was now scowling at them, a fate I didn't wish on anyone.

"Come with me." She grabbed my arm and I had no choice but to follow her, not the least of which because I still couldn't make out more than fuzzy shapes. "Try now," she said once we stopped moving.

It took several more blinks for my pupils to return to normal and the indistinct shapes to solidify. "Thanks, mom. That definitely helped." When she didn't respond, I looked up, blinking a few more times for good measure, but she wasn't anywhere to be seen in the shaded alleyway. "Mom?" A sudden surge of worry tightened my throat and I spun around to look for any sign of her.

"Mom!" I called again. Thinking she might have returned to the restaurant while I recovered, I stepped toward the light. The exit to the alley was still a few feet away when something slammed into the back of my head and the world plunged into darkness.

My head was absolutely pounding when I pushed myself onto my hands and knees. It took a moment, but gradually the last few seconds before I blacked out came back to me. Judging by the grit under my hands, I suspected I was still in the alleyway... and I still had no clue where my mother had gone. Surely, she realized I was missing by now.

30

The Eclipse

I PUSHED MYSELF TO my feet with a groan and blinked rapidly to adjust my eyes. That's when I realized the floor wasn't just gritty, it was dirt. I glanced toward the source of light above me to find a small, barred window. That wasn't right. And neither was the light streaming through it. It had been dusk before, but this looked like morning light. Panic shot through me like an arrow to the heart.

The eclipse.

I spun around, my shoes making an awful scritching sound on the rough ground. When my gaze fell on the clearly locked metal gate—no, not just metal, *iron*—I nearly stumbled backward. "No, no, no. What happened?"

I wracked my brain, but nothing new surfaced. I remembered parting ways with Xander that morning. While he was at the dorm, I confirmed dinner plans with my mother. Then I met her at the restaurant. My father hadn't been there, then the whole disaster with the sun, and then... nothing.

"Good, you're awake."

I ripped my gaze from the floor at my mother's icy tone. She stood on the other side of the gate with a lantern, wearing her typical hunting gear. "Mom, what are you doing?"

A muscle in her jaw twitched, and glaciers were warmer than the look she was giving me. "I could ask you much the same. How could you?" she hissed.

I shook my head, a mistake I immediately regretted. "What are you talking about? I didn't lock *myself* in here. And why am I so groggy? Did you dose me!"

"Don't you *dare* play the victim with me. It's one thing to want to live your own life, abandon your legacy. But this? This is unconscionable!" In all my years, I'd never seen my mother so angry, so hurt.

"Mom, please. I don't know what you're talking about."

She set the lantern on the ground, the up-lighting giving her features an ominous cast, and crossed her arms over her fitted leather jacket. "Are you really going to stand there and lie to me? I'm not a fool, Diana. The light reveals the truth of all things."

The light! "You saw," I whispered, my voice thick. "When the sun blinded me, it caught my eyes." The tell-tale amber sheen would have instantly betrayed me.

She nodded, tightening her arms.

"Then why..." I glanced around at what was probably a holding cell that dated back to the town's earliest settlements, judging by the worn and eaten wood.

"Why are you still alive?" she filled in.

"Not to mince words, but yeah, why am I still alive?"

She huffed and her scowl deepened. "Because you're my daughter. And I did not give birth to you just to kill you." She shot me a nasty glare. "No matter your questionable life decisions."

"Okay..." I stepped cautiously toward the door, but stopped immediately when her gaze hardened. "Then why bring me here?"

"For your protection. As I said, I didn't bring you into this world for you to leave it prematurely." She glanced away from me, her shoulders tight. "We both know your uncle and father will be indiscriminate during the hunt."

"Mom, you can't leave me here," I said as calmly as I could. "You have to let me out. People are relying on me."

"By and by, it would appear your uncle has been having an affair," she went on as if I hadn't just asked to be released from the fucking cage she'd thrown me in. "Some young woman at least half his age he met in a supernatural chat forum. Disgusting, really." She curled her lip in distaste, though I wasn't entirely sure if it was for the unfortunate woman's age or where my uncle had picked her up.

"Mom," I tried again. "You don't have to do this. Let me out."

"No," she said so severely the hairs on my arm stood up. "You may have turned your back on your family, but I will *never*. I'll deal with you once this is finished." She inhaled sharply, then turned on her heel and walked off, leaving me alone with only the lantern and my thoughts for company.

I rushed the gate. "Mom! Please. You don't understand!" I wrapped my fingers around the bars in the slim hope that they'd be weak enough to wiggle free. Pain lanced up my arms and I yanked my hands back. I carefully inched closer and angled my head to get a glimpse of the outside of the bars.

A faint sheen caught the dim light and my heart sank in despair. Silver. She'd lined the gate with magic-imbued silver. It didn't matter if the iron was completely rusted through, there wasn't a chance in hell I was getting out that way. I searched the room for any other means of escape. Aside from the window, that I was positive had a similar treatment as the door, there was nothing. Sure, given enough time, I could probably dig my way out, but it'd be too late by then.

I slumped to the ground and rested my head against the wall. How had I let this happen? Xander was going to be beside himself with worry. *Xander!* I scrambled to check my pockets for my phone. Surprise, surprise, my mother had taken it.

"Well, at least whatever sedative she dosed me with is finally wearing off," I said miserably into the vacant cell.

The light shining through the window continued to shift and I tried to guess what time it might be. The moon had been set to rise around... I stalled. What time *was* the moon supposed to rise? I always knew when. It was one of the few habits I hadn't been able to break once I'd walked away from hunting. So why didn't I know it now?

I squinted through the window to see if I could catch a glimmer of something, any clue that could help. It wasn't until my eyes were watering so hard I had to look away, that I finally admitted the truth to myself. I'd fucked up. *Royally*. I didn't know when the full moon would rise, because there was *no* full moon. Solar Eclipses only occurred during the new moon phase.

A scream of frustration clawed its way out of my lungs and I pulled at my hair. How could I have been so dumb as to conflate a lunar and solar eclipse? There would be no full moon to push my first change. And the others... Xander had talked about everyone shifting way before the eclipse so they wouldn't be caught in a state of vulnerability.

I sobbed and cracked my head against the wall. Had Xander ever referred to today as a full moon? Even once? Or had he simply called it by exactly what it was: a solar eclipse? Which meant the only reason any of them were in danger was because of me. They never would have been outside or shifted if I hadn't warned them of the imminent threat.

"What have I done?" I glanced up at the window again, feeling hopeless, alone, and so fucking guilty it made my soul shrivel. Finally, I wiped my face and pushed myself up to my feet. There'd be time for pity later. "I have to warn them."

I took in my cell again and it's complete lack of escape. Holding a human in here was no problem and the magicked silver on the bars kept me from doing anything remotely useful. My gaze fell once more on the deteriorating wood that made up the wall. More specifically, where I'd hit the back of my head against it and left an indent. Hope flickered in my chest. The room had been designed to hold *humans*. That wall didn't stand a chance against a determined werewolf.

My small flame of hope threatened to gutter out. Without the full moon to help, what chance did I have of changing on my own? I snarled at my own defeatist thoughts. Even a slim chance was better than none at all. We knew the *were* virus had taken hold. My ability to heal had already increased three times over, I was more sensitive to light and sound, not to mention magical silver. Most importantly, I was bonded for fuck's sake. And I'd be damned if I sat around while my mate died.

I barely had a chance to focus on all the tips Xander had given me when my spine crunched so painfully, I collapsed. My chest expanded with heavy pants that seared my lungs and a cold sweat broke out all over my body. I scrambled to get out of my clothes, before what I really hoped was the change progressed much further.

My jeans were nearly free when my leg spasmed, twisting unnaturally as parts of it elongated and others shrank. I cried out as my breaking body snagged in the stiff material and reached with shaky hands to rip the denim free. It wasn't until my nails were digging into the fabric that I realized they weren't nails at all–they were claws. The ruined pants fell away and I collapsed, shoulder first onto the hard earth. Bile rose up my throat as my ribs collapsed and expanded and my internal organs wiggled around to accommodate the new shape. I barely managed to roll to the side in time to be sick. Thank the gods, I'd never managed to eat dinner the night before.

Pain traded places with acute agony shimmering in every nerve-ending. How the fuck did werewolves do this? I tried desperately to regain my bearings, but I wasn't in charge of my body anymore. All I could do was pray to every deity I could think of as I convulsed on the ground. Seconds felt like hours or maybe they were, but the pain never relented. I was a shattered shape lost somewhere between living and desperate to die.

With a pained sob, I prayed to the last deity I could think of–the Goddess of the moon, pure and perfect in her glorious white halo. "Please protect him."

Something inside shifted again and I closed my eyes against a fresh wave of torture. But it didn't come. Or it did, but it was different, an easing of sorts. My muscles relaxed enough that I could finally breathe. Then the sting of a thousand fire ants covered my body. I rolled on the dirt in a vain attempt to get it to stop, not even registering how miraculous it was that I could move at all. Right when I was at the edge of my limits and fully prepared to shred any and all skin I could reach, it was gone.

I lay on the ground in stunned silence, waiting. After a small eternity, I braved opening my eyes and nearly fainted with relief. I wasn't just alive, I'd changed. My legs threatened to buckle as I forced them to take my weight, but I persevered. I did a quick inventory to make sure everything was where it was supposed to be, especially since *nothing* about that transformation had gone at all like Xander said it would.

Reassured that I wasn't missing anything vital, I padded up to the wall. Every fiber stood out in sharp contrast and the sweet, musky scent of decaying wood filled my nostrils. The world of new sensations bordered on overload, but it would have to wait. The single most important thing right now was finding Xander and warning everyone. I scratched at the wall, simultaneously thrilled at the sensory experience and the fact that the wall crumbled easily beneath my sharp claws. I continued to dig with both paws until I'd made a fairly sizable crater. Then I walked back to the gate on the opposite side of the room.

I stole a microsecond to second guess my sanity, then barrelled full force toward the weakened area. My shoulder impacted with the wall so hard I both felt and heard it crunch. For a split second as momentum carried me forward it didn't look like the wall would give. A splintering sound filled the air and the wood beneath crumbled. One minute I was trapped in a rotting cell, the next, I'd punched through into open wilderness.

Triumph filled me from nose to tail. I rolled my shoulder, amazed at how much better it already felt. Not perfect, but better. And I was free. I focused on the light within, that tiny precious bond Xander and I had only recently cemented. Except there was nothing tiny or fragile about it. It was a veritable supernova of feeling seeping into every pore, pointing me exactly where I needed to go. I flexed my claws in the dirt and took off.

I'm coming, Xander.

The earth flew beneath my paws as I zipped between and around trees. I'd never moved so fast in my life. Not even upturned rocks or exposed roots could slow me down. My strides pounded in time with my heart as I ran. A break in the canopy above revealed the sun high overhead.

I stumbled as I screeched to a halt and looked harder. No, my eyes weren't playing tricks on me, a tiny portion of the sun was already blacked out. Time was running out. No way I could get to the pack before my family. Be that as it may, I wasn't giving up without a fight. I redoubled my efforts and pushed myself to go faster.

My lungs were screaming and my heaving sides were begging for mercy when the sound of shouts and snarls reached my ears. I adjusted my course and headed for the heart of the noise. When I burst through the trees, it was onto absolute chaos. About ten wolves were scattered about, snarling and snapping. Mixed among them were my parents and my Uncle Nemo, as well as his mysterious lover.

My mom looked exactly as she had at the cabin in her crimson breeches and matching jacket zipped all the way up. Only this time she had her sapphire blue compound bow aimed at a wolf. She loosed and the wolf dipped to the side just in time to avoid the shot. Not far from where my mother held her ground against two wolves, my father faced off against three. Per usual, he was dressed stereotypically head to toe in black, though he was wielding knives rather than his bow. A quick look revealed it lying discarded and shredded into a hundred pieces. Meanwhile, my uncle seemed to be faring better than anyone. His camouflage cloak rippled as he spun around and fired a deadly shot from his blood red bow into a charging wolf. The wolf's dying cry briefly snatched everyone's attention and I launched myself into the fray.

After my breakneck run from the cabin, I was exhausted and my shoulder ached something fierce. But I didn't let that stop me from body-checking my uncle. He stumbled and his subsequent shot missed a wolf that looked a hell of a lot like Jennifer. He reoriented his broad frame quickly to address the new threat, but I was already out of reach of the dagger he pulled from his belt.

I scanned the chaos for Xander and finally found his dark shape darting back and forth to avoid the fourth hunter. Another wolf lay wounded behind him and I knew without a doubt that even if they'd been shot with a wolfsbane arrow, he wouldn't abandon them. Rather than immediately race over, I attempted to sneak up on the hunter's flank. The closer I got, the more obvious it became that *this* was the hunter that had tried to shoot me.

I was only a couple yards away and doing my damnedest not to draw attention to myself when an arrow flew across the space, hitting Xander squarely in his left haunch. He yelped and struggled to stay upright. The hunter advanced and he snarled, standing his ground as he was no longer able to hop out of reach.

Fury the likes of which I'd never known swelled in my breast. I abandoned my attempt at stealth, cutting through the battle and dodging arrows to get to them. I skidded between Xander and the unknown hunter right as a gust of icy wind blew through the trees, creating an eerie howling effect. The hunter's cowl fell and I reared back with a gasp as their face came into view.

Blond hair that was normally in bouncy waves was pulled back into a severe ponytail and there was a blind hatred in her blue eyes that I'd never seen before. Betrayal broke my heart as I stared in horror at the woman I'd called friend.

Kora sneered and trained her bow on me with a fresh arrow. "I don't even have to guess to know it's you, Diana."

I cringed at the way she said my name and took a tentative step backward. I was still the only thing between her and Xander. He made an agonized cry behind me and I knew it had nothing to do with the poison arrow sticking out of him.

"Oh, yes, I'd know that pathetic look anywhere. I tried so *hard* to be your friend, to get you to let me in, to be part of your world. We could have been sisters! But, no, you and Hyacinth always acted like you were so much better than the rest of us. I thought getting you tangled with the werewolves in the beginning would trigger your hunter instinct. But you ran. Like Prey!" she sneered as she trained her bow on me once more. "You've chosen the wrong side and now you can die like the rest of them."

No sooner did she utter the last word, than darkness descended. Time seemed to stand still as everyone looked up to confirm what we all knew: the eclipse had reached its totality.

A cruel laugh escaped Kora as she pulled the string back. "Looks like you're out of time, too." Her fingers flexed in anticipation of release, then her head snapped to the side and her shot went wide, landing harmlessly in a nearby tree. She continued to stand there as if held up by some unknown force, eyes wide and confused, then crumpled to the ground, an arrow protruding from her skull.

Amazement eclipsed my shock as my mother moved to stand between me and the now lifeless Kora. "Stay away from my daughter, you homewrecking bitch."

"Kora!" Uncle Nemo's cry tore through the air as he ran over.

In the confusion, the wolves still standing—only five now—regrouped behind Xander. The one I was pretty sure was Jennifer even limped up beside him to help steady him as he sagged.

My mother took aim at my uncle and he stopped in his tracks mere feet from his destination.

"Vanessa," my father hissed as he stomped over, fury blazing in his eyes. "What do you think you're doing? This is our chance. We only have another couple minutes while they're weakened!"

"I'm protecting our daughter, Luther." Shock exploded across my father's face as he looked from my mother to me. I inclined my head slightly to confirm his suspicion. Uncle Nemo inched closer and the string of my mother's bow creaked as she tightened her grip. "One more step, Nemo, and brother-in-law or not, I'll put you into the ground too."

My father squared his shoulders, his shock having morphed into disgust. "Drop your weapon, Vanessa." His gaze skittered past her to rest on me once more, revulsion evident in every hard line of his face. "I'll not call any monster daughter as long as I draw breath."

"Luther, in what universe do you think you married a woman that would bend to your will? I have not nor will I *ever* take orders from you. So you can back the fuck up or you can join your delusional brother in the morgue. What'll it be?" She flicked her gaze to my father. At that moment, the light returned, and my uncle surged forward, one of the infamous wolfhead daggers in his hand.

I surged past my mother, knocking her down, and lunged for my uncle's arm. My jaws closed around his bicep with almost no resistance despite the reinforced leathers he wore. Blood pooled in my mouth and he screamed so loud it made my ears ring. I bit down harder until I heard the soft thud of the dagger hitting the ground.

My uncle snarled obscenities as he tried to pull free.

I growled and pulled back, my paws scratching along the ground for purchase. An awful crack split the air and suddenly I flew ass over tea kettle backward with my uncle's arm still clenched between my jaws while he flailed in a shower of blood several feet away. His resulting scream hurt my ears and made my head swim. I was still trying to regain my bearings when Xander limped to stand in front of me, his head lowered threateningly between his shoulders as he bared his teeth and emitted an ominous growl. I didn't understand what he was doing, until I realized my father had picked up my uncle's bow and aimed it at me.

"Don't do this, Luther," my mother said, once more moving to be in front of me.

My father's face twisted into a snarl and he loosed the nocked arrow. The screaming coming from my uncle abruptly stopped and my father lowered the bow. He surveyed our group. Though we were definitely the worse for wear, we still outnumbered him six to one.

"We're done," he declared in the same voice I associated with being sent to my room as a child. "As far as I'm concerned, my whole family died in a tragic hunting accident today." He slung the red bow over his shoulder then retrieved the wolf head dagger. He dusted it off and tucked it into his boot, causing the ruby eye to glint wickedly in the returned sunlight.

"Luther," my mom said softly.

He glanced at her briefly. "Good luck, Vanessa. And if you ever see our daughter again..." Sadness flitted across his face almost too fast to catch. "If you ever see her again, tell her I wish it didn't have to be this way." With that, he turned on his heel and walked into the forest without a backward glance. I didn't know what was more surprising, that he'd chosen to walk away rather than die fighting, or that not a single wolf moved to stop him.

31

---◆◇◆---

A New Future

A SENSE OF PEACE washed over me a millisecond before Xander's unique scent of juniper and petrichor.

"Hey, you," he said from behind me.

I glanced over my shoulder to find him leaning against the door frame for my bedroom, then returned my focus to the disturbing collection of papers, notebooks, pictures, and books. All of it was cause for worry, but the books were the most troubling. Some of them had come straight from the Harker Family Archives. I picked up one of the notebooks filled with Kora's distinctive handwriting.

Xander let me continue flipping through the covered pages for a minute before asking, "Is that all of it?"

"I really hope so. Xander, the things I found..." I shook my head, still unable to believe she'd had all of this werewolf and hunter lore and I'd never even suspected. With a sigh, I tossed the notebook that read like werewolf hunter fanfiction back on the bed.

He left his sentry and walked over to perch on the edge of the bed. "Do you want to talk about it?" He grabbed my

315

hand, which was hanging listlessly by my side, and gave it a reassuring squeeze.

"Yes. No…" My eyes stung with the promise of yet more tears. At this point, I wasn't even sure what I was crying about—that my friend was dead or that she'd betrayed me. I removed my hand from his grasp and used the heels of my palms to wipe away the tears. I'd already cried enough.

"I'm here for you." Xander's gentle assurance warmed my heart, and I gave him a weak smile. He leaned back, grabbed Kora's laptop, and sat up. "I'm surprised they let you out of there with this. Didn't they think you might be robbing her?" He opened it, but it was long dead, mostly because I'd drained the battery, falling down the rabbit hole of her internet history and chat accounts. Figures the one thing I didn't grab was the charging cord and mine wasn't compatible. He set it aside again.

"Actually, no one even batted an eye. A few of her sorority sisters even offered to help me pack her things." My gaze rebelliously latched onto a printout of an online chat she'd had with my uncle. It was horribly graphic—first in how to best kill werewolves, then further on in all the perverse ways they wanted to be together. I cringed as I recalled a snippet about having sex in the hot blood of their fresh kill. "I'm *really* glad I didn't let them."

Xander began forming the loose papers into a stack. "What do you plan to do with it all?"

"Burn it," I said with such heat that I startled myself. Intense emotions were also taking some getting used to, especially anger. "A few things I'll leave intact." I gestured to the two haphazard piles of books. "The small stack on the left I'll mail to my father and the other can go with us to the House to join the library there."

He nodded and moved to secure the books accordingly. "Any updates about Takashi?"

"That's one thing at least I don't have to worry about. Mom assures me that our lawyer is not only clearing my name and making all of this disappear, but also making the intrepid detective seriously second guess his chosen profession." I almost felt bad for Takashi. Almost.

I joined Xander in putting everything away and before long, all that remained was my cell phone. As if knowing it didn't have to compete for attention, it rang.

I barely glanced at the screen before dismissing the incoming call. And I definitely didn't venture into the unholy thread of texts that I still hadn't read.

"Uh, don't you need to get that?"

I crossed my arms over my chest, suddenly feeling defensive. "It's Hyacinth." Xander raised his eyebrows in obvious confusion, and I huffed. "I haven't figured out how to tell her we can't be friends anymore."

"Who says you can't? You could always write letters to her like you'll do with your mom."

I shook my head. "Would never work. I don't trust Hye as much as I trust my mother."

"Is that why you're using a PO Box in Montana to forward the letters?"

He had me there. "My mother understands that we have to keep our distance and be careful when and if we ever meet face to face. Hyacinth won't accept that. I could use a hundred proxy addresses and she'd still find a way to track me down. I won't risk the pack's safety like that."

It wasn't until Xander stood and wrapped me in his arms that I realized how worked up I'd gotten. "Shh, shh. You don't have to explain yourself to me. I just see how hard this is all weighing on you and wanted to offer options."

I squeezed my eyes shut and leaned into him. "I know. It's just, she's my oldest friend. I still care about her and I worry what will happen when I'm not around to help curb her more extreme decisions."

He leaned back to look me in the eye. "You can't be her guiding light forever."

"You're right. I know you're right. It's just... hard."

He combed the hair away from my face. "I know." The chirp of a notification sounded from his back pocket and he let out a resigned sigh.

"So he really did it. Victor called for the Alpha battle."

Xander released me to run his hands through his own hair. "Yeah. I was really hoping I'd have another year, but between what happened over the summer and the murders on campus, he's taking advantage of everyone's shaken trust in my family."

I smiled and cupped his face. "Plenty of people still believe in you and you're going to do great. This is your fight to win and if Victor can't see that, he's even dumber than he looks." The comment earned me a wry chuckle.

"Then I guess it's time. Are you ready?"

We finished dealing with the last evidence of Kora's involvement, then joined Jennifer at the dorm and set off for the House, along with the remaining *weres*. I'd like to say the long drive was blissfully uneventful, but it really just gave me too much time alone with my thoughts. Occasionally, I contributed to Xander's attack strategy, but the bottom line was that the majority of the pack were still strangers to me and I fretted at my reception. By the time we rolled up to the House, I felt more like a tangled ball of nerves than a newly minted werewolf and I wasn't even the one who would be fighting.

We'd barely even opened our doors when Victor stormed out of the plantation style house flanked by his supporters.

"I knew it! How dare you bring an outsider to the Alpha contest!" His shouting had the desired effect and more people than I would have thought possible flocked to see what the commotion was about. He had a victorious glint in his eye as he pointed first to Xander then to me. "You know damn well there are no humans allowed to be present!"

Xander ducked his head to hide his growing smirk and leaned against the hood of the car while Jennifer valiantly fought to suppress her laugh.

"I fail to see what's so amusing about you spitting in the face of all our traditions," Victor snarled. "I don't give a damn if you believe you're bonded or not. No. Humans. Allowed."

"Then I guess it's a good thing I'm not human anymore," I chimed in.

Victor's gaze narrowed. "What did you say?"

I pushed my shoulders back and stepped forward. "You heard me." I raised my voice so no one could miss what I said next. "I'm a werewolf and have every right to witness the Alpha battle. And for the record, we *are* bonded."

Xander slipped his hand in mind and tugged me toward the House. It took more effort than I cared to admit not to childishly stick my tongue out at Victor's flabbergasted face. We'd almost made it all the way up the front steps when his angry voice called after us.

"This won't change anything, Xander! I'll beat you in that ring tonight, then banish both your tails!"

Shocked gasps ricocheted behind us, and I glanced askance at Xander. He subtly shook his head before turning around to address his rival. "May the better wolf win."

Pride swelled in my chest at his diplomatic response and I knew without a doubt that the better wolf *would* win. Xander took my hand once more, and we walked inside, trailed by the excited babble of speculating voices.

Several hours later, the sun had set and every werewolf in the pack was gathered around in a large ring. I danced from foot to foot, unable to shake the feeling that I was sticking out like a sore thumb and worse, that I didn't belong. This was only my third shift, and I'd never been around so many werewolves in my life. My poor brain kept reverting to my old life, and I had to constantly resist the urge to fight for my life–which wasn't in danger–or run for all I was worth–which would do fuck-all to show my support.

I released a heavy huff, and Jennifer pressed her shoulder against me. We couldn't actually talk in this form, nor was there any sort of telepathy despite some of the more ludicrous reports. There was, however, a sense of understanding. So while Jennifer couldn't *tell* me everything would be alright, I still felt it.

I ceased my fidgeting and glanced across the ring. A wolf with bright red fur made eye contact and nodded her head. I couldn't help but grin. While I'd never seen Charline in her wolf form, there wasn't a doubt in my mind it was her. Which meant the hulking blond next to her was David. And if I was remembering right, odds were that the pair of wolves on her other side were Sara and Michael. Like myself and Charline, Sara had also been bitten, though her situation had been infinitely more traumatic.

A sudden hush fell over the gathered crowd and as one we looked toward the treeline where an archway of rocks had been erected. A distinguished wolf with coloring almost identical to Xander's walked to the center of the ring. He took a minute to look around the ring and I shuddered as his gaze fell on me like he was making eye contact with every single person present. Once Alexander completed his circuit, he made a chuffing sound and backed up.

Xander and Victor walked abreast beneath the arch, only stopping once they were in front of the current reigning Alpha. Xander had explained that his father stepping down like this was not only unusual, but unprecedented. He'd also explained that while he and Victor were the main contenders, others could join at any time until only one wolf was left standing. That's where their chosen Betas came in. After having won their own respective Beta battle, their aim was to reduce foul play without overly interfering.

Alexander looked intently at each competitor. Xander remained calm and proud while Victor's hackles rose. After a tense moment, Alexander backed away. Once he'd merged with the ring of impatient witnesses, Xander and Victor moved to opposite sides of the arena. When they turned to face each other, I had to suppress the hysterical desire to laugh at how closely the setup resembled an old-fashioned duel. Jennifer nudged me as if sensing my struggle, and I quieted.

There was no sound of any kind to signal the start of the fight. Victor just sprinted across the ring for Xander. I didn't bother to repress my snarl and was relieved to see that I wasn't the only one so keyed up. Growls and yips of encouragement filled the clearing as Xander dove out of Victor's path at the last minute. Victor spun around and the two snapped at each other's ruff.

They broke apart, circling each other and occasionally fainting and retreating. Victor's faint turned into a lunge, catching Xander off guard and allowing Victor to sink his teeth into the fur at Xander's neck. I moved forward, but Jennifer shifted her leg into my path and gave me a warning look. Cowed, I danced back, agitation making my fur stand up.

Victor forced Xander back, leveraging his size to keep Xander off balance until he was close enough to the ring for one of his supporters to snap at Xanders leg. In the blink of an eye, David was there, muscling the errant wolf back into line. Xander and Victor went back to circling each other as if nothing had happened.

After a few more mildly successful attacks from Victor, Xander went on the offensive. Unlike Victor, he didn't retreat after every attack. He hammered at him again and again, his teeth and claws ripping into Victor. He didn't even relent when Victor managed to get his claws into Xander's side.

My heart was in my throat as their movements became more determined, more savage. Victor sank his teeth into the haunch Xander had been shot in and Xander let out a howl of pain. I let out a furious growl so loud I couldn't hear anything else. The bond might mean the end of both of us if one perished, but if Victor killed Xander, I'd be damned if I didn't see him dead first.

Victor released his grip on Xander, allowing blood to run down Xander's leg and pranced back, his tail held high. It took me a moment to realize the fucker was gloating. Xander stepped toward him and nearly fell to the ground when he tried to put weight on his re-injured leg. I held my breath, sensing the end was imminent.

Xander took another limping step, and Victor lunged. At the last second, Xander swiveled on his wounded leg. Desperate to change his trajectory, Victor stumbled on the torn up earth. Between one blink and the next, Xander's jaws closed around Victor's throat. Victor fought to pull away. Xander let out a muffled yet sinister growl, and Victor went deathly still.

I was fairly positive everyone present was holding their breath, waiting for what would happen next. Time seemed to stretch on forever, until at last, Victor maneuvered just enough to show his belly. Xander dropped his hold and stepped back. It was only then that I realized how bloody both of them were.

Victor struggled to his feet, keeping low to the ground and his head bowed.

Xander threw his head back and howled his victory. Across the way, David emerged and padded up to his side, where he took up the call. One by one, everyone added their voice. Joy that rivaled the bond flooded through me. I tilted my head and let it out to weave with the others in the most perfect song I'd ever heard.

As the last notes drifted off into the dusk, an elation the likes of which I'd never known filled my entire being from nose to tail. I dropped my head and met Xander's gaze from across the quickly collapsing ring. While my newfound pack-mates mingled and celebrated their new Alpha, I only had eyes for my other half, my mate. I slipped past wolves yipping their excitement, barely sparing a glance for the cluster surrounding the defeated Victor. Finally, I made it to where Xander had been standing with David and his parents, only he wasn't there.

I swiveled around in alarm. Surely no one would take him out immediately following an Alpha battle. I'd have shouted for him, but talking wasn't exactly something feasible in my shifted form and, contrary to fan theories worldwide, were-wolves did not communicate telepathically. So instead, my distress came out as a muted whine. Not that it did me much good given how loud the clearing had become.

Someone bodily hip-checked me and I spun to face them, already snarling. In retrospect, I shouldn't have been surprised to find the culprit was Xander. He danced back a few paces, a goofy grin on his wolfy face. Even as an Alpha, Xander was still Xander and I absolutely fucking loved that about him. He glided forward and rubbed against me, this time without trying to knock me over. In spite of the obviously affectionate gesture, I couldn't resist snapping at his tail. Though I was relieved to see that his injuries from the fight were already healing.

We circled each other a few more times before stopping side by side to face the rest of the pack—our pack. We shared a look, then turned as one to walk back through the stone entryway. The second we crossed the threshold, we broke into a run. My exhilaration from earlier returned twofold as our paws thundered on the ground followed by the rest of the North Carolina werewolf pack. I could definitely get used to my new life, especially when I had the man I was crazy about running beside me.

ACKNOWLEDGEMENTS

The world has not been easy these last few years, and neither has been writing this book. That being said, I want to extend a very special thank you to Sam Drake for restoring my faith in this story (even after you initially crushed it). Without your support and friendship, this story wouldn't be anywhere near the amazing one it is now.

I'd also like to thank my good friend Goose for being such an amazing beta reader. You know my worlds better than anyone. So I suppose I can forgive you and Sam for always agreeing with each other's notes and ganging up on me. (I still haven't forgiven either of you for that scene you made me cut. I don't care if you were right.)

Last, but certainly not least, I want to thank Cyd Sidney and Courtney Q for getting the gears going again.

For all my faithful readers, whether you've been with me since the beginning or have just joined the adventure: *May the moon always light your way.*

About the Author

Sam Bolanos (she/they) is a genderqueer author and founder of Chaotic Neutral Press LLC. They believe in love, equality, and the Oxford comma. When not playing with her three dogs, who you can follow on Instagram @austendogs, or spending time with her incredible husband, she's probably agonizing over edits or escaping into her latest fantasy.

Welcome to the adventure!

Newsletter: subscribe
Website: Booksbysbolanos.com
Facebook: @Booksbysbolanos
reader group: Sam's Sunbeams
Instagram: @sbolanosbooks